Praise for
Alyssa Brooks's novels

"A wonderful debut story!"   —*Romance Junkies*

"Once again, Alyssa Brooks creates an enchanting and erotic tale."
—*The Romance Studio*

"Alyssa Brooks has written a charming, bewitching romance."
—*Romance Reviews Today*

"Alyssa Brooks has earned herself not only a few red fingertips from the flames she has produced, but also four Angels!"
—*Fallen Angel Reviews*

"Wonderfully sensual, erotic . . . will leave you wanting more."
—*Romance at Heart*

COME AND GET ME

alyssa brooks

THE BERKLEY PUBLISHING GROUP
Published by the Penguin Group
Penguin Group (USA) Inc.
375 Hudson Street, New York, New York 10014, USA
Penguin Group (Canada), 90 Eglinton Avenue East, Suite 700, Toronto, Ontario, M4P 2Y3, Canada (a division of Pearson Penguin Canada Inc.)
Penguin Books Ltd., 80 Strand, London WC2R 0RL, England
Penguin Group Ireland, 25 St. Stephen's Green, Dublin 2, Ireland (a division of Penguin Books Ltd.)
Penguin Group (Australia), 250 Camberwell Road, Camberwell, Victoria 3124, Australia (a division of Pearson Australia Group Pty. Ltd.)
Penguin Books India Pvt. Ltd., 11 Community Centre, Panchsheel Park, New Delhi—110 017, India
Penguin Group (NZ), 67 Apollo Drive, Rosedale, North Shore 0745, Auckland, New Zealand (a division of Pearson New Zealand Ltd.)
Penguin Books (South Africa) (Pty.) Ltd., 24 Sturdee Avenue, Rosebank, Johannesburg, South Africa

Penguin Books Ltd., Registered Offices: 80 Strand, London WC2R 0RL, England

This is an original publication of The Berkley Publishing Group.

This is a work of fiction. Names, characters, places, and incidents either are the product of the author's imagination or are used fictitiously, and any resemblance to actual persons, living or dead, business establishments, events, or locales is entirely coincidental. The publisher does not have any control over and does not assume any responsibility for author or third-party websites or their content.

First edition: June 2007

Library of Congress Cataloging-in-Publication Data

Brooks, Alyssa.
 Come and get me / Alyssa Brooks.—1st ed.
  p. cm.
 ISBN 978-0-425-21594-4
 I. Title.
 PS3602.R645C66 2007
 813'.6—dc22
                    2007011158

This story is dedicated to my critique partner, Larissa Lyons, who's been my greatest encourager. Thank you, Larissa, for your friendship and all you have taught me. I also want to thank my family, for standing by me even when success seemed like a fantasy, and my editors and agent, for all their efforts on *Come and Get Me*. To all my readers, your support means the world to me.

COME AND GET ME

prologue

Shit. What did Dylan think he was doing?

Sadie paused, her hand in midair. The dinner fork shook and the shrimp dangled from the utensil, ready to fall off. Her breath hitched as a bead of sweat threatened to roll down her forehead and ruin her perfect makeup.

She stared at the shrimp. What now?

Did she eat it? Drop it? Throw it across the fancy restaurant?

If her eyes grew any wider, they'd pop right out of her head and fall on her plate. What the hell was Dylan thinking?

He had dropped to one knee and now rested his hand on her thigh, entreating her full attention. Oh how she wanted to play dumb, to focus on her shrimp, anything besides Dylan.

Reaching in the breast pocket of his sport jacket, he revealed a small, black velvet box.

Oh. No.

Not here. Not now. Not in front of her parents.

Good grief! They'd barely been dating six months. It was too soon! *Way* too soon.

Hell, she'd only just told him she loved him last month.

She wasn't ready for marriage!

Her gaze darted to her mother and father. Their tan, sun-wrinkled, ever-so-pleased gazes beamed back at her. Of course they were happy. They'd been angling for a grandchild for two years now. Every guy she dated was a potential babymaker.

Sadie chalked it up to postmaternal and postpaternal longing. For the past fifteen years they'd been so busy enjoying their millions from the Kansas state lottery, they hadn't had time for raising her.

Now, the money had become boring. Their focus had shifted to wanting a grandkid to spoil. She'd never wished for a sister more.

God, of all the luck. Why did Dylan have to do this in front of them? He should know better. She had dinner with her parents once a week, and for the past two months, he'd escorted her to their restaurant of choice. By now, he was quite aware of the sticky situation she was in.

The wily fox.

Dylan gave her a weak, lopsided smile that punctuated his damn adorable dimples. His dark, almost black eyes shone with love. Opening the box, he revealed a dazzling, downright huge, pink diamond. At least two carats.

"Marry me, Sadie?" he asked in a smooth, velvet voice, sounding so sure of her answer.

A shiver coursed along her spine. In her mind, she imagined her backbone turning to Jell-O.

Dylan had never looked sexier. Bent on one knee in front of her, his hopeful eyes and seductive smile turned her into instant lovey-dovey mush. The *no* she wanted to scream lodged in her throat.

She couldn't do it. She couldn't turn him down.

Her gaze swept his length, wanting him, loving him, needing to say yes. But how could she? It was too soon!

She didn't know what to tell him. Didn't know what to do. Her heart and mind played a fierce game of tug-of-war.

He cleared his throat. His brows furrowed. His forehead creased. Worry etched the lines of his strongly defined face, demanding some sort of answer.

She had to take action. Quick.

Bringing the shrimp to her mouth, she bit into the spicy meat. Again, Dylan cleared his throat. She chewed quickly, cursing herself a hundred times. What a dumb move!

Stupid, stupid, stupid!

Who would take a bite of food in the middle of a proposal? Only her. Now she had to finish eating the damn piece of seafood, while all eyes were on her.

Waiting. Hoping. Demanding.

She loved Dylan. She did. After all, she wouldn't have told him so if she hadn't meant it. He was everything she'd ever dreamt of in a husband. She wanted to become his wife.

But one day, in the future. Not now.

She didn't make a lot of plans in her life. Everything was pretty much easy come, easy go. But there was one thing Sadie had promised herself years ago. She would not marry before thirty. While she wanted to settle down and have a family, she wanted to be ready.

Was she ready?

Her parents sure were.

"Sadie?" Dylan questioned, shifting with nervousness. "Will you marry me?"

"He's been waiting five minutes, sugar," her father pushed. "Give the boy a dang answer already."

"Yes." The response sputtered from her before she could stop herself. "But I want a long engagement."

The moment she blurted the ill-thought-out words, she wanted to kick herself in the ass. Not the most romantic thing to say the moment after accepting a man's proposal.

Why did she keep sticking things in her mouth? First the shrimp, now her foot. What next?

"Of course." Dylan nodded stiffly, wriggling the band on. "As long as you want."

The diamond ring fit so tightly, Dylan had to work it into place. The whole time he twisted it down her finger, Sadie made reassuring promises to herself.

She loved him.

She needed him.

She loved him.

She could get married and give up her freedom at twenty-seven, instead of waiting until thirty, because she *loved* him.

one

"Did you think you could get away with this, Sadie?" The cop's big, exploring hands pressed her down. Forced to lean over the trunk of the police cruiser, her nipples tightened and tingled. Desire dampened her thighs.

Sadie battled the urges pulsating through her body and squinted at the flashing lights. Why was she being arrested?

Everything was a big, nonsensical blur. All she could remember was that she'd been heading to the church to get married. She needed to get married. Dylan was waiting.

Patting her down, the officer moved his hands farther and farther down, over her hips, her rear, toward more intimate regions. His hand slipped under her skirt, his calloused fingers stroking her wet thighs.

Why was she wearing a skirt? She never wore skirts.

She was getting married. What the hell happened to her gown?

The cuffs were tight around her wrists. She couldn't resist him. She didn't want to resist him. Her mind cried no! *Her body insisted* yes!

Three of his thick, long fingers plunged inside of her and a scream escaped her . . .

Suddenly the cop faded into oblivion. She was running, buck naked, through the church. Pew after pew of guests stared at her, their glaring red eyes full of accusations.

Her mind echoed the same chant she sensed coming from the attendees. "Did you think you could get away with this?" The reproachful words grew louder and louder. "Did you, Sadie? Did you?"

Sadie woke in a sweat, bolting upright in the king-size bed, surrounded by dark. A heavy weight smashed her chest, her breathing quick and shallow.

She gasped for air, hardly able to inhale.

Shit. Why couldn't she breathe?

Her hands shook, her left index finger swelling around her engagement ring. Fire prickled her skin as her back threatened to break out in hives.

Oh God. Not again. The last time this had happened—only last week while selecting a wedding cake of all things—her future mother-in-law had practically gotten her drunk on Benadryl from a nearby pharmacy and the reaction had still taken hours to clear up.

Why hadn't she thought to buy any antihistamine to keep at home?

Because she hadn't wanted to accept that she'd find herself panicking like this again.

She needed to get up, watch some television, whatever it took to calm down.

Next to her, Dylan's gentle snores assured her of his presence. Yet he hadn't been the man in her disturbing dreams. Again.

As quietly as possible, so as not to wake him, Sadie tossed aside the comforter. Swinging her legs off the bed, she stood. Maybe a drink would help. A strong one . . .

She took a step and the dampness gathered in the juncture of her thighs rubbed her upper legs, jolting her with a reminder of the desire heating her most intimate regions.

No!

She loved *Dylan*. She was attracted to *Dylan*. They had a good sex life.

So what was with this cop in her dreams? For heaven's sake, their wedding was in thirty-nine days.

At the thought, the weight on her chest grew heavier, her breathing shorter. The walls closed in, suffocating her. She tried harder to get oxygen, but the more she thought about their impending marriage, the dizzier she became.

Oh God . . .

A sharp pain sliced through her. If she didn't know better, she'd swear she was having a heart attack.

Hard, fast panic belted through her. She clutched her chest, gasping for air as she stumbled away from the bed.

She had to get the hell out of here. She had to breathe.

She couldn't do it.

She couldn't marry Dylan.

Just the simple thought of canceling the wedding allowed a rush of air into her lungs. She gulped several welcome breaths, calming down.

So that was it. Deep down, she supposed she'd known the ugly fact all along. Hell, her body definitely did.

Love him she may, but wed him she could not.

Rushing to the walk-in closet, Sadie flipped on the light. She dragged out a suitcase and grabbed clothes off the racks. Only last week, Dylan had succeeded in convincing her to give up her loft and finally move into the home they had purchased together.

From the first night, the dreams and panic attacks had attacked full-force. While she certainly hadn't expected them, she'd sensed all along that the move wasn't right for her. That it was too much, too soon.

Their long engagement had been drastically cut by their meddling parents, who'd pushed and pushed until the two years had been sliced down to six months. Everything had happened so fast, like a giant whirlwind sweeping away her life and her choices, while she cowered from the truth.

She wasn't sure she could be a good wife to him. But she wanted to . . .

As a lawyer, he wanted a wife who could support his career, who could look prim and proper and polite. One who would host fancy dinner parties and be on the boards of too many charities to count. Do the things a lawyer's wife did. She'd seen his mother in action. She couldn't be like that.

Sure, they'd talked about her fears. Briefly. Time and again, when she expressed her concerns, Dylan, sweetie that he was, told her not to worry. According to his promises, everything would be fine. She'd make the perfect wife.

Sadie wasn't as certain. No, scratch that. She *knew* she'd never be a perfect wife.

She had no doubt he was a wonderful man to marry. After all, Dylan was solid husband material. But, every time she imagined herself in the role of his adoring, supporting wife—for the rest of her life—it felt weird.

She had no business living in the New York suburbs, let alone with a high-class workaholic lawyer. No business thinking she could be a wife and mother. Her parents were nuts; her life had always been nuts. She didn't want to drive her husband nuts, or worse, raise nutty kids. She had nothing to go on, no experience, no right to think she could be the person Dylan needed.

She was faking it, kidding herself. She couldn't settle and have kids and live happily ever after. Her dream had just proved it. She wasn't ready.

Dylan was better off without her.

She had to get out of here. Grabbing the brown, oversized photo albums from the shelf, she tucked them under her arm. While most of her photographs were sold at a gallery in the city, these albums held her most cherished pictures, along with favored mementos of her travels and explorations. She needed to add to them, not shelve them in a closet to get dusty. With a shaky sigh, she headed for the bedroom door.

Dylan rolled over, awakened by the light. He squinted at the sight of Sadie dragging a heavily packed suitcase from the closet. What was she doing?

He thought they'd agreed. No more photography trips until after the wedding. Between her larger-than-life mother and his overbearing parents, she had her hands full with the planning. She couldn't just take off to work. Besides, it wasn't as if either of them needed the money. He made more than enough to take care of her, not to mention how her parents threw their well-invested lottery money around like it was inexhaustible.

He sat up, rubbing his eyes. The neon numbers of the alarm clock caught his attention. It wasn't early morning. It was only a little past midnight, and stranger yet, Sadie was leaving in her nightgown.

What the hell was she doing?

"Sadie?"

She jumped, spooked. "Dylan!"

"Where you going, babe?" he asked cautiously as concern rippled through him. She'd been so weird since the move.

"I don't know."

"Come here."

She dropped the suitcase with a sigh, but didn't budge an inch. Standing, he crossed the room to her. She stared at him with crazed eyes, their hazel depths lit noticeably with panic. He pulled her into his arms, wrapping a strand of her short, curly golden hair around his pinky.

Running his fingers over her lips, he lifted her chin. She shuddered, resting her head against his hands.

Need lit through his body, awakening him fully. Leaning in, he claimed her mouth. Slowly, coaxing her mouth open, he slid his tongue over her lips. Tasting salty tears, he caressed the inner recesses of her mouth, kissing her long and deeply.

She matched him, slipping her tongue along his, twining . . . mating. His cock jerked in arousal and grew in his pajama pants.

Moving his hand to her breast, he rubbed his thumb over her nipple. She moaned and leaned in, kissing him harder. He cupped the firm mound in his hand and massaged it in slow circles.

His dick brushed against her thigh. Electric sensation fired through him. The vein along the underside of his shaft pulsed as blood rushed to the area and his cock turned to steel.

Damn, he wanted her.

Wrapping his hand around her hips, he snaked his fingers along her backbone to her ass. Through the thin fabric of her nightgown, he grabbed the fleshy globes and pulled her deeper into the kiss, lifting her.

Carrying her to bed, he laid her on the soft mattress, and she stretched her legs open, welcoming him. He climbed over her and pushed her silky pink nightgown to her chest, baring her thighs. He trailed his touch over the flat of her stomach, to the wisps of black curly hair peeking from under her lacy thong.

He hesitated, longing to use his mouth on her clit. How he ached to taste her. To make her climax with his tongue. His heart leapt at the thought, but his gut twisted in warning.

Would Sadie care for oral sex? He wasn't sure . . .

Maybe . . .

The same old uncertainty held him back, instinct battling with hard lessons learned. In the end, his guilty conscience prevailed. If she wasn't asking, he didn't dare push it on her.

Rather than follow his instincts, he parted her legs, and pulled the scrap of underwear aside. With one hard thrust, he buried himself in her slick tunnel. Her silky wetness wrapped around him, allowing him to easily slide in and out of her.

Her body's quick readiness for his entry made him smile. If anything, at least he knew she desired him.

Sadie cried out and locked her arms around his neck while Dylan pumped in and out of her, listening to her panting moans.

He wished he could make her scream.

He fucked her harder, faster, until his cock pulsed with the threat of an orgasm, though he stifled the urge to come, waiting for her.

Pleasing Sadie mattered more to him than anything.

He rotated his hips and curved his hand around her bottom. He tilted her hips, kneading the flesh of the two perfectly formed globes.

His fingers wandered to the deep crevice of her ass, almost going too far before he mentally restrained himself. Despite how much he longed to act on his increasingly more frequent impulses, his mind insisted they were *dirty, wrong*. That he should be ashamed of himself.

Deep down, common sense told him that he shouldn't think that way, that his feelings were natural, normal, and yet . . .

He pushed away the distracting thoughts and concentrated on Sadie. He fucked her the way he always did, in and out, hard and fast, slow and steady. He varied his speed, but never his actions, because he knew making love this way worked for Sadie.

To his surprise, she came faster than ever tonight. She tightened and a long, relaxed sigh released from deep within her. Her body went limp.

Dylan unleashed his rein and drove into her with three more thrusts. His cock exploded, shooting his seed into her womb.

He collapsed on top of her. Sadie pushed at his chest. "No. No, let me up . . ."

He rolled off her, attempting to draw her into a hug.

Her arms blocked him. "Wait, Dylan."

"Wait?" Unease curled in his stomach.

Why was she pulling away from him? When he'd caught her leaving the room, exactly where the hell had she been headed?

"I'm sorry, Dylan." Sadie fixed her underwear and stood. The hard truth hit him like a punch in the gut.

Sadie was leaving him.

No!

She loved him. She wouldn't leave him. It was something else. It had to be. Something stupid. Another nightmare. Sleepwalking.

He was almost afraid to ask. "Sadie, where are you going?"

She stared into his eyes, searching for forgiveness. "I am truly sorry."

"Sadie, what's wrong?" He swallowed as the knot in his throat became painfully large. "Honey?"

She sucked in a deep breath. "I faked my orgasm . . . and I've been having these sexy, no weird, no . . . damn it . . . they're not about you, that's for sure, but—" Sadie sputtered, looking baffled by her own feelings. "I can't do this."

"What do you mean?" He stepped closer, wanting to yank her into an unrelenting embrace and never let go, yet afraid to touch her for fear she'd reject him.

She provided no response.

He didn't know what hurt more, her revelations, or her silence. All week she'd been acting weird. He'd noticed her waking from sleep in a sweat, but she'd promised him all was fine every time he inquired. Why had she lied?

"Sadie, what . . . ? I'm confused. I love you. Talk to me."

She turned and he jumped in front of her, blocking her path.

"I have to go, Dylan. I'm sorry." She attempted to brush past him, but he caught her by the arm, forcing her to face him.

"At least tell me something, Sadie," he begged, searching her eyes for some sort of answer. "When do you plan to return?"

She lifted her chin, a sudden spark lighting her expression as a slight smile curved her lips. "When you catch me."

With that, Sadie grabbed the handle to her suitcase and headed for the door. She was still in her nightgown, but she didn't care. She had to get out of there.

Desire still ravaged her unfulfilled body, cream dripping from between her thighs. She squeezed her vaginal muscles, wishing the deep need would vanish. Wishing there was some way to fulfill her increasingly lustful, but never satisfied, appetite.

Dylan sure wasn't fulfilling her.

Once again, she hadn't experienced an orgasm. She'd faked it.

Until they'd moved in together, she'd been dealing. Why did his constant presence suddenly make her feel so smothered? Not to mention that damn sexy cop from her dreams who wouldn't stop invading her mind whenever she closed her eyes.

What the hell was wrong with her? Any other woman would be drooling to get on with the wedding, but not her. Hell, she didn't even have a very good reason.

Dylan loved and supported her, but he never pressured her—about anything. Time and again he'd offered her an out from the wedding, or to stall their parents, which she'd declined.

She wanted to marry him. She *did* love him.

So why did settling down seem so difficult to face?

She hadn't climaxed during their lovemaking tonight, but she had realized something important. Like a fire needs oxygen, she needed excitement. As much as she loved him, she needed something more. She couldn't spend the rest of her life faking it.

Part of her almost wished he'd stop her from leaving, that he'd put his foot down, tell her how it was. That he'd take control, be a little masterful.

But Dylan was too nice a guy for that.

This whole situation was too picture-perfect for her. She didn't want to go, but she couldn't stay.

She hoped all she needed was one last fling, a little chance to rebel before the big day. To get her bearings straight so she didn't feel like giving up single life was comparable to relinquishing chocolate. She needed to do something wild, something to remember when life became boring and their flame died out. Something to dream on.

When he'd asked her when she'd return, her plan had instantly formed. They'd play a game, a little sport of hide-and-seek, catch me if you can. Give life a juggle, toss things up between them.

It was that or call off the wedding.

Maybe she was freaking. Maybe she was nuts.

If she were really lucky, the game would even improve their relationship, particularly in bed. Realistically, she accepted that not every sexual encounter could be a blow-your-mind experience, but then not every sexual encounter began and ended in the missionary position. She longed to take their lovemaking to higher levels. She wanted to ask Dylan to go down on her, to eat her out, hell, to fuck her in the ass. Yeah.

Right. Sadie could just imagine the conniption fit her conservative lawyer fiancé would have if she asked for *that* out loud. A hundred times she'd considered calling off the wedding, leaving Dylan, telling him she needed her space. But the thought of *that* tore her heart in two. Whenever she visualized herself going, she'd remember his dimples, some sweet miscellaneous thing he'd done for her, the way his innocent kisses made her feel like a princess. She turned to mush, unable to act.

No. This was the best solution. One last fling. She needed it.

As she dragged her suitcase down the hall, her eyes caught sight of a brilliant red hibiscus flower she'd shot a photograph of in Hawaii. *Perfect*.

She grabbed the photo, carrying it with her. At the front door, she took a moment to carefully prop the picture next to a snapshot of them on vacation. There. Dylan could figure out the rest—if he wanted her.

Dylan sat stunned. Sadie was leaving him? How the hell was he supposed to *catch* her?

In the distance, her car door slammed. The sound crashed through his heart, making him jump.

Damn it! He couldn't just let her go. He had to stop her.

Running naked through the living room, Dylan thought twice about his current state of dress, decided he didn't care, and dodged out the door. "Sadie!"

She backed down the short lane and into the road as he frantically ran after her. "Sadie! Sadie, wait! Damn it, stop the car!"

Tomorrow he'd get calls about waking the whole neighborhood with his yelling. If there was one thing he'd learned since he'd moved out of the city, it was that the suburbs were less forgiving about noise.

But he didn't give a hoot. He just hoped no one looked out their window and got an eyeful.

"Sadie!"

Her black Mercedes sped off, abandoning him.

"Shit!" Dylan slammed a fist through empty air.

He turned and headed inside. What the hell did he do now? He'd be damned if he'd let Sadie slip through his fingers. If only he'd acted faster, maybe he would have caught her.

But he wouldn't make the same mistake twice.

As he walked over the threshold, he noticed the telephone table. On it, a close-up photograph of a brilliant red flower was propped against a picture of them in Hawaii.

Normally, they left messages for each other on the notepad beside the phone. Clearly, she was communicating with him through the photo.

He picked the picture up, realization sinking in. Sadie really did want him to catch her. She was toying with him.

But *why*?

Carrying the picture, he sat naked on the leather sofa and stared at the flower. He remembered clearly where and when the photo had been taken—their vacation to Sadie's favorite little beach, a small, secluded stretch of white sand on the Hawaiian island of Kauai.

He sighed and ran a hand through his hair. Memories of their nine days there played through his mind. Being secluded like that had brought them together in an intimate way, yet . . .

Like always, he'd held back, tempted to try new things, but afraid of scaring her away.

Looks like he'd done that anyway.

He loved Sadie for her wild streak. Sometimes he wished he could break free and be more like her. Sadie had spirit. There was magic in her hazel eyes. It had been her strong character that had drawn him to her, made him love her. She was so different from everything he knew.

He hung his head, resting his elbows on his knees. They were such opposites. Raised by Brothers in a private, all-boys Catholic boarding school, with two attorneys for parents who never so much as cast a flirty glance at each other, he hadn't had much of a chance to be like Sadie. And just look at her parents. They were about as kooky and fun as a couple could be, despite how they tried to put on airs.

Dylan wanted to change. He needed to, as much for himself as for Sadie. No way would he tolerate his wife faking orgasms. He couldn't deny they both needed a little more spice in their sex life.

Sadie always said she loved him because he was so different from her. That he was just what she needed. Now, he wasn't so sure.

He sighed and focused on the picture. Was this simply one of her wild moments or was it something more? She'd made it no secret that she was a little freaked about marriage from the day he'd proposed. Now she was having nightmares, which until tonight he'd thought were nothing more than bad dreams.

But after what she'd admitted tonight, he had no doubt. His fiancé had cold feet.

And it was up to him to warm them up.

two

Dylan faked a cough. "Sorry, Mike, this is one nasty cold. I won't be able make it to court. I could ask for a postponement, but I thought you could cover for me. Any chance?"

He followed with an exaggerated sneeze. He hoped he wasn't as bad at faking it as he sounded. Maybe he needed lessons from Sadie.

He couldn't believe he'd even considered ditching his client to chase after her. But the lawsuit was an open-and-shut case. A drunk driver had backed into a man in a wheelchair. What judge wouldn't award damages?

"The Miller case?"

"That's the one."

Mike half sighed, half groaned as he asked, "The files are in your office?"

"Celia can get them for you. All the information you'll need is there." Dylan coughed again, this time louder. "Celia can take care of the rest of my schedule for the next few days. If I come in, I'll just make everyone sick."

He coughed again, twice.

"You owe me one, Dylan. I planned to take a half day. I—"

"Great. Thanks, Mike." He hung up before Mike could change his mind.

Guilt settled in Dylan's heart. He couldn't believe he'd lied to his partner. Ditched his client on court day. He had to be crazy.

And he was. For Sadie.

Hell, he'd do anything to get her back.

Besides, after a long, sleepless night filled with intense thinking, he'd decided it was high time he revealed the secret side of himself to her. The truth was, he'd always figured once they were married he could talk to her about exploring sex. Things would be more comfortable then, more open. And if she rejected his advances, at least he wouldn't need to worry about losing her.

But now, he was on the edge of losing her anyway.

Maybe he should take the advice Mike had given him a few weeks ago while they were working off some steam on the greens, discussing Dylan's ever-growing stress level. He worked too much and played too little. He needed to let loose, and considering the natural way being an uptight, overworried perfectionist came to him, his best bet was to start doing the opposite of everything normal to him.

Now that sounded like a plan. The more he thought about it, the better it seemed. Perfect, in fact. From here on out, everything he did would be contradictory to his character, disobedient of his thoughts. He might still think like the old Dylan, but he would *behave* like the opposite of himself.

His mind went wild with the possibilities. There were so many things he wanted to try with Sadie—naughty, dirty things he'd never dare attempt. Until now . . .

For starters, he wanted to give his little runaway a good spanking. He was almost positive she'd enjoy getting what she deserved. Maybe he'd even tie her up.

He coughed, half from habit, half from shock at himself. Maybe he'd gotten carried away.

Good. It was high time he did.

Ever since making love to sweet, sweet, innocent Dora, Dylan had been sexually paralyzed.

His mind flipped back in time. Perhaps it had been the alcohol from the dorm party, or maybe he'd become too comfortable too early in their three-month relationship.

And yet, aroused as he had been, he hadn't been able to contain himself . . .

He pressed his prick to the tight bud of her anus, grasping her hips as he prepared to take to her.

She lurched forward, pulling away. "What are you doing?"

Dora threw herself onto her back, crab walking the length of the bed until she pressed against the headboard. She glared at him like he was a rat or worse. "Ew, Dylan!"

His cock instantly melted as embarrassment inflamed his face. "I just thought—"

"Ew!" Shaking her head, she leapt from the bed, quickly gathering her clothes. "My friends told me you'd be just as bad as that nasty roommate of yours. They told me to stay away from this dorm."

Mortified, Dylan watched her rapidly throw on clothes as if poisonous gas had just filled the room.

Dora was the only woman he'd ever been with—all of twice at that—and he'd just made a huge idiot out of himself.

What had he thought he was doing? He wasn't Maxim. Maxim was a player. He wasn't. Maxim dated loose women. He didn't.

Dora was a good girl. Sweet. Innocent. He couldn't pull shit like that.

Damn, damn, damn!

He should have never flipped her onto her stomach. He should have stuck to missionary.

Missionary worked.

"Dora, please. I . . . you . . ." What could he say? He'd fucked up—big time.

"Whatever. I'm outta here." She grabbed her purse from his dresser, slinging it over her shoulder, and walking briskly to the door.

Was that it? It was over?

No!

He caught her arm. "Wait. Dora, don't go. I'm sorry."

"Sorry?" She whirled around, her eyes filled with disgust. "That was really gross. What were you thinking?"

A single tear slid down her cheek, cementing his feelings of guilt and shame. "I'm sorry. I had too much to drink, that's all."

She stared at him so long, so hard, he could have sworn she was about to dump him. More tears rolled down her face and he wiped them away. "Please, Dora, don't go."

She bit her lower lip, nodding. "You kinda scared me. I thought, I didn't know, I—"

"Shhh. It's entirely my fault. I didn't mean to scare you. I wasn't thinking. I missed, that's all." He drew her into his arms and held her tight. "I promise, never again, okay?"

"Okay," she sniffled, softening in his embrace.

Thank God.

Eight months he'd dated Dora. Eight months of the missionary position, afraid he'd touch her the wrong way and upset her again. Afraid she'd dump him.

Eventually, she had anyway, with some mumbled excuse about how they had no chemistry.

All these years and he'd never forgotten the way Dora had glared at him that night. How many times he'd wanted to break free of the missionary position, to touch Sadie in new, more interesting ways.

But he'd been so afraid of losing her . . . so afraid of seeing *that* look again. Disgust.

Damn it, if it was sexual excitement Sadie wanted, she'd get it. In fact, she was in for a surprise. He was going to show her the time of her life, right in his arms.

But Sadie *was* coming home, no matter how he had to persuade her.

The wind whipped her hair, bouncing the short, golden curls in her face. The salty ocean air tickled her senses. Slowly, Sadie guided the rented speedboat into the well-remembered cove nestled between high, pleated cliffs covered in rich green vegetation.

The beach, *her* beach, stretched about a hundred yards wide, the white sands welcoming her like outstretched arms.

Sadie breathed a huge sigh of relief.

Since she'd left Dylan two days ago, every moment of her travels had been filled with self-doubt and uncertainties. Would he understand her message from the pictures? Had he even seen them?

Was he hot on her trail right now? How close?

What if he'd opted to stay home, to end their engagement? He was so obsessive about his work. What if he chose his job over her? She wouldn't be surprised.

She didn't care. This was something she had to do. Her midnight escape was as much a test as a game, a way to see if she could return panic-free to a settled life after a little excitement, but even more, to see if Dylan could cut loose and ditch responsibilities for a little fun. If he couldn't, how could she ever truly be happy with him?

She loved him for who he was. She did. In fact, she'd never seen a sexier sight than when he was dressed in his suit, ready for court. But she couldn't change who *she* was for him.

She dropped anchor and lifted her face to the Kauai sun. Life was all about enjoyment, just like this. She loved the Hawaiian Islands enough to daydream about both of them abandoning their busy lives and starting their family here.

The sudden ring of her cell phone cut through her whimsical thoughts, surprising her. How the hell was it working out here? The commercials must be true.

She laughed to herself. She hated that advertisement with a vengeance. It received no kudos from her, though, because although the beach was secluded, Princeville wasn't that far away, just separated by thick forests and mountainous cliffs. Besides, the boat likely had an onboard booster.

Digging the phone free from her bag, she checked the caller ID. Dylan.

Should she answer?

Anticipation rippled through her and excitement swelled her heart. She couldn't resist.

She punched the green button, holding it to her ear.

"When I catch you, do you have any idea what I'll do to you?" Dylan's deep voice, his tone as hard as stone, asked her.

A thrill surged through Sadie and rendered her speechless.

"When I catch you, dear Sadie, you're going to meet a man you've never met before. A man previously suppressed and now freed." Dylan paused, allowing her a moment to wonder. "I'm going to do things to your body you'd never expect. Touching, caressing, exploring every inch of you in every way I can."

"Oh, really?"

"Really. I'm going to explore uncharted territory. Make you beg. Scream."

"Scream?"

"That's how much I'm going to fuck you," he told her. "Are you ready for that, Sadie?"

Sensation coursed down her spine, and warmth spread through her, her clit instantly pulsing in reaction. Ready? God. Her tongue was tied. "I, um . . . I want to . . . um . . ."

So, she'd never talked dirty before. Well, maybe once or twice in college. But she'd been drunk. Sober, she clearly sucked at it.

As much as she traveled for work, on photography assignments, Dylan had never called her like this. In fact, he'd never even talked to her like this in person.

She gulped, searching her mind for the perfect sentence.

"Ah, sweet Sadie. You think you're so worldly with all your travels." He chuckled, slow and long, sounding dark and dangerous. "I'm going to make you have so much fun you'll grow tired of excitement. Do me a favor, Sadie?"

"Yes?" she half breathed, half squeaked.

"Slide your hand across your breast. Let it slip slowly over that silky skin of yours, running over your nipples." His voice turned deeper, huskier, forcing her to follow his command. "I know those little buds are rock hard right now, aren't they? Are you dripping for me?"

"Yes." She clenched herself as her hands massaged her breasts, sensation shooting around her areolas. "Yes."

She couldn't believe what she was doing. She'd masturbated before, sure, but never at a man's instruction, and certainly not over the phone. Even if he couldn't see her, she felt so exposed. Raw.

"Slide your hand down, Sadie, and touch your pussy."

She shook as she moved her fingers south, compelled by his commands as much as by her body's own need, and dove between her wet lips.

"Dylan . . ."

"Rub your clit, Sadie, in tiny circles. Make yourself hot for me."

"Dylan . . ." A weak protest flitted from her lips.

As if she could stop.

She worked the tense bundle of nerves, her loins flooding with arousal.

"Now, Sadie, slide your fingers deeper. Explore the rest of your cunt," he issued. "For me."

She obeyed him, slipping two digits deep inside her. Her touch was not enough. She needed him like she'd never needed him before. He'd never talked to her this way or used such frank language before. She loved it. Unable to contain the animalistic noise, she moaned, and impatiently awaited his next command.

Silence echoed over the line. "Dylan?"

She slid her fingers free, taking a step back. "Dylan? Dylan?"

No, no, no! The bastard had to be playing a cruel joke on her. Keeping quiet just to tease her.

So he thought himself a wiseass? She'd show him funny.

"Dylan." She took two steps over. "Can you feel me now?" She stepped again. "Can you feel me now?"

Silence.

Damn.

The line *was* dead. Had she lost the signal? Or had Dylan hung up on her and left her hanging? The bastard! Wait until she got her hands on him.

But then again . . .

He'd sounded so different over the line. Sexual. Primitive. Like a caveman.

She envisioned herself as his prey. When he caught her, what would he do? She couldn't restrain her fingers as she reminisced over his commands, imagining herself at his mercy. Her hand slipped between her folds, plunging deeper, moving faster, as she pondered the possibilities.

The tune of her cell phone sliced through her fantasy and jerked her into reality.

Shit.

She yanked her fingers free, the scent of her arousal mingling with the salty air. Heat rushed to her face as if she'd been caught.

Thank God this beach was secluded.

She reached for her phone, positive it was Dylan, the teasing jerk.

But that was too good to be true. Instead, her mother's number glowed on the display. Great.

Sadie chose to ignore the call.

The annoying jingle continued and continued. Knowing her mother, she wouldn't stop. Not when she had something to say or complain over, especially—

Oh shit! She'd agreed to meet her mother for lunch today, and after, they had an appointment with the florist.

Damn.

Feeling guilty, Sadie released a breath of air. Not that she'd been looking forward to selecting the flowers anyway. When it came to the wedding, no matter what she chose, her mother disagreed, and Dylan's mother eventually disapproved as well.

But as trying as her mother was, she'd left her hanging. Again.

The phone continued to ring. Sadie's nerves spilt and frayed. She didn't want to deal with this right now, didn't want to face it, but she *should*.

She had two choices. Answer it or toss the damn thing in the ocean, and she wasn't about to miss another of Dylan's surprising, sexy calls.

Steeling herself for a tongue lashing, she punched the green button. "Yes, mother dear?"

"Where are you, *hon*?" Her mother's carefully cultivated, falsely elegant tone made Sadie want to hurl.

Sadie decided to amuse her mother and play along with the false airs. "Oh, out and about."

"Sadie, reservations at La Shay's are not easy to come by." Her mother released a long, drawn-out sigh as if their life teetered on the edge of a missed reservation. "You'll be at Dolores's at two then?"

"Not quite." Sadie drummed her fingers on the side of the fiberglass boat, sweeping her gaze along the waiting beach. What should she say? She didn't know when she'd be home or where this would lead. Only that she had to do it. "I'm not sure I can make it."

She could easily imagine her mother's already overrouged cheeks reddening to crimson.

"Sadie, you must choose flowers and as soon as possible. It isn't an option. You can't have a wedding without flowers and you barely have more than a month until the big day. What, do you want to end up with plastic floral arrangements? We've postponed this *twice* already."

And so she had.

"Mom, I . . ." She considered telling her mother the ugly truth, that her feet were colder than a corpse's, then quickly changed her mind.

It would sound like she didn't want to marry Dylan, but she did. Then why was she hesitating?

Christ, she was so confused.

"Mom, I'm afraid my choices will suck. I just know I'll pick something tacky. I've got no taste, no class. Not like you." She paused, letting her mother relish the moment. Her mother loved being told she was classy, though in truth, her mother was about as refined as a drunk with an empty beer mug. "Mom, you're so much more tasteful than I am. Could you do it for me?"

Her mother huffed a sigh as if she'd been asked to save the world on a busy day. "I suppose. You'll just pick something out of style anyway, like daisies. I was thinking white lilies . . ."

Lilies? Weren't they for funerals? Easter?

Sadie bit her tongue, because really, she didn't care. Let her mother have her way. This wedding was for her parents more than her and Dylan. Frankly, she'd just as soon get married in a cardboard box. It was the vows that mattered and the commitment after that concerned her.

"Thank you, Mom."

"If you aren't there for your fitting this Wednesday . . ." Her threat trailed off, empty. "You'll meet me for lunch, hon, at Tavern on the Green. We'll see to the fitting then meet with the caterer. It'll be a lot to handle all in one day . . ." She sighed, long and exaggerated. "But what choice do you leave us, Sadie? We're running out of time, my dear. Don't you dare miss Wednesday." With that, her mother hung up.

Sadie stared at the sparkling blue water, anxious to dive in. A sarcastic laugh caught in her throat. Wednesday. Yeah right. She could see that happening.

Dylan cut the engine of the four-wheeler he'd rented. A boat would've been easier, quicker, but also too obvious. He wanted to sneak up on Sadie. Give her the surprise of her life. Besides, the beach wasn't far from Princeville, just very secluded. He enjoyed the rugged conditions.

He crept through the lush forest toward the beach, his eyes soaking in the emerald greens and brilliant flowers of the rain forest. He swatted away yet another mosquito, the thick humid air making his clothes stick to his skin. He couldn't wait to get them off and get in Sadie. She sure as hell was making him work for it.

The tree line opened onto the beach, revealing foamy waves crashing against pristine sands. He crouched, scanning the length of the shore. The skies were graying, the ocean becoming more violent. It looked like it might storm soon.

Near the bright green cliffside, Sadie bent, buck naked, focusing her camera. What she might be shooting, he couldn't make out. Nor did he care. All he could see was Sadie's lush ass, bent, revealing her pink mons, the way the sun had tinted her skin in two days, making her normally golden hue a deep bronze. The deep longing to lick every inch of those long legs grabbed him, making his cock twitch in anticipation.

She leapt backward as a bird fluttered off. *Ah.* So his flighty fiancée was pestering nature again. Quite typical. Her innocent joy for the outdoors was only one of many qualities that made her so very interesting . . . and lovable.

Sadie wasn't a classic beauty. No, she was as unique as they came, with short, spunky hair that framed her face with golden curls and sharp, strong features. Her big hazel eyes veiled by thick, dark lashes, and her wide smile were enough to knock a man out.

She wasn't rail thin nor supermodel tall. Perky curves accented every inch of her average-size frame. Her figure readily grabbed his attention.

She chased after the escaping bird, snapping pictures as he walked from the forest. She caught sight of him and her face lit with surprise. Squealing, she tripped over her own two feet, falling flat on her face in the sand.

He couldn't help but laugh. Sadie had a way of making him smile, even in the tensest of moments. She was quirky, down to earth. Fun.

Sadie rolled over, giggled, and stretched her arms out like an angel. "I've been waiting for you."

He jogged to her, ripping off the sweaty, light cotton tee shirt he wore. Tossing it in the sand, he slowed his run, staking her out. "You could have already had me if you'd never left. Damn it, Sadie, if you wanted a vacation this bad, you could've asked. Not taken off in the middle of the night."

"I couldn't help it."

He stood over her, staring into her squinting gaze. "If you're going to do crazy things at least don't be sorry for it."

"I'm not. I needed to let loose."

"Then I suppose . . ." He straddled her, slowly sinking to his knees. Scooping a handful of sand, he poured it over her chest. He rubbed the grains across her skin and over her areolas. She arched, allowing him access to her hips as he scooted down. "I am going to have to teach you how wild you could be with me, without ever leaving our bed. I guarantee you this: I'm going to get you home, and then I'm going to make sure you never want to leave again."

"Dylan . . ."

"Shhh. No talking allowed, unless it's dirty." He unfastened the button to his khakis, then the zipper.

"But—"

"Shhh." He held up a hand to silence her.

Standing, he removed the shorts and tossed them aside, then crawled over her, pressing his body to hers. His mouth crushed hers, bruising her with a quick, hard kiss. He needed to shut her up, so he could get on with better things.

three

Dylan rubbed sand around her areola and inward to her hardened nipple. The friction over the sensitive skin sent an electric sensation through her, and the bud tightened further, almost painfully.

His hand slid the coarse grains across the mound of soft flesh, across her chest bone, to her other breast. Tingles amplified by the rough, gritty touch jolted from her nipples to her cunt.

Lusty desire flooded her pussy, her clit pulsing for attention. The scent of her arousal floated through the salty air and carried on the cool breeze. She inhaled, relishing the unique scent, turned on by how very much she wanted him, and the thought of making love outdoors.

Warm ocean water lapped her feet with every crash of the waves, which grew more and more vigorous with each passing moment, as did her passion.

She stretched her legs wide, opening her thighs to allow him full access. The gentle gusts of air caressed her intimate areas and she closed her eyes, relishing nature's touch upon her bared mons.

Ever so slowly, he tortured her with his rough yet arousing touch, dipping between her breasts as his hands traveled back and forth, teasing her with the sensuous friction.

He squeezed both of her pebbled nipples, then splayed his hands, running them down over her body. He dragged his sand-covered palm over the flat of her belly, pausing to tickle her navel.

She laughed and rolled away. "Dylan!"

"I couldn't resist." Despite his play, his voice remained deep. Husky. His hand moved farther down, to the top of her pubic hair. He cupped her pussy, the warmth of his touch shooting through her intimate regions. "You want me to love you here, with my mouth. Don't you?"

"Yes," she breathed.

"You want to feel my tongue in you?"

She noticed him gulp and every muscle in her body tightened.

He'd better not stop now!

Sadie arched her hips, pressing her body along his. "Dylan, please . . ."

Shadows danced in his dark eyes and he stared at her a moment, as if making a monumental decision. Slowly, he licked his lips. "Beg me, Sadie." Bringing his mouth to her lower stomach, he suckled and kissed along her shaved hairline. "Scream for me."

His busy mouth drove her insane with the promise of more.

"Oh. God. Please. Dylan I need you . . . ah . . . *please!*"

Placing a hand on either thigh, he spread her legs open farther. His tongue slipped between her moist folds and claimed her clit. He suckled the pulsing nub of nerves, drawing waves of pleasure through her. Ecstasy possessed her body, igniting every inch of her skin. Moaning, she pressed her pussy against his mouth.

She wanted more than this sweet torture. She needed . . .

"Oh! Yes!" She tightened and moaned as his tongue lapped her swollen labia, each stroke longer, slower, and more intense, as he traveled from her nub to her yawning cunt, then to her perineum. He tormented her with his mouth, licking so thoroughly, she could hardly stand his attentions. Anticipation bolted through her, the rush hot and deep.

She was on fire. Blazing. Ready to explode.

"Oh God, Dylan . . ."

To her shock and delight, his tongue continued its path, and gently flicked over her anus.

Every muscle in her body constricted as a lighting-quick zap of passion burst through her. "Oh yes . . ."

At her encouraging words, his appraisal of her intimate areas increased, his tongue greedily lapping at her folds. She lifted her pelvis, rocking to the beat of his mouth. His tongue plunged inside her sheath, tormenting her with the need to be filled.

His fingers joined the play, thrusting into her. Three of his thick, long digits pressed into her, pumping in and out as his mouth nibbled and licked every inch of her intimate recesses.

His oral pleasuring forced her to the edge, and she was ready to burst at any moment.

"Dylan . . ." she pleaded—for what, she did not know.

His other hand joined the game. Wetting his pinky finger with her juices, he smoothed it over her anus and slipped it into the tight bud.

She lost it, climaxing over his plunging fingers, her pussy convulsing in a tidal wave of heat.

Knotting her hands in his hair, she held on. Her breath came in short pants as the powerful orgasm controlled her lower regions.

Never before had she come as a result of foreplay, without a cock embedded in her. Never before had Dylan touched her so intimately. So wonderfully.

In fact, it was the most intense release she'd ever experienced.

He slipped his fingers free as she spiraled downward from her pinnacle of pleasure. Her body relaxed, every muscle limp. Lying in the hot sand, she studied him, trying to think of something intelligent to say rather than just lie there and drool. To her surprise, his eyes still gleamed with lust.

Grasping her hips, he positioned himself at her entrance, and drove into her. Her body stretched to accommodate his width, her loins heating with passion all over again.

Hard and fast, he pumped. The sand beneath her back grated against her sensitive skin and she prickled with awareness. Thrusting into her, he slipped his hand around her hip and grasped her ass.

Once again, his pinky found her rectum and pressed into her. He rammed into her with both his hand and his cock, driving her crazy.

They rolled through the sand and she took control. Straddling him, she propped her feet in the sand and rode him. Her fingers toyed with her clit, pressing the nub in tiny circles.

Ecstasy forced her to clamp her pussy muscles around him. Holding his cock tight, she slowed. Methodically, she moved up and down, enjoying every inch of his length, his finger deep in her anus, her fingers toying with her clit.

Sadie was sure this had to be a dream. That she'd wake at any moment. Straitlaced Dylan wouldn't dare do these things.

Would he?

She wanted to savor every moment of their lovemaking, to make it last and last. Clamping her muscles around him, she leaned forward so that his pubic hairs rubbed her swollen labia, creating friction with her clit.

"Damn it, woman," he growled. "Hurry up!"

Of course he couldn't take much more. If she continued to toy with him, she wouldn't get to come again herself. She unleashed her control, bucking against him wildly.

"Sadie!" His hand tightened its hold on her ass cheek and she tugged on his hair. She shook with an orgasm, intense ecstasy sweeping through her body at once.

Dylan jerked and buried himself deep within her. His cum filled Sadie, mingling with hers.

She relaxed, laying her head on his shoulder. Contentment like she'd never experienced thrummed through her, her body humming with satisfaction, her soul singing.

She didn't feel suffocated. Stifled. Trapped. She didn't want to run or to do something crazy. She felt alive, exhilarated. Happy. Smiling to herself, she wondered at the glorious breakthrough they'd just experienced. Something was different. Unchained. Wonderful.

She'd made the right decision when she'd agreed to marry him, but she'd also done the right thing when she'd left. How could life be any more perfect than it was at this moment?

A sudden, loud clap of thunder crashed through her meandering thoughts and knocked her into reality. Rolling off Dylan, she sat up and faced an ominous gray sky.

Lightning blasted overhead as Dylan sprang upright. In a storm, a beach was a terrible place to be. Sand attracted the electrical strikes like a magnet. Standing, he grasped Sadie's hand and helped her to her feet.

"Run."

As if on command, rain poured down on them. The drops pelted them hard and fast and stung his bare skin. Sadie squealed and followed his lead.

He led them toward the high, emerald-covered cliffs to a spot where he recalled there was a small cave. He'd discovered the shallow, five-foot-high overhang while exploring during their first vacation here. Ducking under a jagged rock, they crept into the cold cave. Sadie plopped Indian-style on the damp sand and gazed outside.

"Wow," she sighed. Astonishment filled her voice.

He gave a quick nod and crouched. "You're telling me. That's one hell of a storm."

Sadie's laugh was low, deep . . . seductive. Her hazel eyes shined with amusement. "No, I was talking about the sex."

Dylan couldn't help his reaction. He puffed up with pride as satisfaction filled him. Her response was exactly what he'd hoped for. Chauvinistic as it was, he wanted to whoop like a warrior claiming victory. He'd busted through the wall holding back their sex life and Sadie was his once again.

He scooted closer and pulled her into his arms. "I think that's the best thing I've heard from you."

"That was the most incredible sex we ever had." She laughed again, pretending to wipe her brow. "Whew!"

He chuckled. "I know. I meant it to be." He lifted her chin and looked into her eyes. "See Sadie, we can have excitement and hell of a lot of it. Even tucked safely at home."

She nodded, rather stiffly. Her whole body tightened, when she should have been melting. She turned her head, focusing on the raging storm.

He turned her chin, forcing her to meet his gaze. "Please, Sadie. I hate that you left. Tell me you'll come back now."

"Dylan . . ." Her words trailed off, filled with pain, regret.

His heart turned to stone, hating what she'd say before she even said it. She was on the run—from him. And thus far, he'd failed to convince her to cease her games.

Damn it. Sadie loved him. She just needed to accept that she couldn't act twenty-one forever. Everyone grew up eventually.

Dylan ran his hands along the stubble that had begun to shadow his jaw. Emotionally, he was pushing her too far, too fast. Clearly, Sadie wouldn't be seduced with endearing words.

Sex was his best friend right now. If he couldn't convince her mind, he could at least convince her body. A concept his cock wouldn't mind one bit, even though his mind did.

Outside, another boom of thunder shook the world and reminded him of the raging storm.

He dropped his hand. "I'm going to get our stuff before it's ruined."

"My camera!" Alarm inflamed her voice.

"It's waterproof and I'll be sure to get it." He ducked from the cave. "I'll be right back."

Sadie watched him go. She hadn't meant to resurrect the walls between them, but her reaction had been instinctive.

The sex had been so great. What he said was so true. Heck, he'd even put his job aside for her. Why couldn't she be happy with the change?

She wanted to talk to him. When she'd arrived in Kauai, she'd promised herself she would go home with him if he came.

But she couldn't. Not yet. She felt as if he was rushing her right back to the way things had been.

Every muscle in her body ached from being tense. Her heart knotted painfully. Her body warred against the overwhelming emotion flooding through her at the thought of going home.

Home.

The thought was torture to her. Part of her wished she'd had the guts to turn down Dylan's idea to purchase the house. She loved their home as much as she hated it. It was the house of her dreams, yellow with blue shutters, a big backyard, and a white picket fence. Perfect for raising a family. Perfect for living out the rest of their lives together.

But every time she imagined their picture-perfect, two-story home, cinder blocks crashed down on her chest.

After only a week of living there, she severely missed her apartment. City life. Single life.

And more than anything, she hated wedding plans with a passion.

She sighed and tried to think positive thoughts, but she couldn't. Pessimism invaded her normally joyous character, threatening to take over.

She was pleased Dylan had caught her, and even more thrilled by the sex. If only he'd never mentioned home . . .

Now she just couldn't shake these awful feelings.

Maybe she was just tired. She had been awake all day, and without coffee at that. She needed to rest. She could think about Dylan, their relationship, and their house tomorrow. Maybe if they talked things over, she wouldn't feel so oppressed at the thought of going home.

Curling into a ball in the sand, she closed her eyes and tried to relax, positive sleep would elude her. Surprisingly, she dozed off almost immediately.

Unclothed, she turned and faced the naked crowd. While the church had been empty moments before, now crowds of unrecognizable men occupied the pews.

All eyes were on her, their gazes unyielding. Hate-filled.

A man with no face rose and walked toward her. Then another. And another.

"*Did you think you could get away with this, Sadie?*" *The chanting surrounded her, haunting her, making her stomach churn with the urge to disappear.* "*Did you think you could get away with this? Did you think—*"

She hadn't, had she?

Her cop reappeared and joined the men surrounding her. Slowly, they closed in on her, until she felt like she'd suffocate from all the man-flesh in her face. Their hands were everywhere, roughly invading the most intimate areas of her body. Grabbing. Pinching. Pulling.

She slid to the floor, overwhelmed by a hot, fast rush of lusty heat she knew was wrong. So wrong.

Where were her clothes?

The men kissed her exposed body, caressed every inch of her skin with their hands. Thick fingers found her clit and rubbed it in forceful circles.

The cop's cock nudged her entrance and pressed deep inside her in one fast plunge. Her pussy screamed in delight at the invasion, accepting him despite her mental resistance.

Another hard rod prodded her lips, stroking the outer rim of her mouth, encouraging her to swallow him. She opened wide and accepted his slow, smooth thrusts along her tongue and cheek.

Another stranger's hands grasped her hips, running over her ass. A pinky finger toyed with her throbbing anus, plunging into the hole. She gasped at the intensity.

The hands of so, so many men touched her all over. Up and down, fast and slow, pinching her, caressing her, spanking her . . .

Pleasure rippled through her body in burning-hot waves. She teetered on the edge of orgasm, so ready, so tempted to lose control . . .

Sadie jerked awake. Her pussy pulsed with desire. She clenched her nether lips, trying to stop the burning arousal, her body demanding satisfaction.

Her mind disagreed.

Panic swept through her. She gasped for air, gulping, sure she would drown in her own fears.

Breathe, Sadie . . . breathe.

After a moment, the attack slowly dissipated, but her qualms lingered.

She glanced around the dark cave. The storm had disappeared and the subtle glow of the moon lit the black sky. In the distance, the song of a bird heralded the impending sunrise.

Dylan lay beside her, his hand splayed on her upper thigh. Slowly, she peeled it away, ever so careful to be quiet and gentle.

She thought about staying, about keeping the promise to herself to talk matters through with Dylan in the morning, but it felt like the cave was closing in on her. At their feet, the bag that held her necessary belongings called to her.

Sadie couldn't take it. She *had* to escape.

She had to run again.

Grabbing her bag, she crept from the overhang and crawled onto the beach, where faint moonlight enabled her to see. She dug through her bag and retrieved her clothes, dressing quickly. Next, she found a small, pocket album and pulled free a favorite picture.

Tuscany. Perfect.

She held her breath as she returned to Dylan and slipped the photo under his hand. Then she stood to walk away.

An empty horizon slapped her in the face. She searched the length of the shore, finding nothing but dark, crashing ocean waves.

Her boat was *gone*.

Oh shit.

She searched the slapping water, alarm flooding through her. The anchor must have given out during the storm.

Oh shit.

Dylan murmured in his sleep and rolled over. She stiffened with alarm. She had to get going, but what the hell could she do without her boat?

Again, the heavy weight of panic began to build. The need to run boiled through her blood, threatening to break through her skin in a very ugly way.

What if she was stuck? What if she could never escape?

No! She couldn't be! She had to go. *Now.*

Turning to the cave, she quietly rummaged through Dylan's pack for the keys to his four-wheeler. Dylan grumbled, tossing over. She stilled until he calmed, then fished out his keys and ran.

four

Damn it all. She'd taken off. *Again.*

He didn't need to search the beach or surrounding rain forest. He didn't need to call Sadie's name. The moment he'd awoken alone in the damp beach cave and found the photograph lying on the sand next to him, he'd known. Sadie was running once again, and she expected him to follow.

She sure as hell wasn't making it easy. Fingering the photo, Dylan studied the ancient stone rise with vibrant green oak trees growing from its top, surrounded by fluffy white clouds in a perfect blue sky. Beneath the cracked tower, the red tile roofs of tiny cottages extended to the base of a mountain.

When he'd found the picture of the red flower on the telephone table, her message had been easy to decipher. But he'd never seen this odd tower before. Dylan had no idea where to start.

Digging through his bag, he found his cell phone, determined to call her. To his utter dismay, the screen blinked with a low battery message.

Great! Why hadn't he charged the damn thing before leaving?

Frustrated, he tossed the phone back into the front pouch and zipped the bag. Gritting his teeth, Dylan continued to study the photo.

Damn it! Was she *purposely* trying to lose him? Maybe this was Sadie's not-so-subtle way of breaking off their engagement.

He'd tried to give her space and accept that marriage was a difficult concept for her, remaining confident in her love. A week ago he'd been positive she was still head over heels for him. But now . . .

Now he didn't want to consider what this stupid game might mean. He only wanted to get his fiancée home and to the altar before he lost her.

Dylan secured the canvas straps of his bag on his shoulders and crawled from the shallow cave, reaching to the morning sun as he stood. Warmth enveloped his body as he stretched. Clenching his hands at his sides, he lifted his face and inhaled the ocean air, trying to release his annoyance at his runaway lover. At himself.

After several deep breaths, he relaxed his fists and marched across the beach, his bare feet moving fast over the hot sand. He wanted to be hot on her trail by the afternoon, right after he ate and figured out where the hell she'd gone.

Sadie might be trying to vanish from his life, but there wasn't a chance in hell he would let her. He loved her too much to allow anything to destroy their relationship. He'd prove that to her, no matter what measures he had to take.

He couldn't imagine them having better sex than yesterday's explosion of unslaked lust, and yet, there were tons of things he wanted to try and otherwise wouldn't have dared. Now, it wasn't a matter of insecurity anymore.

If she wanted more, boy would she get more . . . more than even she could handle. Though the thought of acting on his repressed urges made his insides quake with a strange mixture of unease and excitement, he knew the only way he'd bring her home was to seduce her, body and soul.

Yes. He'd prove to Sadie that *she* was the grounded, sane half of their relationship. That life with him would never be boring. In fact, as soon as he found her he'd—

No!

His four-wheeler was gone.

"No, no, no!" Dylan brushed aside tall ferns, searching the woods with his gaze.

Could he be looking in the wrong place? He had to be.

"This isn't happening . . . no freaking way!"

Dylan spun around, studying every inch of the thick, green forest. His only way out of here had vanished into thin air.

What the hell had happened to the four-wheeler? Who the fuck could have taken it? He had the keys.

Unless . . .

Frantic, he dug through his pack. The keys were nowhere to be found.

Sadie.

"You've got to be kidding me!" Flinging foliage out of his way, he burst onto the beach, anxiously running to the water's edge. Sadie's boat was nowhere to be seen. Neither were her footprints. Dylan backtracked. Sure enough, Sadie-sized footprints were engraved in the sand from the cave to where he'd parked. No doubt, she'd taken his four-wheeler.

But why?

And if she had, then where the hell was her rental boat?

Dylan wasn't sure he wanted to know. Sadie's behavior just kept getting crazier. Wilder.

"This is ridiculous," he muttered to himself. "It's like you're trying to test me, Sadie. Trying to piss me off." A wry grin formed on his face as he shook his head. As soon as he found his way back to civilization and to wherever on the damned planet she'd disappeared to, he'd give her the spanking she so richly deserved. The punishment she was clearly vying for.

Visions of her firm little rump displayed lushly across his knees possessed his mind. Dylan relaxed in the hot sand and unleashed his fantasies.

God, he wanted to make her pant. Beg. Scream. He wanted to see her backside bent in front of him, Sadie at his mercy, and loving every moment of his paddling. Then he'd fuck her from behind, holding onto her sweet ass and really pounding into her, hard and fast, so she never, ever forgot. So she never dreamed of another man. Of leaving.

His prick grew, swelling with need as he imagined every stroke into her tight tunnel. The way she'd scream his name. Beg.

Dylan chuckled to himself, actually beginning to feel pretty damn good about the whole situation. Oh yes, Sadie would get what was coming to her. He'd even tie her up if the moment were right.

And when he finished fucking her, running would be the last thing on her mind, if she could even walk. She deserved as much—and so did he.

A glass of orange juice, please."

Too bad she couldn't order something stronger. Feeling edgy, Sadie smiled at the stewardess, determined to calm down as she leaned back in her cushy first-class seat. Needing to relax, she'd splurged on this flight, knowing it would be a long one. Nonetheless, her mind raced, racking her nerves.

What had happened to her boat? Would that little folly catch up with her?

No doubt.

Luckily, she had rich parents to pay for damages, monumental as they'd be. Depending on them to fork out for utter carelessness on her part made her seem spoiled rotten—hell, this whole trip made her feel like a real brat—but some matters couldn't be helped.

Until this week, she'd always used the money they gave her for charity, wanting to be independent and untouched by wealth, but every once in a while a woman deserved to be selfish.

But what if she'd pushed Dylan too far this time?

What if he couldn't pinpoint the location in her photo?

It shouldn't be that difficult to find a picture of Torre Guinig in a travel book or encyclopedia, at least not if he really looked hard. The old tower with trees growing from its top was a popular sight for sightseers in Tuscany.

Yeah right, she thought. Have you ever looked in the encyclopedia for that particular picture?

Okay. She hadn't. She'd assumed, possibly ruining the best thing she'd ever had.

Talk about regrets. Man!

But she couldn't go back. Wouldn't go back. Not until she was ready.

Her game wasn't just about sex, though the passionate way Dylan had made love to her on the beach had awoken her to at least part of their problem. Dylan was restraining his true desires. As many times as they'd slept together, he'd never touched her so intimately, nor climaxed with such passion.

Why? What was he afraid of? *Her?*

Right now, there were huge barriers, sexually and emotionally, between them. Perhaps she was a victim of fanciful thinking, but if she married him, she wanted no walls in their relationship.

What if she hadn't run? Would he have married her, and never, ever touched her like that their whole lives? She couldn't bear the thought.

The stewardess returned with her orange juice. Over the intercom, the captain urged passengers to fasten their seatbelts and prepare for takeoff. As she pulled the strap over her lap, her cell phone vibrated in her pocket, creating a sensation along her hipbone.

Technically, no electronic devices were allowed to be on, but she hadn't been able to stomach turning hers off, too hopeful Dylan would call.

She retrieved the phone, flipping it open. "Hello?"

"Sadie, hon, I trust you have very valid excuse. Though nothing short of you being mangled and left in a coma by a horrid car accident would excuse your absence today." Her mother chomped on gum, a true sign she was *very* annoyed. Chewing bubble gum wasn't classy according to her mother, who considered it a rude habit, which said a thing or two about how she felt toward Sadie at the moment. "The seamstress is *through* with you. Christelle is well sought after, and as you're aware, she hasn't time to waste on games. We may be rich, but you're not Arnold Schwarzenegger's daughter, you know."

Sadie sighed. "I know. I'm sorry, Mom. Something came up."

Her mother scoffed. "Something came up? Is that the best you've got?" Her usually subdued country accent mangled her words as she roared into the phone. "At this rate you'll end up wearing some ill-fitting gown from a discount rack!"

Sadie bit her tongue, knowing better than to protest when her mother was on a rant.

Her mother continued, not showing any signs of slowing. "Do you want me to take you to the dollar store for your wedding? Would that make you happier? We can afford these things now, Sadie, and you should appreciate them more. What am I going to do with you?"

"I'm sure we'll find something, Mom." Sadie indulged her, feeling guilty that she wasn't enjoying the wedding plans and the chance to bond with her mother more, as a daughter should.

"I don't want *something*! My God—" Her mother choked back an overdramatic sob, sounding hysterical. "You aren't going to embarrass me in front of the whole world, are you?"

"The whole *world* doesn't give a damn about my wedding." Sadie drew a deep breath, aware of the stewardess standing over her, looking rather impatient. "Mother, I really have to go."

"Go? Where are you? I demand to know exactly where you are! I am coming for you right now. You'll stay with me until the wedding. You'll—"

"Mother, please!" she whispered, sheltering her mouth to the phone. "I can't come home right now. I'm doing something very important."

Sadie drew a deep breath. "I promise I'll come home with a gorgeous wedding dress. Meanwhile, I give you my full permission to plan anything else you want, however you want, even if Dylan's mother hates it."

"Dylan's mother is out of the picture?"

"Mother, I give you full reign over my wedding plans. Take it, please."

"You may come to regret this, Sadie," her mother laughingly joked, then hung up the phone, no doubt fleeing out the door to shop for tacky wedding items.

Sadie folded her cell shut, hesitantly lifting her gaze to the stern-faced stewardess.

The woman gave her a look that didn't leave room for argument. "Please, turn your cell phone off. Completely."

The stewardess pointed to a sign, then waited impatiently for Sadie to shut off the phone. Sadie did, then shoved it into her purse, leaning back.

Once the woman disappeared, she gulped at her orange juice. To her surprise, alcohol wasn't necessary. After a few mouthfuls of the tangy, sweet liquid, her eyelids became heavy. After all, she'd hardly slept the night before.

Sadie chugged the remaining orange juice, hoping she would sleep soundly. She really didn't need anymore sexy nightmares right now.

Excuse me, miss." A heavy hand landed on her shoulder, waking her with a jolt. Sadie jerked, spinning to face her cop. His black eyes bored into her, dark and accusing, as he grasped her arm. "Did you think you'd get away with this, Sadie?" He slowly shook his head. "Not on my plane."

"But . . ."

Grasping her arm, he pulled her to her feet. "I'll show you what happens to women like you on my plane."

Dragging her down the narrow isle, the cop led her to the rear of the aircraft, and shoved her inside one of the tiny bathrooms.

Pinned against the sink in the small confines, Sadie wriggled as he pushed his hips against her behind. His large, intrusive hands roamed along her body and his callused fingers slid under her clothing.

Her shirt disappeared, leaving her tingling skin exposed to his stroking. As he moved farther south, her slacks also vanished, allowing him full access to her private regions.

Seizing her wrists, he cuffed them behind her. His thick, rigid member rested against the small of her back, and he lifted her, sliding his erection between the clefts of her cheeks. He entered her in one forceful thrust, driving her body against the sink.

His fingers found her mons and delved into her moist folds. With hard, punishing strokes, he pumped his cock in and out of her, driving her into a fervor.

Her channel rippled around him, tightening with intensity as he toyed with her swollen clit. Sadie bucked, thrusting her bottom against him, wanting more, needing more from this uniformed man she didn't even know . . . didn't want to know . . .

She had no control of her body. She was a slave to his thrusting sex, her core peaking with a climax so powerful, she screamed, her cry echoing in the tiny confines of the plane's restroom.

Her cop chuckled as his hands cupped her wet, betraying mound. "Ah, dear Sadie, have I not proven the truth to you? You won't get away with this . . ."

The bathroom disappeared from around them, swirling as if the room were being flushed down a toilet. Suddenly the church surrounded her, the pews filled with laughing men. At the front, Dylan stood, his arms crossed as he shook his head, waiting impatiently for her.

All around her, the protest echoed in her mind. She couldn't get away with this . . . She couldn't get away with this . . . She couldn't get away with this . . .

Screaming, Sadie jerked upright. Sweat beaded on her forehead, her body aroused to its fullest state.

She glanced around the plane and her eyes collided with many strange stares. Oh God.

What had she said? Done? Oh shit. What if she'd been bucking in her seat, or worse, talking out loud?

Red-hot embarrassment flushed her cheeks and Sadie bit her bottom lip. She could run from Dylan, she could circle the planet trying to escape him, but she couldn't hide from her own mind.

She shifted uncomfortably, reached into her purse, and pulled out her wallet. From its leather folds, she retrieved a picture of Dylan. She traced her fingers over his smile, wishing she could touch his lips. Damn it, he was so perfect, so handsome, so much what she needed. Why did she keep rejecting him? Feeling so distant?

Studying his face, she deliberated over the choices she'd made in the past week. Either she was making the best decision of her life, or the worst; she just hoped it didn't equate to losing him.

While she was running from the prospect of being his wife, having kids, settling down in general, those were the very things she yearned for most in life. Dylan was the epitome of her desires, both physically and emotionally.

Growing up, she'd never had stability. Normality. Her mom and dad were flaky at best. To say the least, they weren't exactly winning any awards in the parenting department.

Though she longed to live the suburban life, she didn't know how to be a soccer mom, how to be normal, how to live an average, quiet existence. What if she screwed up? Or worse, messed up their children?

What she wanted, she feared the most. Better said, it *terrified* her.

No way could she marry Dylan while having these dreams or feeling as if their relationship was incomplete. She'd called this adventure she was leading him on a game, but it was so much more. It was about healing—for Dylan, for herself, for their relationship.

Crazy as it was, she had to be doing the right thing. She refused to have any more second thoughts. She'd go through with this. She had to.

She'd be ready to go home with him when she *knew* she could go home and stay home with no more doubts. Tucking the picture back into her wallet, she glanced out the window at the fluffy white clouds. Three more hours and she'd arrive in Tuscany. How long would it take Dylan?

She hoped he hurried.

five

This was impossible. Absolutely hopeless.

Pinching the photograph between his thumb and forefinger in a knuckle-whitening grip, Dylan scrolled the Web site page, past slow-loading picture after slow-loading picture. When he found no match, he pounded the table with his fist. "Darn it, Sadie!"

"Shhhh . . ." A little girl reprimanded him, placing a plump finger to her pursed mouth. "Shhhh . . . you're in a library, mister."

Dylan couldn't help but smile, the edge of his anger smoothed by her audacity.

"Sorry." He winked and turned back to the computer, drumming his fingers on the table.

For what seemed like days he'd been sitting in this tiny, sunless cubby in the back of a poorly lit library, searching online for a tourist destination that compared to Sadie's picture.

After a long-ass hike back to civilization, he'd discovered his hotel was without power and the telephone lines were down from the storm. Impatient to find Sadie, he'd rented a car, which he'd been sleeping in ever since, and gone on a search for any place with power. Eventually, after lots of driving, he'd found himself in this library. Meanwhile, he'd seen on the news that the power and lines of communication had been restored in Princeville. What rotten luck. Had he stayed there . . .

Better yet, if Sadie had stayed, they could have been making wild, passionate love in the sand and surf, enjoying his stolen time from work.

Oh yeah, she was in for it when he caught her . . . *if* he caught her.

One thing was for certain: Google wasn't helping. Maybe he should turn his search to good, old-fashioned books. The truth was, computers weren't a talent of his. He had a secretary that handled such tasks. He hated e-mail and preferred to deal with clients directly, a fact he'd never been more grateful for in his life. He swore he'd been through about every sluggish Web-page on Google's list of tourist sites, positive Sadie would've chosen a spot people frequented, but damned if he could find it.

Groaning again, he rued the moment he'd turned the librarian down for help on his first day here. Though he kept promising himself he'd find the tower, he hadn't, and it was time to swallow his pride. That, or hop a plane home.

He stood and sulkily approached the desk. "Okay, I forfeit. I need help."

The plump, slow-moving native Hawaiian cast him an all-knowing smile. "As hard as asking for directions, eh?"

"I never imagined finding something on the Internet would be this difficult, not to mention how slow your computers are. No offense meant."

"None taken." She waddled over to his computer. "We can't reach the modern world on this section of the island. No DSL, no cable, just plain dial-up and lots of complaints to go with it."

She lowered her large body into his chair and he handed her the photograph. "I'm trying to pinpoint the location of this tower."

She nodded, a sly grin curving her cheeks as she looked over the list of sites he had on the screen. "Did you try to search 'old tower with trees'?" she asked as she typed the words into the search field and hit enter.

Immediately a much more prospective list of potential destinations popped up. Dylan's face and neck heated with embarrassment. "I . . . uh . . . thank you. I think I can take it from here."

She winked at him. "I'm sure you can. *Now.*"

She chuckled as she stood and shuffled away, her body shaking with amusement.

Feeling like a world-class moron, Dylan sunk into the seat and scrolled the page, clicking on a few links before, just like that, there was a match to his photo.

"Bingo!"

He practically jumped out of his seat, and was again shushed by the little girl who was intently reading a book way too thick for her age.

He held the picture to the monitor, comparing the two images. The photos had been taken from a different angle, but it was definitely the same tower. Sadie was hiding in Lucca, Tuscany, and he was off to catch the next flight to Italy.

As he stood, his cell vibrated in his back pocket. Grabbing the phone, he noted it was his beloved runaway, and sat back in the chair. Though anxious, he let it ring a second and third time before he picked up, so he could compose himself.

"Yes, dear?" he answered, trying to sound cool and calm. "Any particular reason you're calling?"

"Okay. So maybe I miss you," Sadie admitted, her laugh throaty. Her tone hinted to despair, albeit self-imposed, which frustrated Dylan.

"Tell me you're close," she begged.

"Close?" Staring at the picture on the computer screen, Dylan played dumb.

The connection got fuzzy and he quickly rose to his feet, in an attempt to not lose her. This far from civilization, he was surprised he had any reception.

"Oh, come on. You're getting ready to board a plane here, right?"

Excitement tingled in his stomach. So she missed him. Good. Served her right. What he didn't get was why she kept running off on him, when she clearly wanted to be with him.

"Where's 'here'?" he asked in an interested tone, sounding as if he truly didn't know. He didn't want her to realize he was aware of her location. With any luck, his arrival would be pure surprise.

"No . . . !" Sadie groaned in protest. "Do you want a hint?"

"No thanks, sweetie. Just do me one favor."

"I'd do almost anything," she purred.

Dylan wrinkled his brows, perturbed by the response. "Except come home."

"Except come home," she confirmed in a softer, guilt-laced tone. "I will, Dylan, I just can't right now. Not yet. I need . . . I need you to please come and get me."

Well, at least he knew she felt bad about what she was doing, which only added to the puzzle of why she'd run away again. "Just stay where you are, Sadie," he told her, then hung up. Snapping his phone shut, he muttered under his breath. "I'm coming for you, babe."

Today was her sixth day in Lucca. Sadie tapped her fingers on the small, marble-top café table, counting the days. Almost a week she'd waited for Dylan, watching for him out of the corner of her eye, mistaking strangers for her lover. She saw Dylan everywhere, yet nowhere.

Feeling hopeless, Sadie traced her thumb along the curved rim of the dainty, porcelain cup filled with steamy, black coffee. Maybe he wasn't coming. Maybe—

Wait! There he was!

She leapt from her seat, toppling the ornate cast-iron chair over with a loud clunk. Running from the café into the street, she jumped on Dylan's back, and bear-hugged him with a piercing squeal.

"You need serious help, lady." An angry voice reprimanded.

The annoyed man, who was totally *not* Dylan, peeled her hands from his shoulders, dropping her to the ground as if she was dangerous. Whirling around, he glared at her with blue eyes so cold they were icy.

"This is the second—no, third—time this week," he snapped, followed by a few choice words. He shook his head, motioning to a beautiful blonde standing next to him. "And again, please meet my wife, who's bound to think I'm cheating on her if you continue to pounce on me like this."

Where was a hole when you needed one?

It was the third time this week she'd mistaken this man for Dylan, and he didn't even look like her fiancé! Apart from his dark hair and build, the two men were nothing alike.

She was going crazy. Most definitely.

"I'm sorry," she muttered, her face flaming as she backed away. "It won't happen again."

"Are you sure?" He frowned at her, his eyes accusing. "This time?"

Sadie couldn't help the little laugh that she choked back. Why did she always do such stupid things? This was insane! "I promise . . ."

Another chuckle caught in her throat and she spun on her heels, rushing away.

Oh God. She shook her head. No more leaping on men this week! If she thought she saw Dylan again, she would *not* do a damn thing about it except wave until his identity was confirmed.

If he even showed. Maybe he wouldn't. Maybe when he'd told her to stay where she was, it had been because he didn't want her back, not because he was coming to get her. The heavy thought quieted her laughter. Still flushed with embarrassment, Sadie walked back to her presumably cold coffee, stopping in her tracks when she looked at her table. It wasn't empty.

She had to be seeing things. Crazy.

She gawked as Dylan grinned at her, reached into his pocket, and pulled out his cell. Still watching her, he dialed a number. Her phone rang.

Sadie dug the phone from her pocket and opened it. "Dylan?"

"Caught ya."

Sadie's humor resurfaced, and she laughed out loud. Even from this distance, she noted the way his eyes glimmered with ravenous hunger, lust unlike any she'd seen in their depths before.

The laughter caught in her throat, fading under his stare. He was looking at her like a man looked at a woman when he meant business. Sexual business.

Anticipation tickled her skin and curled in her womb. Warmth rushed through her lower regions, fiery excitement possessing her body from head to toe.

Dylan stood, prowling toward her in wide, deliberate strides, like an animal scouting prey. "I'm hot on your heels and maybe just a tad pissed about you leaping on strange men while I'm chasing you around the world. You better run, sweet Sadie. Run."

SIX

*H*er stomach fluttered and she spun on her heel, darting past curious gazes as she sprinted into a narrow alley she knew would lead her to the outskirts of Lucca, where she'd rented a small stone cottage.

As fast as she ran, Dylan burned up her trail. Both the exercise and the exhilaration left her breathless, but she pressed on, knowing her destination—the bed—was not far.

Reaching into the tight pocket of her slim-fitting jeans, she dug for the key, fumbling as she hurried up the dirt path to her front door. No sooner had she reached the entrance than Dylan's arms wrapped around her, drawing her against his well-muscled chest.

Laughing, she relinquished the key as he lifted her into his strong embrace. He unlocked the cottage door and carried her over the threshold, kicking the door shut with his foot, his tight hold never slacking.

She melted under his rapacious glare, which threatened her body in the best way. This man was going to devour her, and oh, how she wanted to be eaten.

"Think you're ready?" he whispered in her ear, nuzzling the lobe, then pulling the nerve-tingling cartilage into his mouth. He suckled the sensitive flesh, sending prickles across her skin as her body electrified. Working his way down, he kissed and teased her neck, tracing tendons with his tongue, laving her with his desire.

She leaned into his attentions, relishing the way his lips felt on her neck. "I've never been more ready for anything in my life."

"I don't think you know what you're getting into," he threatened with a velvety chuckle.

Carrying her into the bedroom, he cupped her mons and ran his forefinger along her folds, teasing them through her jeans. Her pussy flooded with fervor and the muscles in the lower half of her body tensed in response.

"You were a bad, bad girl, Sadie." He licked along her collarbone, tightening his grip around her waist so that her body smashed against his.

His fingers pressed against the thick fabric of her pants, running along the crease of her cunt, and nudging her silky thong panties between her labia, the touch rough, intrusive, demanding, yet oh so arousing.

"Oh goodie. I'll admit, I was going for bad . . ." She spread her legs wider. Breathless, she moaned aloud from his arousing rubbing. "But what's a good boy like you going to do with a bad girl like me, huh, baby?"

Dylan chuckled, and set her on her feet, promptly swatting her bottom. "To the bedroom." When she didn't move right away, he slapped her again. "Move."

"Oh yes, sir," she giggled, hightailing it into the back room of the tiny, rustic cottage. He followed close behind, stripping his clothes off as he walked.

Sadie practically leapt onto the four-poster bed, sprawling across the soft mattress, her legs wide in invitation. Naked, Dylan sat on the edge of the bed, turned, and unbuttoned her jeans, then slowly slid the tight-fitting pants off.

"Come here," he commanded, rubbing his palm along her leg, the contact of his hands setting her thighs and genitals on fire.

Sadie scooted closer, her clit throbbing, the excitement rippling through her body so intensely she wanted to leap on his lap and take what she needed—his cock, deep and hard.

She nuzzled against his shoulder and pressed her breasts into him. To her surprise, he caught her arm, dragging her over his knees, bottom up. His left hand on the small of her back pinned her, while the other hand moved to stroke the exposed mounds of her bare behind.

"You know what I think, Sadie?" He traced his finger along her thong, between the crevice of her buttocks. "I think you have too much freedom. I think you're out of control. And I think you know it."

His pinky caressed her anus, sending a pulse of wanton yearning through her. All the muscles in her body constricted and she moaned, unable to respond otherwise.

"I think," he continued. "You need to be taught a lesson. I think you *want* to be taught a lesson, don't you, Sadie?" His tone demanded an answer.

"Yes," she whispered, hardly able to speak because she was paralyzed by desire, because her answer was raw truth. She wanted Dylan to take control, to be a caveman, to be rough and fierce. To show he loved her in an invincible way.

Sadie sucked in a deep breath as his hand connected with her backside, sending stinging thrills through her, freeing her from her hesitation. No longer muted by fear of what he'd think of her, she cried out, "Oh yes, Dylan, I need it!"

He slapped her ass again and again, causing her to rear up, arching for more of his sweet punishment. "Yes!" she cried out, inviting his spanking. "Please Dylan, please. *Yes!*"

He met her bucking with more punishment, slapping each of her cheeks alternately as she cried for more. With his other hand, he reached under her and cupped her left breast, kneading the fleshy mound. His hand landed on her bottom with a final soft smack.

With tender strokes, he caressed the hot, burning globes of her ass, sending shivers up her spine. Again, his finger traced the length of her thong strap as he dived between the cleft of her buttocks, running his finger over her anus to her cunt.

He toyed with her clit, rubbing the bundle of nerves. Pleasure bolted through her, and she clenched her vaginal muscles, longing to be deeply filled.

"Dylan, I need . . ."

"Shhh . . ." He patted her ass. "You'll get what I give you. What *I* think you need."

He returned to toying with her pussy, stroking the wet folds and teasing her pulsing nub. With two fingers, he entered her, fucking her vigorously with his hand.

Sadie cried out, closer than ever to experiencing an orgasm simply from foreplay. Bucking against his hand, she pushed for more.

Dylan slid another digit into her slick depths, then another, filling her with four fingers. His hand pumped in and out of her in a steady rhythm, matching the thrusting beat of her eager hips as his thumb pressed the tender area between her rectum and slit.

Sadie clutched the sheets, on the brink of explosion, when Dylan withdrew his hand, swatting her behind. The muscles of her vagina pulsed, her abandoned pussy yearning to be filled again. Every inch of her loins tingled, alive with pleasure.

Need.

Satisfaction.

This was exactly what she required to erase her nightmares.

At the reflection, images of her cop and the things he'd done to her in her dreams raced through her mind, heightening her arousal. She hated the fact that she was so attracted to this nonexistent man, yet the yearning she felt at the simple thought of him was uncanny.

Dylan's hand ran softly along her side, leaving a trail of sensation as Sadie slid from his legs so her face was in his lap.

She grasped his long, thick erection and licked the precum glistening on the wide mushroom helmet, then kissed the tip, running her tongue down the shaft ever so slowly.

From his balls to his apex, she licked him, paying special attention to the sensitive, soft spot below his head, then the thick blue vein along the underside of his cock.

Dylan knotted his fingers in her hair and guided her to swallow him. Following his lead, she took him in her mouth, relaxing so that he easily slid down her throat. She wrapped her tongue around his thickness and savored his salty taste.

"Damn," Dylan ground out between his teeth. "So good."

His body tensed as he used his grasp on her short locks to guide her, increasing the pace at which she pumped his length into her mouth. Faster and faster she swallowed him, relishing the sensational feel of his rod running along her cheek and tongue.

His grip on her hair tightened and he tensed, informing Sadie he was close to a climax. Slowing her pace, she slipped him from her mouth, kissing the tip good-bye, then lying back on the bed.

Dylan opened her thighs and dipped his tongue into her moist folds, lapping her labia with eager strokes. Spreading her wide open, he made love to her with his mouth, delving into her depths.

Sadie arched as he withdrew his tongue and suckled on her clit. Glorious ecstasy burst through her and she constricted her nether muscles, trying to hold back from the orgasm that threatened her.

Her body would have none of it. She shattered, her pussy spasming as she bucked against his mouth, coming so hard she forgot to breathe.

She collapsed, sinking to the mattress. Dylan smiled, stroking his fingers along her thighs as he stood and gazed down at her. "Do you have any idea how beautiful you are in this moment?"

Sadie laughed. "I'm sweating."

"I wish you could see it." He wrinkled his brows, looking rather serious about the matter. "Wait—you can!" His eyes darted around the room. "Where's your camera?"

"On the kitchen table, but—"

Dylan pointed at her. "Don't move. Don't change."

He disappeared from the bedroom, but was back in a jiffy, sporting her camera. He immediately snapped a photo of her and she rushed to smile.

"No, don't pose. Just lie back. Relax."

Yeah, right, that was likely. Relax on command? Not possible if you asked her.

Dylan sat on the edge of the bed, slowly tracing his fingers over her tense body. Diving between the swollen lips of her mons, he stroked her silky opening. He really wanted to capture the moment. Spanking her, he'd been so nervous. Afraid she wouldn't like it. That she'd get mad, or worse, laugh at him.

It had taken all his nerve to shove aside the hesitation controlling his mind and act on his inner urges. Sadie's reaction had helped. The more she'd panted and begged, the more he'd forgotten his hesitation.

Now he felt free. Comfortable. *Sexual.* All he could think of was trying more games. Taking things even further . . . hell, as far as Sadie would go. But first, he wanted to capture this moment forever, like the media had captured the fall of the Berlin Wall.

He continued to stroke her pussy, loving the way she melted under his attention. "Relax. Don't think about the camera. Just think about my fingers."

He plunged into her glove with three of his fingers, sliding his pinky into her anus, and fucked both holes with his hand.

"That's it, baby. Move with my fingers," he encouraged as she bucked against him. He lifted the camera with his left hand, the motion awkward, and shot a crooked picture of her, then another.

He needed more. Setting the camera down, he slid his fingers free, and took her hand in his. "Touch yourself for me."

"Dylan—"

Placing her hand over her mound, he urged her, "If I can bare myself to you as I have, you can do the same for me." He cupped her hand with his, forcing her fingers to massage her vulva. He refused to give up. Not now. "Don't make me spank you again."

Sadie chuckled, arching with pleasure. "I might just disobey you on purpose." With a half smile, she moaned and obeyed him, sliding her fingers into the depths of her lush flesh.

"That's perfect, Sadie." Licking his lips, Dylan stood, and stepped back as he readied the camera. As she pumped her hand in and out of her dripping cunt, caressing her thumb over her clit with arched hips, he snapped photos of her.

At first he captured her entire body, then just her head, her neck, her flushed breasts and hard nipples, working his way farther south along her form, piece by piece.

The body as a whole was a gorgeous creation, but never before had he realized how very sexy each individual part was. How sexy she was.

All this time, he'd had a goddess at his disposal. The woman of his wildest dreams and he'd wasted her. But now, he intended to worship her the way she deserved. Never again would Sadie be left wanting. Never again would *he* be left wanting.

Kneeling, he took a close-up of her wet center, of her fingers pumping in and out of the tight tunnel, ensnaring the swollen redness of her desire. The way her arousal glistened like dew on a flower. Honey spread on fruit.

Her aroma teased his senses, compelling him to taste her, but he resisted, and stood to shoot photos of her arched legs, so smooth and long, and her dainty ankles, even taking pictures of her tiny toes, so delicate and painted with red polish.

Only after he'd photographed every last inch of her alluring frame did Dylan succumb to his increasing, almost unbearable, hunger for her. Setting down the camera, he wrapped his hands around her thighs, spreading them wide open.

With one thrust, he plunged into her warm depths, enveloped by ecstasy. His lust overpowered logical thought and his actions became involuntary. He drove into her with a force so hard he moved the bed, ramming in and out so fast and furiously he lost track of all else. Sadie panted and arched beneath him, meeting his thrusts with her own, gyrating and bucking against him as she cried out, begging for more, begging for mercy.

Her vaginal walls shook, tightening around his cock as she dug her nails into his back. She released a scream, coming, and he drove into her with finality, ejaculating.

seven

Sadie woke in Dylan's arms, snuggled in the massive bed, her nude body molded against his. The Tuscan breeze blew over her skin and delighted her senses. She inhaled deeply, the fresh but otherwise plain fragrance of the air invoking a deep-seated inner peace, the kind of serenity one couldn't explain, and rarely felt.

She assumed Dylan opened the window sometime after she'd fallen asleep, for which she was thankful. By and large, she'd chosen Tuscany as her next destination because of the tranquil, harmonious atmosphere. She had only to inhale, to lay eyes on the rustic stone buildings and rolling fields of lush green, and her soul was soothed. Considering the mess her mind was in, she needed some solace. Okay, a lot of it.

Her mind flooded with options she didn't want to face, and she groaned, attempting to roll over. Dylan's strong arms held her unrelentingly, as if he were afraid she'd run off on him . . . justifiably so.

After all, that was the plan, wasn't it?

Peeling his palm from the small of her back, she gently laid his hand on his hip, then rolled over, her heart and mind a mix of emotions as she stared outside. Dylan groaned from the disturbance and again wrapped her in a bear hug. He pulled her body tight to his, pressing his cock to her bottom, and heating her bare body with the warmth of his skin. A moment later, his breathing returned to a slow, steady pace.

Sadie sighed in relief. She needed time to think. After all, her original game plan had been to leave him after each joining, leading him on a sex-filled chase, one that would provoke him to explore their relationship deeper.

But this time, she couldn't.

A piece of her wanted to run, needed to, but indecision held her where she was. One good thing: she hadn't dreamt last night. It had been weeks since she'd gone a night without a visit from her cop.

Was it a sign? Was she ready to return home and be married?

A slight twinge of doubt knotted her stomach and Sadie quickly stifled the thought. Maybe she wasn't sure about running away again, but she definitely wasn't prepared to consider going home today. She simply wanted to enjoy Dylan. Tuscany. Life.

With a sigh, she wriggled against him. He moaned and nuzzled her neck.

"I guess you want a little more of this," he whispered in her ear, using his tongue to toy with her lobe. He rotated his hips, nestling his cock between the crevice of her ass. "You're still here."

"Not for long." Sadie giggled, relaxing into his delicious attention.

He suckled hard at her neck and tingles danced over her skin. She curled her toes in natural reaction. The kisses were tantalizing, so damn good, she could easily give in to his advances, if it weren't for her jumbled mind and growling stomach. His large palm cupped her breast and his thumb slowly rolled across her nipple. "Oh? That a fact?" He rotated his hips, rubbing his shaft along her bottom. "I'm not letting you go."

Desire ravaged her body, making it so very hard to protest. "Not even for . . . hmmmm . . . how about foccacia sandwiches? Real, Italian foccacia?"

"Mmm . . ." he moaned. "Foccacia." His kisses increased, his mouth devouring her from her neck to her collarbone. "You know I have a weakness for Italian sandwiches. But as soon as we eat, it's right back into the bedroom, young lady. I have some lessons to teach you." His fingers traced her ass, hooking the separation between her cheeks. "And I mean it. I *want* you, Sadie."

Excitement curled in her stomach, and she grinned, obligingly pressing her rear against his palm. His hand caressed her bottom, and she welcomed the touch, consciously using his lust to ensure she'd get what she wanted.

"Oh, come on. I thought we'd rent some of those old bicycles— they're so antique it's fun—and then we can go have a picnic in the countryside," she begged, truly craving some downtime with him. "We can pack a blanket," she added as an afterthought, realizing she didn't want *that* much downtime.

"Vixen." Dylan swatted her behind and rolled out of bed, stretching toward the ceiling. "Actually, sex outdoors sounds damn good to me. Be sure to bring your camera and extra batteries."

Sadie frowned and extended her arms, allowing her body time to wake as she pulled the knots from her shoulders. "What's this sudden obsession with my camera?"

"This isn't a dream, Sadie. It's real and I want the proof. I don't ever want to forget, but more importantly . . ." He paused and several slow, awkward moments passed in silence while she waited with bated breath for him to finish his sentence. Wishing she could read his thoughts, she stared into his cocoa eyes and studied their dark depths. A war waged in his gaze, as if he had something quite important to say, but couldn't.

What was he thinking? What could he be deliberating over so intensely? "Dylan?"

He gave a short nod. He looked more serious than she'd ever seen him, and that was pretty damn serious.

Finally, when she was ready to stomp her feet like a child and scream at him, he spoke again. "I want *you* to see your desire for me. You think you can run. Hide. But you can't, Sadie. You're mine. *Always*. Circle across the world and it won't change a damn thing. We were meant to be together."

Without allowing her the chance to respond, he stalked to the bathroom, his words final. A moment later, the hiss of the shower cut through the silence of the cottage.

Sitting on the edge of the bed, Sadie stared into blank space, contemplating his words. Never before had he spoken to her in such a manner. Those words had been from his heart, not his mind, despite all his deep thinking.

She didn't know what to think of him. Of them.

Then her mind clicked with realization. A smile broadened her face and she chuckled. The more she thought about it, the more perfect this was turning out to be. The giddier she was about her decisions of late.

She threw her head back and outright laughed. Oh, indeed how correct Dylan was! She was his, no matter how far she ran, no matter her doubts.

But it wouldn't stop her from leaving again. Not a chance. This game was bringing them closer than ever. In all reality, if she wanted to continue to get closer to Dylan, she needed to keep fleeing from him.

A part of her couldn't wait to get home and develop those pictures, but she was still scared to death of marriage and couldn't resist the prospect of taking a few more photos here in Tuscany, then getting on the move. She wasn't done with Dylan's heart yet. Not by a mile.

Now that he was relieved from the painstaking task of frantically searching the streets of Lucca for Sadie, Dylan took notice of the churches. Small and large, built from lasting stone, and all so ancient, medieval, they littered the small town. Cold as they appeared from the outside, they beckoned one to come inside with the warmth only a church could offer.

They must have passed at least twenty as they lazily pedaled from town on terribly old-fashioned bikes, the roads so bumpy, they couldn't have gone fast if they wanted to. Of course, here, no one did.

Dylan sighed, gazing over terra-cotta roofs. The points of several more places of worship jutted into the pristine blue sky. Had Sadie chosen this destination because of the churches?

Even if the thought hadn't been conscious, she had to have. She'd traveled here before and it wasn't as if one could miss so many churches in such a small town. Hell, perhaps this whole game was a ruse to get him here, so they could have a quiet wedding, without their nosy, overbearing parents intruding. Wouldn't that be wonderful?

Unfortunately, his wishful thinking didn't explain her weird dreams or her lack of orgasms before the trip.

Dylan knew one thing for sure—Sadie hadn't left this morning. Whether her current presence was because of his bear hug through the night or something deeper, he still had her, at least for now. With any luck, he'd proven himself to her. Convinced her to give up this silly game and come home, where they could continue their sexual exploration from the comfort of their own bedroom, without him worrying over losing his job.

Ah yes, he needed to fully sway Sadie and he intended to exploit every opportunity he could to persuade her.

A large, tree-lined stone wall surrounded the city, a remnant from the medieval period that had since grown over with lush foliage. Through a wide opening, they rode from the enclosure and pedaled through ever-thinning archaic neighborhoods of stone cottages and villas.

Eventually, they left all of Lucca behind, taking a smaller, dirt road—more accurately a farmer's path—into a brilliantly green rural area. As they reached the peak of the gentle hill, a shrill police siren cut through the peacefulness of the countryside.

He practically leapt from his skin before realizing it was simply the new tune he'd programmed into his cell phone. A week ago, bored in his travels, it had seemed funny, but now that he'd almost had a heart attack, maybe not so much.

Dragging his feet, he slowed to a stop, and debated whether to answer. He probably shouldn't, he knew that. But a hundred responsibilities prickled at his nerves, reminding him of all the things he'd left undone by chasing after Sadie. Christ, what did his partners, his peers, his family, think? He'd risked *a lot* on this crazy mission.

What could answering hurt?

Ahead of him, Sadie skidded on the dirt road, rolling into the grass as she brought the barely moving, but still barely controllable, bike to a stop.

"Yoo-hoo," she beckoned, her short blond hair bobbing as she whirled around, the sexiness of the casual move reminding Dylan why he should not be reaching for his cell. "Forget—"

The piercing siren compelled him, demanding he answer as if this call was a true emergency. He couldn't ignore the ringing. Whoever it was, he promised himself he'd keep the conversation short.

Dylan raised his hand, halting her protest, and retrieved his phone. Her father's number blinked on the small screen, making him grimace at the bad decision he'd just made.

"It's your dad," he called to Sadie.

No way would he answer. The ringing stopped then started again, stopped then started again, stopped then started again. Bill wasn't giving up easily.

Dylan released a frustrated sigh and glared at the phone. Bill would just keep calling until he answered. Sure, he could turn his phone off, gaining peace for a little while and a pissed-off father-in-law for life.

His thumb hesitated over the green button. If Bill needed to speak with him this badly . . .

"Bad choice, baby," she warned him, impatience burning in her hazel eyes. "Don't answer the phone!"

But of course, he didn't listen. The last thing he needed was to get on Bill's bad side. Besides, this trip, this damn "game" of hers, was about the most irresponsible thing he'd ever done. Allowing their parents to worry wasn't fair.

Hitting the neon green button, he answered. "Hello?"

"Listen, punk," Bill barked, his country accent warped with threat. "I want some answers, and dammit, I want 'em now. What have you done with my Sadie?"

"She's right here, Bill." Dylan whirled around, intending to have Sadie holler a hello to help pacify the angry man, but she *wasn't* right there.

She was gone, along with her bike.

Shit. No way!

Fuck, fuck, fuck! He'd lost her again!

Dylan searched the surrounding green fields with frantic eyes and barely caught sight of her tiny image escaping through a patch of red wildflowers on her bike.

He'd be damned if he'd let her escape this easily.

Dylan cleared his throat, so anxious to catch her he could hardly speak, but he still had an angry father to cope with.

"Everything's fine, Bill, but I've got to hang up. Dinner's being served and—"

"Boy, her mama is fit to be tied, and I've gotta say, I'm downright pissed as well." He inhaled deeply, and Dylan could just imagine him puffing on one of his vanilla-scented cigars, the self-rolled tobacco stick smoked down to a red glowing butt. "The Hawaiian State Police called. Sadie rented a boat, and they found it adrift—no Sadie. I want answers, boy. Where are you? You better give it up right now, or I'm off to file a missing persons report, and believe you me, you'll be the first person I mention as a suspect."

Sadie pedaled out of his sight and Dylan stomped his foot, aggravated. "Tuscany!" he unintentionally shouted into the phone.

"*Tuscany?*" Bill's confusion was as clear as the sun on a bright day.

Dylan released a deep breath and urged himself to be patient. They were a long way from anywhere. He'd find Sadie. Easily.

If he didn't deal with Bill, the man would likely report him as a kidnapper. The last thing he wanted was to end up on *America's Most Wanted*. He had enough troubles right now. And as a lawyer, the last thing he needed was nasty legal issues blemishing his record.

"I suppose you could say we're taking an early honeymoon. Sadie was anxious about the wedding and this trip was a surprise. Of sorts. But everything is fine, I assure you. We're working—"

Bill chuckled with glee. "Oh ho, you mean you're off making me a grandbaby? Well, thank the stars. Why didn't you just say so? You two waited so damn long I thought I'd be chasing after the kiddos in a walker. Now listen, boy, let me give you some good advice."

Dylan's stomach rebelled at the thought. "Advice? No, I think I'm good. Truly."

"Yeah, I'll bet. How long was the engagement my daughter insisted on? Two years? We parents had to make y'all push up the date. You sure as hell haven't swept her off her feet, and I'd wager it's because you haven't been persuading her in the bedroom."

"Sir, I—"

"Forget manners, boy, this is important. If you want to get a gal pregnant, first you've got to get them horny. You know, get their juices flowing."

"This is ridiculous. I'm hanging up," Dylan threatened.

"Are you sure she's having orgasms? Because we want her to be—"

"Yes!" Blood rushed to Dylan's face and he groaned, wishing to God that he could take back time and the ugly fact that her father was right. "God, I did not just answer that!" No way could he allow this conversation to continue. "Ok. I'm hanging up now."

He jabbed the red button with all his force, tempted to throw the phone. Instead, he jammed it into his pocket.

Shit! What in the hell had that been about?

Bill had always been a little rough around the edges, but where did he get off trying to discuss orgasms with him? Normal people don't *talk* about orgasms!

"Crazy shit!" he swore at the top of his lungs, then grabbed his bike so quickly, he tripped over the rusted frame, landing face first in the dirt.

"Fuck!"

He practically threw the bike upright again and hopped on, pedaling after Sadie like a madman.

Your father asked me if you were sexually pleased. He's convinced we're on a baby-making mission," Dylan proclaimed from behind her, "and that I need advice."

A bubble of laughter escaped Sadie. She should have known her peaceful moment couldn't last.

The sun's brilliant rays blinded her as she opened her eyes and rolled over on the blanket. She'd discovered the perfect spot for their lunch on the crest of a hill overlooking an olive grove. Behind her, a field of fragrant red wildflowers scented the air with their gentle perfume.

Lying there, waiting for Dylan, she'd fallen into a tranquil trance, but here came reality and a healthy dose of its wonderful, albeit wry, sense of humor.

"I hope you didn't divulge too many details," she giggled. "My father tends to gossip."

"That isn't funny, Sadie. They found your boat, adrift, and without you."

Sadie stifled her laughter, though it was hard. "You shouldn't have answered the phone. You should have kept right on pedalling."

"You know, your father is threatening me with police reports and *America's Most Wanted*. If I hadn't answered, I would now be the main suspect in your kidnapping." Her mouth formed an *o*. Thank goodness he'd answered, right? How stupid she was for being annoyed at him.

Who was she to complain? She could never stand to let her phone ring either, which was why she'd left hers at the cottage for the day.

Even so, one of her biggest fears was that Dylan would eventually put her and their potential family second to business. Sure, he was young and just getting his career rolling, but he tended to put work first a lot. She'd never been on a date with him where his cell hadn't come along.

Really, why had he even brought his phone if today was supposed to be special? It showed where his mind was.

She wasn't mad—far from it—but when she'd ridden away, she'd ridden away irritated. She didn't want to believe he'd ever place her second, yet sometimes, when he acted like that, she was scared.

Deep down, she realized she should share these concerns with Dylan, not hide her feelings and run, as she had with so many issues. But though she'd tried to on several occasions, she never found the right way or the right time.

This comical episode might just give her the opening. If she could talk without laughing.

"I'm sorry," she told him in all seriousness, not sure where the giggle that followed came from.

"Oh yeah, this is so funny, Sadie." Dylan paced back and forth. "You know, your father asked me if I gave you an orgasm. An orgasm! Who *talks* about orgasms?"

Sadie couldn't resist the urge to roll her eyes. "Lots of people, silly."

"That's ridiculous," he ground out, continuing to stalk back and forth like a prowling wildcat. "I can't believe you think that."

Wow. She knew he was a tad suppressed, but he was taking this a bit hard, wasn't he? Defensively almost, like a kid caught with his hand in the cookie jar, but still not willing to 'fess up.

Clearly her father had struck a sensitive chord in Dylan—being comfortable with sex. Good. In her opinion, he probably needed a healthy dose of embarrassment and recovery if he was ever going to stop being so damned introverted about their love life.

Dylan ceased his pacing, laying one hand on the angled bone of his hip. "I'll tell you one thing, Sadie, my parents would never say such a thing. My parents don't even have sex."

She raised a brow. "Then how did they make you?"

"They—" He moaned in defeat, threw his hands up, and resumed pacing.

"You know, Dylan, I'd rather be like my parents, a little crazy and too open to be average. Quirky. Fun." She paused, pondering her new train of thought. "That's odd, because all my life I've been so embarrassed by them. But I've got to say, after meeting your parents, thank God."

He scoffed. "What's wrong with my parents? They're normal."

"No, Dylan, they're not." She chewed at her lower lip, hoping he wouldn't get angry at her honesty. "That's partly why I ran, you know. If they're normal, if that's what you want from me, I just can't do it."

Dylan stopped pacing, looking at her hard. He swallowed and his Adam's apple bobbed.

Great. He was mad.

"I'm not sure that's fair," he replied in a low, even tone. After another moment, he strode over and sat on the blanket next to her. His hand rested on her knee. "But it's honest."

"That's what I'd hope our marriage would be."

"Growing up, it always seemed so odd when I saw other parents touching. Mine rarely smiled at each other, and yet, they were rock solid. Nothing has ever shaken them. So in some ways, their relationship bothers me, but in others, I idolize them." He sighed and looked to the sky. "We aren't my parents, Sadie; we're who we are, and that will never change, marriage or not. But I did think we wanted certain things in life."

"I'm not talking about *things*, Dylan. I'm talking about the fact that I've never seen your parents hug, much less kiss. They don't ask for grandkids. They do nothing but work, all the time. There's no dirt in their house. No problems. No excitement. Slot A goes into slot B. Every single one of their days is the same."

"Whoa. One at a time." His hand slid from her knee, and he stared at her, his dark eyes difficult to read. "I had no idea you felt this way."

Sadie plucked a blade of grass, tearing it into shreds, nervous now that the truth was released. "I'm not trying to criticize your parents, Dylan, though it sure sounds like it. If they're happy, they're happy. To each his own. But don't you see? I can't be happy like that."

Silence hovered between them for so long, Sadie was ready to leap to her feet and bolt out of there. He might very well reject her for feelings she couldn't help. What then? Though she'd said what she had to, she couldn't stand the thought of losing him.

Perhaps she'd said too much, too soon.

Finally, he wrapped his arm around her, and drew her close. "You didn't have to run to tell me this, Sadie. I'd have listened, anywhere, anytime."

His fingers stroked the bare skin of her shoulder, a gesture that should be soothing. But it wasn't.

The connection between them was so delicate, so raw, it touched her too deeply. She began thinking of all the things she was terrified of . . .

"As long as you weren't busy." When she should have been snuggling closer to him, she looked away. "I just—it's overwhelming to me, Dylan. You're so much like them—always working and preoccupied and sometimes I don't know if I can do it. I want to be with you. I want to marry you, have kids, all that good stuff. But I don't know if I can live like that."

What she didn't say was that she was ready to run, run, run, and controlling the urge wasn't easy. Her breathing became shorter.

Her heart pounded. She was so close to fleeing in that moment, she didn't know how she remained seated.

Except deep down, she wanted to have this conversation. She wanted to heal their relationship. She *wanted* to stay.

Dylan cleared his throat, staring straight ahead. "Sex is like that for me. Overwhelming, I mean. I want to . . . I think these things . . . you know, sexual things, but when I go to do them, it's like, I can't. There are these strings tied to my hands that keep pulling me back no matter how hard I push forward."

Surprised by what he'd just admitted, Sadie jerked around to face him. "But you've broken the strings, haven't you?"

"I guess . . . mostly. Honestly, touching you is almost terrifying at times. But I want this and, by God, I'm doing it." Dylan cupped her jaw, stroking the fine bone with his finger as he stared deep into her eyes. "Sadie, we can never be like my parents, simply because we aren't my parents. We're fun. Our life together will be fun, messy even."

She chose to ignore the fact that he'd just said touching her was terrifying, and go with the bigger topic at hand. "How can we be sure? How do we know it'll work, that we'll work?"

"We can't. But we can do our damned best to work together." Lowering his head, he caressed her lips with his. "Please don't run again. Stay. Talk to me like this. Promise me, Sadie."

"I can't," she whispered.

At least she could be honest. There was no guarantee to her feelings. No way would she vow not to run from him again, not when she wasn't certain she could stay. What if she had another dream, another panic attack?

"Then I'll just have to keep convincing you," he murmured, the heat of his breath blowing across her lips.

eight

His hand at the small of her back, Dylan lowered her onto the picnic blanket, eager to prove to her once again how very much he loved her. "My God, you're so beautiful. Take your clothes off for me."

Nervousness fluttered in his stomach. Fantasies pent-up far too long stampeded through his mind. Though he'd already tried so many new things with her, he could easily think of ten times more that he hadn't. Today, he wanted to take her from behind, to thrust his cock into her tight asshole and . . .

The notion was overwhelming.

The one other time he'd attempted anal sex, he'd been humiliated. But that wasn't with Sadie.

How would she react? What if she hated it? What if she hated him?

That was ridiculous. Clearly, Sadie liked to play dirty. He had to forget his worries, to somehow unknot his stomach, and just do it.

Dylan shook with nervousness as he stripped, his cock already long and thick with need, his determination steely. As requested, Sadie quickly disposed of her jeans and blue peasant blouse. He devoured the beautiful sight of her body from head to toe and gulped, drawing her camera from the pack.

Reminding himself of his "do the opposite" plan, he stood over her, his legs straddling her. Enough with the sweet requests. The new Dylan commanded, and the new Dylan wanted Sadie face down.

"Roll over. Place your hands above your head."

To his delight, Sadie obeyed, and turned over. She stretched her hands above her head, interlacing them, then spread her long, tanned legs. The sight was too glorious to deny. With a deep breath, Dylan swallowed his fear and acted the part he'd always wanted to play.

Sadie listened to the almost-mute click of the camera as he photographed her over and over again, feeling so desirable. Stepping backward, his bare feet brushed her hips and legs as he shot her backside, from head to toe.

Though he hadn't laid a hand on her, having such acute attention paid to her body was arousing, and every inch of her sun-warmed skin screamed for his touch. His fulfillment. All her willpower was barely enough to prevent her from pouncing like a hungry kitty.

Finally, he finished with his picture taking and knelt, leaning over her. His body stretched along the length of her back, his hard shaft pressing against her bottom.

"I love you," he whispered in her ear, nibbling the sensitive lobe. Fireworks of desire blasted through her as he suckled the cartilage, moving down her neck, and across her shoulder blades to her backbone.

Licking her spine, he ignited every one of her nerves. Sparks shot through her as he followed the disks towards her buttocks. When he reached her tailbone, he cupped the round cheeks of her ass, molding the globes in his palms, and kissing every inch of her rear end.

Sadie clenched her feminine muscles, flooded by hot, wet need. Sticky moisture drizzled down her thighs as her clit pulsed, craving his touch. As if he could sense her need, he lifted her hips and raised her to her knees. He parted her and dove into her cunt with his expert tongue.

Uncontrollable, desperate lust belted through her and she bucked against him. "My clit, Dylan. Suck my clit."

"Beg me." He lapped at her, purposely not coming into contact with the throbbing bundle of nerves she urgently needed his mouth to claim.

Sadie knotted her hands in the blanket and bucked against him. "Oh God, Dylan, please! Please suck my clit." When he did not reward her, she screamed, her cry piercing. "Please!"

Relishing the taste of her passions, Dylan took the swollen nub in his mouth, suckling hard, then swirling his tongue against the sensitive flesh. She cried out once again and reared against him.

Dylan didn't intend to simply give her head; no, he wanted to eat her out *thoroughly*, to give her oral pleasure, licking every inch of her intimate areas.

He just needed to gather his nerve. By now, he understood her well enough sexually that he could suppress his hesitation with a little inner encouragement.

This time, he was in charge and there was no stopping him.

Oh yes. He was *positive* Sadie would enjoy having him devour her, front to back.

"Dylan!" she cried out again, thrusting her cunt against his mouth. "Fuck, Dylan, please!"

His fingers dug into her hips as he ceased all her wiggling and deeply probed her with his tongue, enjoying the way her pussy contracted around him. Her sweet juices flowed into his mouth, and he lapped at them, inching his mouth farther and farther upward, until his tongue stroked her perineum, then her anus. She jerked, the muscles of her bottom tightening. Slowly, he kissed around the edges of the puckering bud.

He loved every inch of her private regions until she teetered on the edge of an orgasm, her body quivering.

"Yes!" Sadie panted, moaning and begging for release he refused to give her, at least not yet. "Fuck yes!"

He had a stronger climax in mind.

Straightening, Dylan rubbed his cock along her folds, and drove into her with one thrust. Her tight moisture enveloped him, sheathing him like a glove.

He pumped in and out of her, hard and fast, and she writhed under him. As her hips bucked in rhythm with his, she cupped her left breast with her right palm, and played with her nipple, tweaking it in slow, rolling movements.

His prick throbbed in her cream-lined tunnel as her pussy squeezed his shaft. The motion filled him with pleasure so intense it was almost painful. Groaning, he measured his movements, grinding into her hard and deep.

He spread apart her ass cheeks, revealing the puckering bud he wanted to sink his cock into. Laying his thumb over her rear entrance, he pushed ever so slowly. "Sadie? Would you like it if I . . . took you this way?"

She arched against his hand. "Yes, Dylan. Fuck me in my ass."

Dirty woman. Leave it to her to be so blunt. So inviting.

"I'll be gentle," he promised.

Pushing deep into her sheath one last time, he withdrew, and very slowly pressed the tip of his pulsing head into the tight depths of her anus.

"More!" Sadie cried out and gripped the blankets as he entered the virgin tunnel. When he'd fully penetrated her, he paused, allowing her body time to adjust to his presence.

After a moment, she pushed her body against him, inviting him to ride her ass. Dylan thrust into her with slow, controlled movements, scared that he'd hurt her. Her rectum held him so firmly he could hardly stand it, but she continued moving against him, clearly enjoying his rod in her ass.

Wrapping his hands around her hips, his fingers found her pussy. He explored the slick folds then rubbed her clit in tiny circles.

Groaning from the immense pressure constricting around his cock and filling the rod with ecstasy, he increased his pace, though only slightly. He did not want to hurt her, considering they'd never tried this before. He intended to make sure she enjoyed herself as much as he did.

Shifting his weight, he grasped her wrists, and lowered her from her hands and knees to lay flat on the blanket. Propped on his elbows, he hovered above her, slowly, almost lazily moving in and out of her, so that their coupling was relaxed, despite pleasure so intense he could hardly control himself.

He'd waited so damn long to experience anal sex. He wanted to savor the moment, to relish every stroke and sensation. Despite the fact that he'd thought himself dirty for yearning for her this way, the act was truly beautiful. He had now taken Sadie every way a man could, fully, deeply, and she had welcomed him. Pleasured in him.

He planted kisses along her spine, wrapping one hand around her torso to tease her nipple. He pinched the tight, hard bud, tweaking it. She sucked in a deep breath. He continued his attention, wanting to drive her crazy.

As he played with her nipple, her asshole tightened around his shaft and she bucked against him. He slid his hand lower and lifted her hips just enough to allow room for him to once again sink his hand into her moist depths. He plunged four fingers into her pussy, caressing her clit with his thumb.

Fucking her with both his hand and his cock, he increased his pace, his thrusts becoming wild and animalistic. Beyond control.

Sadie shifted onto her knees, displaying her firm tush to him. With his free hand, he smacked her inviting bottom, spanking her as he fucked her thoroughly. With each slap, Sadie screamed out, begging for more, and ramming against him. Every one of her muscles constricted around him, shaking as she climaxed in a series of convulsions over his hand.

She collapsed onto the blanket, causing Dylan's cock to slip out. He quickly sank his rod back into the tight depths of her anus with one final thrust, driving himself into a jerky, uncontrollable orgasm. His vision went white as his seed shot into her heat, his mind blanking from the extreme pleasure.

As soon as he regained awareness, he rolled off her, panting from the climax he'd just experienced. Never in his life had he come like that. Felt so fulfilled. Felt so damn good.

"Wow."

"Mmmm," she murmured. "Wow is right." Sadie curled against his body, pressing against him. "Talk about feeling dirty. I hope you brought some tissues. I'm soaked."

The reference pricked at his nerves, considering how he didn't want to think of anal sex as dirty.

Of course, he realized Sadie hadn't intended it that way. In actuality, she sounded comfortable with what they'd done and the fact that they'd indeed gotten a little dirty doing it.

"Even better. I grabbed some wipes from the restaurant because I had a feeling . . ." His voice trailed off, too embarrassed to admit he'd planned to claim her anal virginity. Reaching into the front pocket of his pack, he grabbed a handful of wipes. "You're okay?"

"Of course."

"No. I mean with what I did. The—"

"I loved it," she reassured him, placing a hand to his shoulder. "I've always wished you'd fuck me in the ass."

He shook his head at her crudeness, almost turned on by her casual words. "You're something else, Sadie."

Opening two of the foil packs, he wiped his hands, then his cock clean. When he finished, he opened a few more, positioning himself between her legs. Spreading her thighs wide, he wiped the cum from her pussy, awed at how none of this bothered Sadie. Amazed by how, despite his anxiousness, he was pretty damn impressed with himself for going this far.

The sex was fantastic, but her mind was a mess. Torn between her fears and her love, Sadie didn't know what to think. She only knew how she felt and she didn't want to dwell on it anymore, at least not for the moment.

She sucked in a deep breath, sat up, and reached into the picnic basket. She withdrew the foil-wrapped foccacia sandwiches, disappointed that they were now lukewarm. "The sandwiches are cold, but I'll bet they're delicious. I can't wait to sink my teeth into one. Sure, you can buy them back in New York, but Italian food in America can't compare to a meal fresh from Italy. Are you still hungry?"

The mouthwatering smell of roasted turkey, artichokes marinated in homemade sauce, and mozzarella atop fresh baked bread wafted through the air and it took all of Sadie's efforts not to gobble down both sandwiches herself.

"Famished." Dylan sat behind her, encircling her waist with his strong arms. The skin-to-skin contact warmed her. He rested his chin on her shoulder, kissing the arch of her collarbone. "I should take you skydiving."

"What? You better pretend like you never suggested that. I know I'm a crazy at times, but not certifiably insane." Grimacing, Sadie removed the cork and poured them both a glass of wine. "Besides, you've never even gone skydiving before."

She turned and handed him the sandwich.

He held her gaze, his dark orbs piercing. "But I know what it feels like."

"Oh? And how is that?"

"Like loving you." He cupped her chin, stroking her face as he stared deep into her eyes. "Loving you thrills me to the very core. Skydiving, roller coasters, bungee jumping . . . nothing can compare to the way I feel when we make love the way we just did."

Sadie relaxed in his embrace and leaned her face against his palm, loving the way his fingers felt on the delicate skin of her cheek. "Now don't you wish you'd—"

"Done it all along? Yes," he iterated with passion.

Sadie smiled, lifted her face from his hand, and straightened. "You amaze me."

He flashed a cocky grin and sunk his teeth into the sandwich. Sauce smeared the corner of his cheek, and she reached up, wiping the mess for him.

His hand caught hers and she pulled away, returning to her waiting lunch. If she wasn't careful, they'd be making love all over again, and she really was hungry. She bit into the sandwich, her taste buds impressed by the incredible flavor. The creamy sauce was so rich, so spicy, it was almost a turn-on.

She concentrated on eating, downing the meal in a few bites, then regretting the sandwich was gone. Slowly, she licked each finger clean. "So tell me, what are some of your fantasies? The deep ones, the ones you'd otherwise never tell."

"Ohh . . ." He sucked in air through his teeth, clearly not comfortable with answering. He stalled by slowly finishing his sandwich.

Oops. Too much for Dylan? Perhaps she'd push him even farther then. Grinning, she wrapped her arms around her knees as she gazed out of the olive grove, awed by the beauty of the setting sun. Orange and pink colors streaked through the sky among the clouds, the sun a blazing yellow ball dipping below the horizon.

"I won't let you avoid the question, Dylan." When he didn't respond, she continued. "No matter what you say, I won't judge you. In fact, I'll forget within an hour, guaranteed. Come on, what do you want, even if you'd never do it? Share with me!" she begged, twisting around, and pressing her breasts to his chest. "Do you need a little French maid, Dylan, to service your dirty needs?"

Though his humor was strained, he chuckled and stroked her hair. "Cute. Real cute." He wrapped his finger in a curl, tugging on the ringlet. "Why don't you tell me yours, little Miss Bold and Brassy."

Sadie released an exaggerated breath. "Oh, where shall I start? The list is so long . . ."

"Funny."

She licked her lips. "I'd like to try a little food play, become a Sadie sundae and be licked clean."

He chuckled in delight. "I could deal with that."

So he was game? Time for shock value!

"I'd like to have a threesome—not with a woman, though. I want two men." She cleared her throat. "Maybe three."

"Three men!" Dylan gasped, astonishment entwining his words. He stared at her with wide, dark eyes. She couldn't tell if he was awed or disgusted.

"I didn't say I *would*. Just that I've fantasized about the notion."

"Three men!" He poked at her side, tickling her. Laughing, Sadie rolled into a ball and wrapped her fingers around the camera strap, which sat on the blanket in front of her.

Time for some payback for his explicit, very thorough, picture taking. She rolled away, dragging the camera with her.

"Maybe four," she squealed and leaped to her feet, escaping his teasing fingers. She ran down the hill, almost stumbling through the thick grass, Dylan hot on her trail.

Darting naked through the olive grove, she barely avoided him, dashing in and out of the rows and around the many trees. Her feet squashed the fallen dark purple fruits, slipping on the tiny pits embedded in their flesh.

She lifted the camera, preparing to snap a photo of Dylan lurching unsuccessfully for her, when her feet slid from under her.

Her foot twisted sideways as she crashed to the ground in a jerky, unstoppable movement. Pain burst through her ankle and she cried out, bracing her fall with her forearms.

In agony, she squeezed at the only thing in her hand, the camera. Her fingers accidentally pressed the shoot button, snapping a shot of the olive-laden ground before she rolled onto her back to stare up at Dylan, wondering how on earth she'd be able to run from him again when her ankle was most likely broken.

nine

I'm sorry, Mike," Dylan pleaded with his business partner. "I know I've left you hanging."

He was answered with frustrating silence.

Stifling a groan, Dylan cast a glance into the bedroom at Sadie, who lay in bed, her twisted ankle propped on fluffy pillows. She sipped a glass of white wine, looking rather unimpressed with life at the moment.

Dylan leaned against the door frame, feeling guilty. From the sound, or rather the lack of sound from Mike, he was almost glad her ankle was injured. Now he could get her home without a battle and return to work before he wound up damaging his career in a very permanent way.

Still, at bare minimum, it would take a few days to get home and he had another very important court case that he needed Mike to cover. He needed to level with Mike, friend to friend, man to man. He couldn't continue to make up excuses and he sure as hell couldn't continue claiming he was sick. "Look, Mike. I haven't been completely straight with you."

"No shit, Dylan. You might have fooled me the first time, but considering you've been gone, hell, for almost two weeks, I'm not buying the whole 'I'm sick' lie. You know, what I don't get is why you won't be honest with me about what's going on." Mike paused, sighing with frustration. "We partnered up because we trusted each other. Now, if you're in some sort of trouble, or pulling some sort of scheme, I've got to say—"

"No," Dylan interrupted, cupping his hand over the receiver as he walked into the next room. "Man, I shouldn't have left like that. I'm sorry. The truth is, Sadie and I are having problems."

"Dammit," Mike groaned. "You should have told me, Dylan. I'd have been a hell of a lot more understanding."

Embarrassed as he continued his explanation, Dylan felt heat flush his face. "Yeah, well, point blank, she left me. I'm getting her back. There's a lot I can't explain."

"You don't think maybe you should let her go if she wants to leave?"

"No," Dylan almost shouted at his friend, frustrated for having to reveal such private particulars. Not that Mike was to blame for wanting answers, but Dylan felt about as comfortable sharing relationship details as he did talking about sex.

"Okay." Mike cleared his throat. "Okay. Then as your friend, I'll cover for you, but not for much longer. You're going to have to get her and bring your butt back here."

Dylan nodded in a silent vow and walked back to the doorway. "I will. Promise. Just give me a week and I'll be home."

"We need to talk about the McDougal case tonight. You would not believe some of the phone calls I've received from this man. He's pissed. His court date is in two weeks and you've disappeared."

"Sure." Dylan glanced at Sadie once again, concerned by the way her brow furrowed. The way her smile had vanished. The way she stared at him. "But let me call you back in about an hour."

"Don't forget, Dylan." Mike instantly sounded annoyed. "I'm serious."

"I won't. I'll call you in an hour and be home within a week. Swear it on Sadie." He paused, remorse gnawing at him for letting matters go this far. "And Mike, thanks."

Mike sighed for at least the fifteenth time. "No problem. One hour, Dylan."

"One hour, swear," he assured Mike, then hung up the phone. Crossing the room, he sat on the edge of the bed. "Sorry, but I'm all yours now, at least for an hour. Promise." He gathered her swollen foot in his hand, massaging the tender area.

Sadie grimaced, speaking through her teeth. "Promise, huh?"

As if fate were out to prove him a liar, the siren of his cell screamed through the room once again. Dylan groaned, knowing he really should ignore the call, all things considered. But how could he?

"Just as soon as I take this call, on my life." Standing up, Dylan quickly answered his phone, without thinking to check who the caller might be. "Hello?"

"Boy, you don't sound out of breath. Not a good sign," Bill chuckled. "How's the grandbaby-making coming along?"

"Uhhh . . ." Dylan cleared his throat as blood rushed to his face. "Sadie twisted her ankle."

"Whoa, doggie, y'all are really enthusiastic all of a sudden, ain't ya?"

"Ahh . . . no." Dylan cleared his throat once again, this time so hard it made his windpipe sore. "No, sir." He leaned forward and rested his head in his hands. He could *not* handle another conversation like this.

"Sadie fell running through an olive grove, Bill, and she's laid up, so no baby-making going on here. None at all. Not for a long time. But Sadie is awfully hungry, so let me put you on the phone with her, so I can go—"

"Don't be a fool. Your woman is in bed and can't get out. Perfect time to knock her up."

"Oh God," Dylan groaned and Sadie laughed out loud.

"That's what you get for answering," she whispered. "Again."

"Don't be shy. Now listen, I was thinking about the whole boy versus girl issue. Not sure what sex you want, but here is a little well-meant advice for the two of ya. If you want a girl, have her stand on her head after sex." Oh God. Dylan was going to be sick.

Dylan knotted his fingers in his hair, downright ready to pull it all out. "Stand on her *head*?"

"Absolutely. And if you want a boy, put her on top. Aim's got to be right, you see . . ."

This was *definitely* advice Dylan couldn't take. He was so mortified, his face was on fire and his insides tied in so many knots it hurt. Being open with Sadie was one thing—her father was another.

Dylan quickly hung up the phone, clenching it in his fist. "Shit."

Sadie's stomach cramped from laughing. Stand on her head? Oh God. Too funny!

"Well, a headstand would keep me off my feet," she chuckled, punching him in the shoulder. "Are you done with the cell phone now? Or are you waiting for my mother to call?"

"Cute. Real nice, Sadie." A little laugh slipped from him, despite how he tried to remain disgruntled. "What I want to know is why you're getting off so easily. They're your parents. They should be calling you."

"I'm smart," she offered with a sarcastic, but good-humored, roll of her eyes. "My cell phone isn't on."

"Smart, huh?" Dylan pocketed his phone and crawled over her, pinning her wrists. His dark eyes threatened her. "Better watch it. I just may start taking some pointers from your father. When you find yourself upside down, we'll see how funny this is then."

"Don't you dare!" Squealing, she wriggled under Dylan, pressing her breasts against his hard chest. "This is torture, you know."

His grip on her wrists was unrelenting as he gently kissed along her neck, nibbling the sensitive flesh. "I think you like torture, don't you, Sadie?"

Sadie relaxed, relishing every magical touch of his mouth. Sensation ignited in her lower regions, her breasts flushing. "Only if it's the right kind . . ."

He devoured her stomach, licking and sucking at her belly button as he slid her underwear around her knees.

"Do you want me, Sadie?" His forefinger dove between the already-dampening folds and stroked her clit. "Do you need me?"

His fingers dove deep within her, making her cry out. "Yes!"

"Good." He withdrew, abandoning her. "Think about that while I'm gone."

Sadie's pussy protested at the abandonment. "What?!"

Dylan crossed the room and slipped on his shoes, then straightened, grinning. "I'm going to get us some takeout and a nice bottle of wine." He winked. "Miss me now."

With that he walked out, leaving her body wanting and her mind racing. Sadie leaned back, relaxing in the plush, soft pillow and shutting her eyes. Her phantom cop instantly appeared, dangling the cuffs in threat. She wasn't even asleep! Sadie bolted upright, her heart racing in panic.

The dreams had disappeared! Why were they back now?

No!

All at once, the craving to escape bubbled within her, uncontrollable and wild. Sadie's mind raced, reason telling her to stay, an unyielding urge pushing her to run.

This was ridiculous. Her ankle had her laid up, for heaven's sake. Besides, she was having a really *nice* time with Dylan. Why would she want to go now?

Yet the thought of staying grated on her nerves. The phone calls, the fact that Dylan would ask her to go home soon, and especially the looming wedding plans, closed in on her.

Sadie knotted her fingers in her hair, groaning as she thought of the fact that she still needed to find a wedding dress. How many of her mother's calls had she missed? How could she ever stomach returning them?

Could she really walk down that aisle?

Crap.

Her skin crawled with the threat of another hive breakout. Dread and doubts tied her in knots, choking her very soul. The weight on her chest was too great, too suffocating. She felt as if she were having a heart attack, her blood was beating so fast with panic.

Oh God. She had to breathe.

Sadie wiped sweat from her brow, drawing shallow gasps. Why now? Why again?

In the back of her mind, she'd always planned to continue the game, but for more positive reasons. She'd thought she'd done away with the panic attacks as well as the cop.

She had to get out of here.

She couldn't take this awful feeling. There wasn't much time until Dylan returned, and with this ankle, she'd better hurry. Sitting up, she swung her legs over the bedside and limped into motion.

Where was she going? She had to leave him a picture clue so he could find her.

On the end table, the cottage owner had left several travel and history magazines. She grabbed one and flipped through it, frantically searching.

Just like that, she knew exactly where she'd go. Cairo. She tore the page from the magazine, studying the picture of the Citadel, a massive limestone enclosure, much like a castle with huge, round towers. She'd always wanted to see the ancient structure as well as the rest of Egypt.

Favoring her ankle, Sadie gathered her luggage as fast as she possibly could. All the while, she made lighthearted mental notes to herself of the things she'd do in Cairo, trying not to think of Dylan and his reaction when he discovered her gone.

Until now, he'd followed her quite obligingly, but this time, she wasn't sure he would. She'd heard him on the phone with his partner—he'd told Mike he'd be back in a week. He'd sworn it.

Dylan was a man who kept his promises. This time, would he choose his job over her? How much did she mean to him? She knew he loved her . . . but he loved being a lawyer too. A lot, based on the way he worked dusk to dawn.

A sob caught in her throat, followed by quick, hot anger. She couldn't stand the thought of him being fired because of her. How selfish of her was it to make him lose something he cared about just to keep her?

She was horrible to be doing this to him. To them.

Why the hell couldn't she stay? Why couldn't she be a normal, complacent fiancée, and quit ruining his life? Why did she keep feeling this deep need to push him?

While her initial reasons for this game had been legitimate, the fact was, the past few days with Dylan had been incredible. She should be satisfied, shouldn't she?

It just went to show—maybe she couldn't do this. She was fooling herself and him. Maybe this time she shouldn't leave him a clue.

And yet, how could she not?

Another sob racked her chest. If he came after her, he came after her. It was his decision.

Sadie squeezed her eyes shut, stifling her heavy thinking. Happy thoughts . . . happy thoughts . . .

She wanted to go shopping in an old-world, Egyptian marketplace. The Khan, she believed they called it. Ever since she'd watched *Aladdin*, she'd wanted to meander down sandy streets, negotiating with vendors over fine silks and exotic fruits.

And she couldn't forget the pyramids. Who wouldn't want to see them?

On and on her mind raced, her true, heavy feelings suppressed as she convinced herself what fun a jaunt to Cairo would be.

ten

Dylan stared at the empty bed in shock. The sheets were rumpled and tossed aside. The television program Sadie had been watching still played. But his lover was nowhere in sight.

Once again, Sadie had run out on him.

On the pillow lay the absolute proof, a small torn magazine page sporting his next picture clue.

Damn it! He should have expected this. He should have known she'd run again.

Groaning, Dylan dropped the carryout on the nightstand and flopped on the bed. He grabbed the picture, scowling at the hint to her whereabouts.

This time he knew exactly where she'd taken off to. Cairo. The photograph was of the Citadel, a spot he'd toured numerous times. After all, his parents loved vacationing in Egypt, where their long-time American family friends, the Coxes, ran a very prosperous hotel.

In fact, their son, Maxim, had stayed with Dylan's family for four years while he'd attended college. The two of them had become like brothers, and though he hadn't seen Maxim in years, they'd kept in contact, calling each other when they had big news to share, like his recent engagement.

Did Sadie remember his ties to Cairo? Had she chosen this photo because of them?

Did she think choosing a place he was familiar with changed the fact that she'd left him?

Not that it mattered.

While the thought of following her was fun, he couldn't keep doing this. Mike was expecting him back in a week. Tops. He'd promised.

His mind exploded with memories. Lifelike visions of all the romantic moments they'd ever shared, of the great sex they'd had the past couple of weeks, of every silly little reason he loved Sadie, flashed through his mind. Would it ever end?

If he didn't go after her, would she come back? Then again, if he *did* go after her, would she come back?

He had to go home. He couldn't go after Sadie again. Not this time. He just didn't see how it was possible.

The handcuffs were cold and unyielding, locked around her wrists as she marched down the aisle. Naked. All eyes were on her, appraising her body, accusing her very soul.

Did you think you could get away with this, Sadie? Did you . . . get away with this Sadie . . . get away with this . . . get away . . . get away . . .

The chant echoed in her mind over and over as the church faded and she was thrown into a jail cell. The cop slammed the iron door shut with a rever-berating bang. She backed away as he cornered her, stumbling to the floor.

Landing on her knees, her face met his long, thick cock. Uncontrollable longing stormed through her. Her nipples tightened into hard buds and her pussy flooded with creamy desire as her body prepared for his loathed, yet arousing, touch. Opening her mouth, she swallowed his length, his shaft pressing deep into her throat.

He pumped in and out of her, shoving his rod down her throat, too far, too fast . . .

She was choking, gagging . . . she couldn't breathe . . . she needed air . . . she needed to get away . . .

Oh no . . . she'd swallowed more than she could handle.

Sadie jerked awake, her mouth wide open. A bead of sweat rolled down her forehead as she glanced around her hotel room. She could still feel the cop's cock in her mouth, rubbing up and down her throat, large and uncomfortable.

The other dreams she'd struggled to understand, but this one she got.

Indeed, she'd swallowed more than she could handle by agreeing to wed Dylan. The thought of marriage was suffocating her.

God, why couldn't she be normal?

All she wanted to do was call Dylan. To hear his voice. To be close to him. Yet she couldn't. The dreams had returned and were worse than ever. Three times tonight she'd been jolted from sleep, or lack thereof.

Maybe she'd been mistaken. Maybe it wasn't excitement she needed. Maybe it was freedom.

Rolling over, she wiped away nonsensical tears and sat up. Her flight to Cairo left in less than three hours. She might as well get to the airport. As long as she was moving, she wasn't thinking, or dreaming, neither of which she wanted to do very much of right now.

Counting to ten, she limped around the room, throwing on some clothes, her heart racing, her stomach sick.

Hours later, Dylan paced the floor of the Pisa-Galilei Airport, ready to pull out his hair. Clutching his plane ticket home, he reiterated to himself that he was making the correct choice.

Of course he was.

If it wasn't for this damn delay, due to dense fog, he'd be in the air already. He wouldn't be having all these crazy ideas and second thoughts. Hell, he'd probably be asleep.

Yeah right. Didn't he wish?

As it was, it was almost eleven at night and he'd spent hours considering his decision. He couldn't even sit, much less retire to the airport hotel for some shut-eye, as suggested each and every time he double-checked at the customer service desk that the monitors were indeed correct.

What if something happened to Sadie? He loved Egypt, but after all, she was headed into the Middle East. The culture was different. Sadie hadn't prepared for her visit. She didn't know the taxi cab drivers would try to rip her off, she didn't know the language even the slightest bit, and she certainly didn't realize the greater dangers . . . like tourist kidnappings by Muslim radicals.

The chance of her being kidnapped was unlikely, but anything was possible, especially with Sadie.

Sadie's a big girl. She's fine. Stop getting carried away.

Yeah right. Sadie was a pro at getting herself into trouble.

Dylan glanced at the clock. Could it hurt to call Maxim? Maybe his old friend would keep an eye on her. Perhaps hire a private detective to stay on her trail, but . . .

He didn't want to spy on Sadie. He simply wanted to know she was safe.

Taking a seat in the almost-empty terminal, he dug through his bag and found his Palm Pilot. He flipped through his address book, located Maxim's number, and dialed him on his cell.

Maxim answered on the third ring, the sound of music blaring in the background. Women's giggles drowned out his friend's voice. "*Sa'ida!*"

Dylan cleared his throat. "Hey, old buddy."

"Dylan!" Maxim switched to accented English. "Ladies, turn that down!" A moment later, the background noise quieted. "Sorry, I'm having a little gathering, if you know what I mean. And old? I'm not old! Look in the mirror."

Dylan cracked a smile. He didn't think he'd ever known Maxim to have less than two women on his arm, or in his bed, though how he found himself constantly in such situations befuddled Dylan. He couldn't imagine himself ever being in a similar position. The thought was unconceivable. Multiple-partner sex was a fantasy, not something a person actually engaged in.

But Maxim did. His ability to land himself in female sandwiches was mind-boggling. Sure, he was rich and handsome, but his aptitude with women went beyond that. It was his suave personality. His commanding presence. He was skilled in the art of seduction. Women simply didn't tell him no—not that he'd tolerate a refusal.

As much as Dylan admired him, he couldn't help but wonder if his friend planned to live the rest of his life this way. After all, he was almost thirty. "Still no notion to settle down and tie yourself to one lady, eh?"

"Not me, no way. There are too many beautiful tourist ladies for me to choose from. Sometimes, like tonight, I have to bring them to bed in teams."

Dylan laughed. "Still as cocky as always."

"Of course."

Dylan could just imagine Maxim's chest puffing and laughed again, knowing he'd made the right choice by calling. Maxim's live-large attitude was exactly what he needed right now. Hell, he wished he'd been smart and listened to Maxim back in their college days, instead of being such a stick-in-the-mud. Of course, he'd become a lawyer and Maxim had grown up to be a womanizer, career choices Dylan wouldn't trade for the world.

"I haven't heard from you since you got engaged. Are you calling about the wedding? Tell me the affair is still on. I've been looking forward to the visit. My trips to America are becoming less and less frequent. My parents are trying to dump managing this hotel on me so they can open another in Africa."

Poor guy, Dylan thought with a shake of his head. Yeah, it certainly sounded like Maxim was having a ton of responsibility unloaded on him from the female party in the background.

Dylan sighed. "Well, I hope the wedding is still on, but my fiancée has run off on me. For the third time. Not in the literal sense per se. She hasn't left me," Dylan rushed to assure Maxim, and himself. "But she's run off on me and she expects me to follow and—"

"I think *I* don't follow. There is a difference between run off and left?"

Dylan groaned. "I can't put the situation into words. I guess you could call this a game—at least it is to her—but one I simply can't play anymore. She's on her way to Cairo."

"And your wedding is in a few weeks."

The reminder smarted, singeing his fragile nerves.

Dylan stood, pacing again. "I'll cut to the chase. I need a favor."

"Want me to show her a good time? Anything for an old friend."

"Maxim, touch her and die."

"You could join us, you know."

"Funny." He shook his head, laughing it off. "Gross. It would be like sleeping with my brother."

"Some people might think that was kinky."

"Knock it off."

"All right, all right. You know I love getting your goat. So what do you really need?"

"Sadie can be rather reckless. I'm afraid she'll get herself into trouble."

"And you'd like there to be a watchful eye on her?"

"Yes."

"Done," Maxim stated in a tone that left Dylan no doubts. "You're right to have called me. I know everyone who's anyone in Cairo. E-mail me a photo and her info, and I'll have her followed."

"Good. I appreciate it."

"It's no problem. Your family is my family, and besides, I still owe you for all your homework help in college."

"Help?" Dylan cracked a wry smile. "Far as I remember, you never did a drop of work. I did."

"And you made my parents very proud. So proud, they think I can run a hotel alone." Maxim gave a sarcastic chuckle, then sobered. "Your little lady will be well watched over, so don't worry."

"That'll be a feat. The woman is walking trouble." Dylan shook his head, running his fingers through his thick hair. "You know, Maxim, I just can't believe she's pulled this stunt again. I've already chased her to Hawaii, then Tuscany. She teased me, pleased me, then disappeared in each spot. It's not much fun anymore. I'll be lucky if I have any clients left by the time I return home."

"Well, maybe something needs to happen to her, something to jar some sense into her." Maxim's voice softened. "You know I'd never suggest you hurt a woman—I love their gender far too much—

but perhaps a little scare might make her see the light? Whatever you need Dylan, say the word."

Ideas spun in his head. "No, no . . ." Dylan cleared his throat, unable to believe he'd even paused for a second to consider Maxim's suggestion. "Just keep an eye on her."

"Let me know if you change your mind."

"I won't."

"I would, if I were you. I would."

"I won't."

"Just keep my offer in mind and I'll watch for your e-mail."

"I'll call to check in tomorrow, when I arrive home. Thanks."

Dylan hung up, more a mess than when he'd called. Maxim's suggestion stampeded through his mind, torturing him with ideas he'd never go through with. Not in a million years. Or would he?

Teach Sadie a lesson? He should. He absolutely should.

But he wouldn't. He was going home and he could only hope she would follow.

Hope. That was all he had left to do.

Hope Sadie didn't get herself in a tangle. Hope she still loved him. Hope their wedding would actually happen.

eleven

Sadie couldn't shake the feeling that someone was following her.

She'd spent the day at the Citadel, limping up and down ancient corridors, observing the same Egyptian history over and over, all the while hoping Dylan would show. But he hadn't.

Every corner she'd rounded, there was this guy, damned sexy, in a dark and dangerous way, but creepy. He kept appearing, too often for it to be a coincidence. The way he glared at her with his black, piercing orbs, watching her every move, devouring her body with his sexuality, gave her chills.

By early afternoon, her nerves had been so fried, waiting for Dylan a moment longer had been intolerable. She'd gotten out of the old royal fortress and grabbed a taxi to the Khan, in hopes of finding a silk concoction in the bustling market suitable to present to her mother as a wedding gown.

Nerves still on edge, Sadie meandered through the moderate crowd, craving cool evening air, but thankful it was still the afternoon and not too packed. She'd always imagined Egypt as a tranquil place, but in reality it was a dirty city full of life and movement. Horns constantly honked, children ran wild, and a merchant was always calling out, trying to grab her attention. Still, there was something uplifting about the city, and as she shopped, the unease over the creepy man and the lack of Dylan's presence lifted.

She approached a vendor and fingered a glorious piece of ivory silk, her mind floating to her engagement as she caressed the fabric. For months this wedding had loomed over her, and she hadn't wanted a thing to do with the plans, but suddenly she felt compelled to be knockout beautiful on her big day. She wanted to steal Dylan's breath away.

If there even was a wedding day . . .

"Three hundred *paistres!*" The vendor barked at her in broken English, bumping her from her thoughts. "A deal. Good deal. Yes?" He lifted the piece of folded silk, urging it to her.

Pressured, Sadie didn't have time to think. "Yes . . . but . . ."

"A good deal! Going soon!" he threatened.

She had no idea if the deal was good or bad, but she didn't have the time to spend on having a dress made from scratch. Though it was nice to dream, she should find something she could actually wear. Perhaps something with a strong Egyptian influence. That would give her mother a jolt.

Sadie shook her head. "No thank you."

She started to move on, but he shadowed her. "Red." He lifted a bolt of brilliant red cotton, thrusting it at her. His dark eyes implored her, insisting she like the choice. "Red your color."

Really? Sadie glared at the fabric. She'd never worn red in all her life. She'd never considered it. Staring at the too bright fabric, the realization that she'd never tried many things slapped her in the face.

Here she was, about to be married, and she'd never worn red. She'd never done lots of stuff.

She sucked in a sharp breath, eying the cloth as she debated the purchase, then shook her head vigorously. "Not my color at all."

Some things she probably shouldn't consider. Or try.

She moved on to the next merchant and purchased a silk scarf she thought would be gorgeous with a little black dress and a few extra for souvenirs. Her mother and friends would love them. Carrying the small bag, she turned, thinking she'd return to her hotel room and take a nap. Traveling had taken a toll on her body and her sore ankle smarted. For days she'd refused to slow down and the choice was catching up with her, but she sure as hell couldn't stomach hanging around in her empty hotel room for hours every night, where her cop was free to possess her mind, body, and dreams.

No, she was avoiding him at all costs. She—

There he was again!

Sadie spotted the disturbing stranger who'd stalked her all afternoon, resting against the weathered brick corner of an alleyway, his eyes focused solely on her. Her stomach flip-flopped, panic pouring through her body.

Oh God. Something was off. Too weird. When he'd been following her through the Citadel, it had been eerie, but that he'd pursued her here was downright scary.

Every hair on her body stood on end as she glared at the man with the black, hungry eyes, mentally defying him. Whoever he was, whatever he wanted, she wouldn't let him best her.

She needed to get the hell out of here and ASAP. Whirling around, she dashed through the crowd as fast as her twisted ankle would allow, which wasn't nearly quick enough. All she could do was awkwardly limp-run, and with all the people shopping, she was getting nowhere and rather slowly.

Glancing back, she was relieved to find he hadn't trailed her. Still, he hadn't stopped staring either, his gaze focused directly on her. Sadie could feel the silent threat.

The sooner she made it to her hotel room, the better.

The thought of taking a back alley was daunting, but she needed to lose the creep and fast, so she dashed into the narrow, precarious passageway between buildings, instantly regretting the decision.

On the opposite side of the alley's opening, a black, expensive-looking luxury car squealed to a stop, blocking the way.

The most muscular, well-dressed Egyptian she'd seen to date leapt from the driver's seat, running straight at her. Instinctively, she knew she was in more shit than she could wade through. Gasping, she whirled around, only to find her stalker blocking the other exit.

As the men closed in on her, Sadie screamed, stumbling backwards until her rear end slammed into a wall. "Heeeeeeeelp! Heeeeeeeelp!"

Who was she kidding? No one would help her in time. If they even tried. She charged like a bull, attempting to maneuver past the men, but she couldn't move fast enough. Her escape attempt practically threw her in the bastard's arms, rather than bring her close to freedom.

Terror knotted her stomach, her mind racing with fear as one of their large, unshakable hands clamped around her wrist. Inwardly, she screamed for Dylan, outwardly, she screamed for anyone who would save her. "Help! Someone help me! Please! Help!"

But of course, Dylan didn't come and neither did help. The next thing she knew, her bag of souvenirs was snatched, then her purse. She prayed her money was all they wanted, but to her dismay, a powerful arm encircled her waist, and she was yanked against the second man's hard body. His tight, unrelenting grip smashed her stomach, making breathing difficult as he dragged her.

Kicking and bucking against him, she fought with every ounce of her ability, but he continued to pull her toward the running vehicle. Her stalker threw a burlap bag over her head, all the while muttering under his breath in rapid Arabic.

"Quiet, woman," one of them commanded in fairly good English. "Quiet!"

Her other captor responded in Arabic and they shared a hearty laugh. Like hell she'd shut up! Making good use of the moment, she screamed as loudly as she could, sucked in a deep breath, then released yet another piercing cry. The man holding her jerked her hard against his chest, whispering as he nibbled at her earlobe through the bag. "The boss said you were a wild one. He'll have fun taming you."

She curled from his disgusting touch, pulling her ear free from him. Tame her? They didn't know who they were dealing with! "I don't know your damned boss!"

"You will," he chuckled. "I promise you that. Us, as well."

"Never! Kiss my ass!" she screeched, her cry cut off as he clamped a hand over her mouth.

She bit into his flesh, her teeth puncturing his skin through the nasty tasting burlap and drawing blood, but he didn't relent.

The men forced her into the front seat of the car, sandwiching her between their bodies as they sped off. She punched blindly at them, hoping to make them stop the vehicle, or hell, even wreck it. Anything so she could escape!

Her hands were caught and coarse rope tied securely around them. The bastard squeezed her cheeks, forcing her to open her mouth, which she did, screaming bloody murder. He gagged her through the bag and tied the cloth at the back of her head. His strong arms wrapped around her and held her tight against his body, preventing any further violence from her.

Hot tears streamed down her face, the urgency within her to escape so great, words couldn't describe her terror.

The fabric gagging her was almost impossible to breathe through. Forced to draw shallow, stale breaths, she fought harder and harder against the rag. Her mind whirled with panic, fear overtaking reason.

She needed oxygen! She couldn't breathe!

The more she struggled, the harder breathing became. Fright-inducing visions raced through her mind. Would they rape her? Sell her? Sacrifice her?

Murder her?

Her fright stampeded over her wits and all sensible thoughts were crushed under the weight of her fear. Desperately as she battled, her brain failed and darkness claimed her.

twelve

Worming away from the cop's touch, Sadie attempted to twist free, determined not to permit him to ravage her one more time, despite the unwelcome arousal flooding her body.

How urgently she yearned to scream, to pound him with her fists, to demand her release, but her hands were tied and her mouth gagged.

Arching up, she smashed her body against his solid chest, half in an attempt to push him away, half frantic to feel her skin pressed against his hot, bare muscles.

With unyielding power, he grasped her hips, tilted her pelvis, and drove his thick cock into her wet pussy, entering her with such force that her body lurched.

A tidal wave of pleasure and need swept through her. She screamed, clawing her nails into the skin of his shoulder blades as he drove in and out of her, hard, fast, fulfilling.

His rigid member pumping into her tight tunnel was so good, so damn rewarding, but deep down, Sadie knew this was wrong. She battled his touch, and at the same time she fought for more of it.

An orgasm convulsed through her body and she thrashed, scarcely able to withstand the deep waves of pleasure rippling through her.

Her sheath contracted and released in quick rhythm and she gave up. The ecstasy was too great to deny. Relaxing, she melted into the cop's arms and accepted her fate. She turned her head to draw a deep breath, shocked by what—no who–she found watching.

Cross-armed, Dylan stood in the corner, glaring at her with dark, hate-filled eyes.

"Did you think you'd get away with this, Sadie? Did you?" he ground out through clenched teeth, his voice growing louder and louder, until it echoed around her, so intense his words shook her very heart. "Look around you. Look what you've done."

A blurred mess of visions flipped through Sadie's mind like a slideshow . . . beautiful blond-haired children . . . minivans . . . romantic dinners . . . glorious sex with Dylan . . . and roaring orange-red fire and smoke as it all burned to black ash, then disappeared into thin air.

For the first time in her dreams, she found herself able to speak. "No . . . no . . ." Her whisper exploded into a scream. "No! No! Nooo! Nooooooooooooo!"

Noooo!" Sadie jerked awake. She was in a strange, dark room, her cry muffled by the gag filling her mouth, her natural reaction to thrash her arms stifled by the shocking reality that her hands were bound, that she was *trapped.*

The kidnapping rushed back to her and she fought the rope securing her wrists. Swift, terrifying panic raced through her and the thudding of her heart echoed in her ears, her mind spinning in a million directions.

Oh God! Oh no, oh no, *oh no*! Who were these awful men who'd captured her? Worse, what would they do with her? *To* her?

He'll have fun taming you . . .

Oh God. Sadie gagged, repelled. The man's insinuation left a lot to the imagination, but there was *no* question that their plans for her involved sex. She'd heard about illegal brothels and harems in the Middle East, on Oprah or some show, but she'd never pictured them as real, not truly. Not until now.

They certainly had money, probably from selling women. She could think of no other logical reason why she'd been stolen in broad daylight. Besides, if the men had only intended rape, wouldn't they have done it by now?

Maybe not. Maybe they were waiting for their boss, or worse, waiting until she came to. Maybe they wanted her kicking and fighting so they had a sick excuse to beat her up.

Oh God.

Her head throbbed from the possibilities and she tried to will them away. Chills shook her body.

She didn't want to know!

Son of a bitch, she had to get out of here and fast. Choking back a sob, she attempted to use her fingers to work down the gag, but her bound wrists made the task impossible. The coarse fabric burned her lips and tears welled in her eyes.

Dylan . . .

She'd give anything not to have left him. Anything to be with him now.

Worse, unless she found a way to escape, he'd never find her. When she wasn't at the Citadel, he'd probably believe she'd run off for good.

Damn this stupid game of hers! Damn her dumb notions!

Screw the pain. She refused to give in to the fiends. Tasting blood as she tugged with all her might, she delivered the gag a final wrench and yanked it down. Gasping for fresh air, she sat.

Unsure in the pitch-black room, she slowly lowered her feet, finding the floor, and stood. She held her hands in front of her and felt around the room, discovering she'd been placed in a twin-size bed on a wooden frame. There was nothing else in the room. No dresser. No chair.

No windows. No weapon.

Her fingers found a light switch and she flicked it on and off, disappointed when it didn't work. Damn it!

Grasping the cold metal of a knob, she rattled it, then banged against the door. She wanted out of this room. Out of this mess. Let the men come back and bring it on. She'd beat the bloody hell out of them.

She slammed her body against the hard wood and screamed with all the strength of her lungs, hoping to knock the damn door down, to draw a neighbor's attention, anything that would free her from this small, dark room and the terror of being trapped within it.

Loud footsteps closed in on her dungeon, moving closer and closer until they stopped directly outside her door. Overcome by adrenaline, she forgot her fear, and rammed against the punishing wood once again. "Let me out of here, damn it! Let. Me. Ouuuutttt!"

"Calm down," Dylan's composed, even voice commanded. "Go sit on the bed and we'll talk."

The world ceased to spin. Sadie stared into the dark, flabbergasted. Dylan? Dylan was here?

Dylan was behind her kidnapping?

Good God.

Dylan was the boss!? But then, who were the men who'd abducted her? Damn him!

How? *Why?* None of this made sense.

She inhaled deeply, taking in several shaky breaths as she attempted to figure the situation out, and instead developed twenty more questions. And whole hell of a lot more anger.

"Lay down on the bed," Dylan demanded in an inflexible voice once again. "Or I'm walking away."

"Screw you!" she screamed, outraged beyond reason. Her breaths came in heavy pants as she once again threw herself into the door. How *dare* he scare the shit out of her like this?

Sharp pain shot through her shoulder, so she kicked the door with her good foot, nailing it dead in the center with her heel, over and over. She didn't want to hear a damn thing he had to say! The lousy bastard!

In fact, he had no clue how damn lucky he was that she wouldn't listen to him, because she swore, once he came through that door, she'd pound the hell out of him. She'd—

"Settle down, Sadie, and go lie on the bed," he ordered, too coolly, too calmly. "While I don't want to leave your wrists tied, I'll walk away if I must."

"Erhhhh!" she cried out, stomping the floor. "I can't believe you did this. I can't believe you, Dylan! You bastard!"

He chuckled lightheartedly, actually had the nerve to *laugh* at her like she was a joke, then walked away. Balling her fists, Sadie listened to his steps fade, so angry she was close to combustion. How dare he leave her locked in a dark room with her wrists tied?

He couldn't do that . . . she *knew* he couldn't do that. Not Dylan.

He'd come back any moment and heaven help him when he did.

Who the hell did he think he was, turning the tables on her like this? He had no right! This was *her* game . . . this was *her* . . .

Oh God. No.

Realization struck her hard. She'd totally asked for this. She'd pushed Dylan too far, too fast.

She'd created a monster.

Dylan clenched and released his fists, his hands hanging at his sides in defeat as he stalked to his chamber. He didn't like leaving Sadie in the room, still bound, but she left him little choice. Maybe he deserved to be attacked, but he wasn't inclined to having his eyes clawed out. As soon as she settled down, he'd return.

Even now, as the plan progressed, he had trouble believing he was really going through with this. He felt strangely out of body, like he was watching some other man, rather than doing these things himself.

But while his mind was stunned by disbelief, his heart and soul knew this was real. His cock knew this was real. He was finally acting with passion, rather than thinking with plain, boring reason.

As much as he thought he should've, Dylan hadn't been able to go home. Good choice, bad choice . . . in the heat of the moment, it hadn't mattered one damn bit.

Oh, he'd tried, and he'd failed. Miserably.

For five hours after his phone call to Maxim, he'd moped around at the airport, even missing his flight home as he'd hatched a crazy plan he'd known he'd never, ever go through with. Then he'd bought a new ticket home. When it came time to board, his feet refused to move.

Despite all sense, he'd found himself stalling, damn sure he couldn't return home alone, he couldn't go after her again, and he sure as hell couldn't do the insane shit in his mind.

Then just like that, he'd remembered.

As he'd promised himself, he was supposed to be doing the opposite of everything normal to him. Everything.

No, not in any way, shape, or form would he previously have considered kidnapping Sadie, holding her hostage, or making her his sex slave, but damn it, he was doing things differently on this trip.

So he'd hopped the next flight to Cairo.

To his great relief, Maxim had handled the details from there. Like an all-knowing sexual superman, his good friend had swept down on his problem and the next thing Dylan had known, he was staying in an impressive, old-world mud-brick house just outside of Cairo, near the pyramids, hatching plans to sexually seduce Sadie.

The day after settling into the rented country home, Maxim sped up the sand drive with a crammed-full Lamborghini, sporting his rather outspoken, almost tacky, personal "assistant," an older woman named Nafrini, and two of his friends, wealthy, young Egyptians who were all too eager to *help* and so darn handsome he had to worry.

The rest was history. Nafrini prepared for Sadie's arrival, taking a survey of his preferences, and hers, and a huge chunk of cash to finance the fantasy, then the men had set off to kidnap his fiancé.

So here he was, in an inconceivable situation, and behaving in an inconceivable way.

Crossing through the threshold into the master bedroom, he strode to the French doors and threw them open, allowing in a waft of oppressive, dry air. He sucked in a hot, deep breath, amazed at how it soothed him. He was a winter man himself, had never cared for summer, but here, the hot weather was somehow stimulating.

Gazing over the expertly landscaped, lush-green palm grove garden surrounding the house, to the contrasting stretch of desert in the distance, he basked in the heat of the sun, and wondered at the vast change in the land, and the change in himself.

Being in such a different place made him truly feel like a different man. From the inside out, he'd been renewed. The hesitation likened to the old Dylan had vanished.

At least for the most part.

He refused to give his doubts room to grow. If he didn't allow them to exist, they wouldn't. After a few more moments under the scorching sun, Dylan sought comfort in his huge, king-size bed. He sank into the plush pillows and soft cotton sheets, his fingers running over the empty spot where Sadie would soon lie next to him.

In time.

Perhaps he should feel guilty about scaring her as he had, but he didn't, in the same way that Sadie possessed no remorse for running away from him. She'd pushed him this far . . . and he was pretty damn sure these were the results she craved. Whether she knew it or not.

"Did it not go well?" Speaking in almost perfect English, Nafrini materialized in the doorway, her tiny, orange-and-blue pattern–covered body weighed down by the amount of heavy jewelry she wore. Her gracious, full smile lit her dark eyes. She carried a large, brown paper bag and from the logo he gathered it was from a pharmacy. "I should speak with her, perhaps?"

Dylan sat and inhaled a deep breath. "No. I can handle her. I know how to handle her."

"The compassion of another woman would calm her, yes?"

"Are you kidding?" Dylan shook his head. "Sadie would scratch your eyes out."

Nafrini lifted her chin, a twinkle in her eye. "Let her try. I don't care."

"No?"

An evil grin curved her cheeks. "Remember, I'll be overseeing her bikini waxing." Before Dylan had time to laugh, Nafrini plopped the bag on his lap. "Pick which you prefer."

Dylan peeked inside, noting several bottles of perfume and more condoms than even Maxim could use. "Of which?"

"Both."

"Why?"

"These are very important details. The wrong condom, less pleasure. The wrong scent, less attraction."

"But Sadie and I don't use condoms."

"In a ménage, you do."

"Oh."

"You pick. If you like, I can step from the room and you can try some on."

She rose from the bed and Dylan held up a hand. "Don't go."

"Do you need my assistance?" she purred, her brows high as she glanced at him in a sarcastically lustful way.

"No. Hell no. I mean, I know what I want." Dylan dropped the bag, refusing to allow himself to laugh. "Smart ass."

"Better than being a stupid ass, yes?"

He didn't know where the hell Maxim had found this woman, but she was worth every penny he paid her. Her attention to detail and her flamboyant sense of humor put him at ease.

"Pick," she demanded. "Now."

Did he mention her determination? With Nafrini around, he couldn't skip out on this plan of his even if he wanted to.

He peered into the bag, noting every type of condom known to man, from chocolate and fruit flavored, to ribbed, to glow in the dark. There was even one that produced warm sensations.

The perfume choice was easy. He simply didn't care. Grabbing one of the bottles, he presented it to her. "This will do nicely. As for the condoms, leave them. We may use a variety."

"The chocolate ones are tasty and calorie free."

"I'll keep that in mind."

She snatched the bag and dropped it on the nightstand. "Now, you go reason with her again. This time, do not fail. I'm drawing her bath."

She strode from the room, leaving him to his condoms. Was Sadie calm yet?

While she was quite angry, he had no doubt her surrender would come shortly. Sure, she'd fight, she'd claw, but once he pressed his body to hers . . .

His prick twitched at the prospect. Standing, he crossed the room to the bar and retrieved a decanter from the refrigerator below. He poured a fine crystal tumbler to the brim with chilled, rich, red brandy and swigged the burning liquid.

The cold drink warmed his throat as the fluid traveled south and settled in his stomach, granting him courage.

"Opposite, opposite," he whispered to himself, determined not to waver now. He took one last sip and slammed the glass on the counter. "Ready or not, here I come."

Sadie lay flat on the hard mattress and stared into the dark, seething in anger. Damn Dylan! The nerve of him. The gall!

Didn't he realize he'd scared her to death? She could've had a heart attack!

Perhaps she should be relieved her captor was her lover and not a vile rapist or worse. But she'd almost rather be facing a stranger.

Where did he get off terrifying her as he had? Surrendering her to the mercy of strange men? Tying her up? It was inconsiderable . . . abhorrent . . . detestable . . .

He was behaving nothing like the Dylan she loved. No, his actions were more akin to the chauvinistic, sexy cop that stalked her in her dreams. The man she admittedly fantasized Dylan *could* be, but never hoped he *would* be. They were notions, not real!

Right?

Damn it! She wanted to pound the living daylights out of Dylan. She was caught in a way she'd never been caught by a man before. He'd figured her out. He'd gotten the better of her.

Dylan had control now, a fact she did not appreciate, and didn't know how to face.

Even when she'd allowed him to spank her in Tuscany, ultimately she'd been in charge. Now she didn't have the upper hand, or even the lower hand. She had no hand at all. She was in this room at his mercy.

Why did that seem to turn her on? Why was she anxious to have him return and continue their battle? What the hell was the stirring in her stomach about?

She drew in a shaky breath, aware that her thoughts made little to no sense.

Dylan's unmistakable knock pounded on the door and she bolted upright. A neon light flickered on, illuminating her surroundings for the first time. Squinting, she gave the empty room little regard, on edge to jumpstart her confrontation with Dylan.

"I'm on the bed, damn it. Now come in." The moment she spoke, she leapt to her feet, determined not to let him dominate her.

As the door swung open, she leapt through the air, and plowed the surprised Dylan backwards. Pounding on his chest, she screamed bloody murder. "You bastard! You no good jerk!" She took a wallop at his face and missed. Damn the ropes around her wrists! Her blows were not near as strong as she'd prefer, not that she'd let them stop her. Taking swing after swing at his face and shoulders, she attacked him with all she had. "You asshole! How dare you? How *dare* you? I want to know! Answer me! Damn you. *Damn* you!"

Dylan stumbled against the door and grabbed her wrists. Enveloping her hands in his, he held her tight, and forced her to walk to the bed.

"Stop fighting me," he ground out, his tone threatening. "Don't make me hog-tie you."

She twisted against him. "You wouldn't dare."

"I would." He pushed her onto the mattress and sat on her, his strong thighs holding her in place, despite her twisting. "You're in my possession now, Sadie. The rules of the game have officially been changed. By me. You don't want to go home? Then fine. But you won't leave here until you're ready to become my wife."

"Bastard." She spit at him, his threat making her even angrier, though her libido begged to differ.

So maybe she was slightly turned on by the fact that he had her pinned. That he was demanding her love.

She was still pissed and he could kiss her ass.

Dylan held her to the bed, his legs straddling her waist. With one of his hands, he restrained her. With the other, he pressed the hardened bud of her nipple. Electric desire shuddered through her body, awakening her every nerve to his touch. Arousal flooded her, the wave hot and fast.

She squeezed her vaginal muscles, disgusted by the creamy desire lining her tunnel. Her body had some gall! Sadie clenched her teeth. She was not getting turned on. She refused to.

Dylan caressed her areola with his thumb through the thin fabric of her peasant blouse and bra. She arched, moaning.

Okay, *maybe* she was a lot turned on. But only physically, and it was ridiculous!

Dylan gyrated his hips against hers. "You want me, Sadie. You can't deny it." The hard length of his cock pressed against her cunt and he knotted his fingers in her hair. Tilting her head, he forced her to face him. His lips hovered over hers as he harshly whispered. "You keep pushing me and pushing me and now matters have gone further than you ever expected, because now *I'm* pushing *you*, aren't I? Guess what? I intend to make you face your fantasies, and fears, the same as you have me."

Sadie's struggles deflated and she crumbled into a ball of defeat. Despite herself, she couldn't fight his advances, no more than she could fight her cop.

"Dylan . . ." she whimpered, her clit swollen with need, her body awash with hunger for him. "Please untie me. Please."

He slid his hands from her hair and seized her chin so she couldn't look away. "I'll untie you, but only if you promise not to be naughty."

"Naughty?" She wriggled her lower half against his rigid erection. "When am I ever?"

He mashed his hips against her. "You are very bad, woman, running from me the way you have. You deserve to be properly punished."

She whimpered, struggling uselessly against his pressing cock.

"Promise," he demanded.

"This isn't fair," she pleaded.

He worked at the tight knots securing her wrists, loosening them. "Of course it is. It's just as fair as when you left me, in the middle of the night mind you, and forced me to chase you halfway around the world." He chuckled, deep and low. "But like I said, I've caught you now, and matters between us are going to change. Starting now."

He gave the rope one final tug and it came undone. Pulling her hands away from him, she rubbed at the sore skin around her wrists, staring at him. "What if I don't want to go along with this? What if I'm through with you?"

His fierce glower dared her to try to run. Slowly, he shook his head. "You're not, Sadie. We both know it."

With a gulp, she searched his eyes for answers. "What will you do with me now? You can't leave me in this room forever."

"Of course not. I don't even intend to lock the door. Now that you're calm, you won't run. After all, where would you go? The desert? Not likely. You won't leave me now, will you?" He raised a brow. "You wait until after the sex for that, correct? It's part of the game."

"The rules have changed."

"So they have. But you haven't. Nafrini, whom you'll find quite helpful, is on her way. She'll see you are prepped and prepared to my liking. When you're ready, I've two men waiting to escort you to my room." His evenly spoken words seemed crazy. Impossible. "Think of this like a harem Sadie, except there is only one woman, and two men, and you are *all* at *my* disposal."

Sadie gulped and stared at him, shocked beyond words. What he was telling her was insane! Was this a dream? How could any of this be real?

Dylan would never do this. He couldn't do something like this. Breaking the law, being mean, participating in a ménage, it was all beyond him.

He climbed off her and stood, his jaw set as he spoke through his teeth. "Know that I intend to guarantee you are thoroughly sated by the time you leave this house, Sadie, whether it involves two men or five, whether it involves one day, or ten. There is no length to which I won't go. Not this time. This time, I'm in charge."

He stalked from the room, leaving her lying there in absolute shock.

thirteen

Her nerves were so fried, Sadie swore each and every last one literally burned in protest. Drawing a deep breath, she stood and answered the gentle knock.

Dylan hadn't just left the door unlocked, he'd left it hanging open. Yet, he'd been right. While she was sure one of the men would stop her if she attempted escape, deep down, she hadn't had it in her to run.

So she'd closed the door completely, shutting herself back in the small room, deciding Dylan hadn't just lost his mind; she'd lost hers.

Not knowing who, or what, to expect now, she swung the door open. Heat whooshed into her quarters and she sucked in a deep breath of the fresh but horridly dry air and focused on the older woman standing in the threshold. Small and boldly dressed in vibrant colors and beads galore, the Egyptian smiled in a very satisfied way. "You're pretty. Good."

"What business is it of yours?" Sadie snapped. Squinting from the brilliant burst of sunlight that bombarded her room, she noted the shadowed frames of two men on a nearby bench. As her eyes adjusted, she realized they were the mean-spirited thugs who'd kidnapped her.

Beyond them, a narrow hallway with several large, open-arched windows were lined with vibrant green plants she didn't recognize, but itched to photograph, despite how silly the notion was at the moment. The corridor was so bright, so airy, it seemed like a pathway to heaven.

"I am Nafrini and these wonderful men who escorted you here are Nassor and Ziyad." Her English was slurred and occasionally hard to understand, but better than most Sadie had heard in Cairo.

Not that she liked what the woman was saying. *Escorted* was hardly an interchangeable word for *kidnapped* or *forced*. And she disagreed with *wonderful* as well.

Nafrini took her arm. "If you'll come with me, please, madam."

What choice did Sadie have? Nafrini tugged her along, walking briskly into the brilliant light, the click-clack of her sandals filling the quiet air around them. Sadie narrowed her eyes against the bright light and peered out the windows. A small garden of lush plants surrounded the home, but beyond it, white sand stretched forever. Dylan hadn't been lying. They were secluded as hell.

They crossed into another section of the gargantuan home and Sadie glanced back down the corridor. The room where she'd been kept was in a separate section from the main house and she gathered the wing was the servant quarters. Another insult added to injury.

Her dearest husband-to-be could have locked her in a nice room. But he hadn't. The jerk. Rather, he'd chosen to terrify her in that dark dungeon of a box. Did he enjoy his display of dominance? She wouldn't allow him to get away with such behavior, not for long.

He could kiss her ass. Aroused or not, no man would ever get the best of Sadie Williams. Not on her life. She'd simply develop a new game plan. One that really got him good.

Nafrini released her arm, walking ahead of her. Despite her age, the older woman had a rather sexy sashay to her walk. She glided over the marble floors, leading Sadie through the richly decorated home with such grace she appeared to be floating.

Throwing open a large door, Nafrini held it for Sadie, ushering her into a massive, white marble bathroom already steamy from hot running water.

"Take off your clothes, please." The woman didn't skip a beat.

Sadie jerked her head around and glared at her. "What?"

"Take your clothes off, my dear." Nafrini walked to a giant tub overflowing with bubbles and tested the temperature. "Perfect."

Sadie inhaled the floral scent of jasmine floating through the air, glad to smell something other than her sweat. Too bad there wasn't a chance in hell she'd get in. While the water looked inviting, no way was she stripping in front of a stranger.

"I'm not in the mood." Sadie's gaze wandered to a bench on the left of the room, its cushioning lined with crisp white towels. On top of it sat a large pile of cotton strips, and next to it, some sort of warming pot on a hotplate was plugged into the wall. "And what in the hell is that for?"

"Waxing."

"Waxing?"

Nafrini stood, smiling. "Yes, dear. Waxing."

Oh no he didn't! "Who . . . and *what* . . . do you plan on waxing?"

Dylan knew she didn't wax and especially never those areas. She'd tried once in her younger days, and the pain had been so severe, she'd stopped midway through and vowed never again. Dylan had hinted at her getting a bikini wax, but she'd refused.

She still refused.

"Your husband has requested—"

Damn him! He had! "No way, and he's not my husband."

Nafrini's dark eyes sparkled, as if she knew she was pushing Sadie's buttons and got off on the fact. "Your *husband* has requested a complete head-to-toe wax. He desires your intimate areas to be bald."

"Oh . . . no way." Sadie took a step back. "No, no, no!"

"But I told him that was impossible the first time. We'll go only as far as we can." Grinning, Nafrini waved her to the tub. "Come now. I won't bite, just wax. Your *husband* is anxious for your presence, and you must be famished after your ordeal. Let us get this over with."

"I am not taking my clothes off in front of a stranger."

"My dear, I am not attracted to the female gender, and besides, I'm much too old for you. Come now, before I call for help."

"Help?"

Nafrini lifted her brows, clearly aware of the fact that she'd struck a chord. "You wouldn't want Nassor and Ziyad to help, would you?"

"Dylan wouldn't dare."

"Madam, I do have your husband's instructions."

"Fine!"

Loathing the thought of having strangers' hands on her body, Sadie slowly removed her light, ankle-length floral skirt and sleeveless, lacy peasant blouse as well as her bra. Standing only in her pink thong, she felt more naked than ever, but she tugged the slinky underwear off as well.

Sadie crossed her arms over her breasts, clutching her shoulder where it ached from ramming it against her door. Rubbing the sore spot, she stood there like a dumbass. Never had she felt more exposed, knowing this woman was not only seeing her, but intended to bathe and wax her.

God only knew what else.

"Well, for a shy one, you don't mind standing there naked."

Right. Why the hell wasn't she in the tub already? Sadie made haste and stepped into the water, sinking into the hot depths. Bubbles rose to her chin, the heat enveloping her sore and tired body. Soap bubbles tingled against her skin, popping as they came into contact, and she leaned back in an attempt to relax.

The bath did feel awfully good. She refused to enjoy it, but thought she might as well make use of the opportunity. The streets of Cairo were filthy, and after spending the day exploring them, dust and dirt formed a layer upon her skin.

Sadie scooped up some suds and washed her arms, unpleasantly surprised when the woman joined in, washing her with a heavily scented bar of soap. Gathering her hair, Nafrini lathered her short locks vigorously and massaged her scalp.

The attention felt so damn good, Sadie found herself leaning into Nafrini's hands, inviting more. The moment she realized she was relaxing, she snapped upright.

"Should I ask what else Dylan has requested?" Sadie ground out, determined not to be anything but mad.

"Your husband—"

"*Dylan.*"

Nafrini moved her hands to Sadie's neck, kneading the tensed muscles. "Your husband requested that you be pampered and relaxed before being delivered to him."

The dumb lug. Did he really think he'd throw a hot bath at her and she'd succumb?

Sadie rolled her eyes. "How kind of him."

"Indeed." Nafrini worked the soap in her hands and washed Sadie's back, gently scraping the skin with her nails. "He is a good man, your husband."

"Pfffhhh . . ." Sadie wanted to scream to the hills, but her weak protest never gathered form. Instead, she sank under the hot water, feeling beaten.

Dylan was winning.

As much as she really, really wanted to hate this bath, to hate him, she couldn't. The rebellious part of her ached to take his actions and use them as an excuse to escape marriage, but it was beyond her.

She was actually, unforgivably, excited.

Blowing air bubbles into the soapy water, she swished her hair around until she could no longer hold her breath, then rose. Gasping for air, Sadie wiped her eyes, noticing Dylan and his two sexy goons standing in the doorway. Their gaze connected for a brief moment, the heavy tension between them forcing Sadie to swallow.

Quickly, she jerked her gaze away. The best punishment she could give Dylan was to lead him on.

"Let's get on with this, then." Sadie rested a hand on Nafrini's knee, wetting the soft fabric of her pants. Slowly, she scooted her fingers upward. "I'm ready for you."

There! Let him have that!

She'd allow this woman to wax her and whatever else Dylan had in store. She'd pretend to thoroughly enjoy every moment. Let him watch. Let him be turned on. Because when they made it behind close doors, her legs would *not* be opening.

At least that's what she promised herself.

Go ahead, turn around. Look," Dylan suggested to Nassor and Ziyad, stepping back from the door frame to allow them a view. "She's a beautiful woman and I'm proud to share her."

He clutched his second glass of brandy, trying far too hard to play it cool. An erection filled his soft cotton pants from the sight of watching Sadie strip. The slow, seductive way her blouse and skirt had slipped from her lush frame, revealing her gently curved back, her narrow waist, her lush, firm bottom and finally, those lengthy legs, had made him harder than steel.

His will working overtime, he battled the urge to plow into the room and bend her over right then and there.

He was sorry these men had missed the view. Sadie was hot, plain and simple *h-o-t*. He wanted to share that. The thought of these men lusting after his woman turned him on. Big time.

Nassor folded his brawny arms, his dark, frowning eyes devouring her form as she rose from the bathwater. "A fighter."

"Wild." Ziyad nodded in agreement. "I almost thought we'd have to let her go to prevent her from hurting herself."

Dylan cast a discreet glance downward, curious to see if these men were as turned on as he was. The tents in their pants didn't disappoint.

Good grief. He was officially a weirdo. Checking out other men's cocks . . . What the hell was wrong with him?

Heat rushed to his face and he took a swig, then another. Since he'd already helped himself to one glass of liquid courage, the alcohol went straight to his mind, excited tingles pulsing through his veins.

He tapped his teeth with his tongue, searching for something to say.

"You men did great, you know, with the nabbing. I have to tell you, I appreciate it. Thanks for looking out for her too. I can't imagine what she thinks of you two, but . . ." Dylan took another gulp, savoring the feel of the burning liquid. He toppled a little sideways, grinning. "So, you two want to fuck with me?"

Nassor shot him a look. "Easy on the liquor."

Ziyad nodded in agreement, chuckling. "Yeah, we'll fuck with you. Maxim didn't suggest we come over here to play children's games. We said we wanted to participate, and trust me, we aren't the types to change our minds." Placing his fingers to the rim of Dylan's glass, Ziyad pushed the drink down. "But slow down on the alcohol. You want to get it up when the time comes, eh?"

A knot formed in Dylan's throat despite his buzz. "I'm nervous."

But damn it, he refused to stay this way! He was going through with this and there was no stopping him. No way.

"Don't be. Consider us pros."

Dylan couldn't leash his humor. "Professionals . . . in what?" he laughed.

"Ménages." Ziyad's black eyes danced with pride. "Sex."

"Is that a career these days?"

"It is when you don't need money but you do need sex. What can I say? I'm a hungry man, and it's my job to fulfill myself."

"A hard life you live."

Nassor raised his brows. "Indeed. So, what does your little lady like?"

What did Sadie like? Hmm. He'd discovered quite a lot about her desires the past couple of weeks, but he'd never actually examined her preferences or listed them.

Perhaps he didn't even know everything she'd like in the bedroom. No, on second thought, he *knew* he didn't. But he was learning.

He just hoped he got some right.

"She likes to be spanked. And as I'm learning, she likes a man to take control." He cleared his throat, which was rapidly constricting. "I think we have that down pat."

He took yet another swig. What the hell was his problem? The old Dylan had flown home! He was the opposite man, and he should be playing it cool. Enjoying the ride. Not near panic.

Damn it.

Okay, he was going to count to three, and then he was going to answer them, honestly, and without feeling stupid.

Yeah right.

Shut up! He shoved aside the doubtful, inhibited voice in his head.

One . . . two . . . three!

"She likes to have her ears nibbled and her belly kissed. I find she also enjoys having her clit rubbed, and being finger fucked," he fired in rapid succession, feeling winded by the hasty confession.

But the men acted like he'd just ran through a list of his favorite television shows.

"And . . ." Dylan started to add more, but stopped.

"Have you taken her in the ass yet?" Nassor asked.

Anal play, the only turn-on he hadn't mentioned, though it had been right on the tip of his tongue. While he suspected Sadie enjoyed it a lot, uttering such a truth was almost impossible for him.

He nodded stiffly. "I . . . I believe she . . . enjoys . . . you know."

Nassor grinned, "Good." Grabbing his crotch, he jiggled his balls. "She'll be ready for Nassor's big cock then."

An unexpected surge of anger plowed through Dylan and his spine went ramrod straight. He glared at Nassor, staring him dead in the eyes. How dare the man-slut speak of his fiancée like that?

Ziyad laid a hand on his arm. "Easy, boss. No need to get angry."

"Sadie isn't a piece of meat," he ground out through his teeth.

"We know," Ziyad said. "She's a nice woman. Actually, that's why we're so eager to participate in your little fantasy. The women we regularly see, they've known plenty of men. Your wife, she's new to this. Fresh. Different. Unlike them, we might actually be able to please her. Nassor meant no harm, and I think the liquor is doing some speaking for you."

Dylan's sudden fury melted and he blew out a frustrated breath. "You're right."

Nassor jerked his head in a quick nod. "What about you? What turns you on?"

"Sex."

Big secret! Wow, he'd really admitted something there.

New plan: he needed to start thinking before he spoke. One of his greatest fears was coming true. He was making a complete ass out of himself.

"I, um . . . I think I'd like to watch for a bit."

"We can handle that."

To his great relief, the men didn't appear shocked by his request, and that fueled his fire. "I want to take pictures and I don't want you two to fuck her without me. I want us to take her together."

Dylan watched Sadie stepping from the bathtub, her beautiful body glistening wet. Actually visualizing another man's hands upon her body was difficult, despite the situation he found himself in.

He cleared his throat. "As far as the sex goes, her pussy is mine. You men can have . . . other areas."

Obviously mesmerized by the sight of Sadie's naked form, Ziyad nodded, and spoke in a distracted tone. "How about this? You give the instructions, and we'll follow. Whatever you say, we do."

Dylan polished off his drink. "I say . . . that Sadie is in for one helluva trip."

Nafrini helped her from the tub and Sadie stretched, allowing the woman to pat her dry from head to toe with the softest towel to ever have touched her body.

Then, Nafrini led her to the table and Sadie climbed aboard, propping up her legs and spreading them wide. She peeked at Dylan, hoping he was looking. He was. So were the two thugs who'd kidnapped her. And they were all hard. Too hard.

A knot lodged in her throat and a spark of excitement curled through her body. Preparing for the wax took Nafrini forever, leaving Sadie exposed to their stares, and feeling more and more naked. Bare. Aroused.

Sadie wanted to leap up and scream and toss an embarrassing fit, but if this was Dylan's game, she'd play along.

She passed the time by counting to ten. Over and over and over.

Finally, Nafrini spread the first piece of cloth along the stray hairs that grew south from her navel, the gentle touch soft, almost arousing, as Nafrini spread the wax strip on, but there was nothing gentle about the way she ripped the hair from her body. Nafrini quickly tore the cloth away and Sadie had to grind her teeth to keep from crying out.

Damn it! Exactly why she didn't wax!

"Waxing is an ancient Egyptian practice," Nafrini informed her as she spread the second piece closer to Sadie's thigh. "The royal and well-to-do look at hair removal as a way to remain young and forever beautiful."

"Well, I hope Dylan is enjoying this," she muttered under her breath, locking her jaw as Nafrini wrenched more hairs from their roots. "I'm sure not."

"Ah, but does it not give you pleasure to please your man?" Nafrini's words were spoken lightheartedly as she gently spread another torturous strip on.

This time, Sadie couldn't contain her squeal of pain. Damn Dylan!

"You've got to be kidding me." Sadie gripped the towel beneath her. "Tell me you're kidding."

"Of course." Nafrini continued working, her touch oddly sensuous and brutal at the same time. "I was just seeing if I could make you believe it."

Eventually, Dylan and his goons disappeared. Sadie supposed watching a woman writhe in pain wasn't their thing. To her surprise, the waxing passed much more quickly than expected. When nearly every retrievable strand of hair had been torn from her lower half, Nafrini had Sadie shower, then proceeded to massage her with oils, which was followed with a manicure and pedicure.

Nafrini swept Sadie's hair into a style she never wore, a mass of curls atop her head, and applied more makeup to her face than she'd ever considered. Finally, Sadie was dressed in a brilliant gown of red silk that clung to her every curve.

Nafrini led her to a body-length mirror and Sadie stared at herself in shock. Dylan had really gone all out . . . for himself. Goodness. She looked a little sluttish.

Was this what he really wanted?

Sadie spun around, admiring the glow of her skin, the way the dress fell against her generous curves.

Maybe red *was* her color.

"Are you ready?" Nafrini questioned, smiling as if very pleased. "You look beautiful and your husband awaits."

Sadie cast a second glance at herself. Was she ready? For what?

Great sex? A fight?

She didn't know how to feel right now. She was still annoyed at Dylan, but found her anger weak and wavering in the blur of emotion swirling in her mind. He'd been so selfish, so reckless in his actions, but the more she thought about it, the more she realized the game had been about her from day one. She'd needed Dylan to chase her, to open up sexually, to give her the things she so deeply craved.

While she'd told herself he needed to be pushed, that this was improving their relationship, the truth had been simple. She'd been fulfilling *her* needs. Now, Dylan was doing the same. Could she really hate him for that?

Sadie sighed. None of her anger mattered anyway.

She couldn't hate Dylan, not ever.

Sadie gave a quick nod and pasted on a smile. "Take me to him."

Heading to Dylan's room, Sadie couldn't resist attempting to mimic Nafrini's sensual walk, the way the woman swung her hips ever so slightly, her strides long, proud.

The combination of her high heels and a still slightly sore ankle spoiled Sadie's efforts and she stumbled, landing on her rear.

Nafrini turned, her grin widening as Sadie scurried to stand. Brushing her skirt into place, Sadie shook her head. "Too much wax on these floors."

"They are marble." Nafrini smiled brilliantly.

Sadie had no idea what that meant, considering she hadn't cleaned in years. "Exactly!" She lifted her chin, limping after Nafrini, all hopes of a graceful walk dashed.

Nafrini chuckled and opened the massive, exotic wooden doors to Dylan's chamber. Waving Sadie in, Nafrini stepped aside. "Marble is not waxed, my dear."

But *she* was. Sadie groaned inwardly, feeling like an idiot.

Sadie stepped into the small alcove enclosing the doorway, sweeping her gaze across the lush interior of the master bedroom and easily locating Dylan. Sitting in a huge chair next to a table filled with fruit, he gazed out open French doors, taking small bites of a strawberry.

"Come. Join me," he issued without even looking at her.

Cocky.

Sadie frowned. Even his voice sounded different. Deeper. Harder. Not at all like Dylan.

Both irritated and intrigued, she drew a deep breath for courage. It wasn't as if she could walk out now. Dylan certainly had her attention if nothing else.

Gliding across the room, she stood before him. He'd changed and the clothing he wore was a far stretch from his normal daily attire. White and thin cotton, his pants resembled a breezy, comfortable pair of pajamas, the shirt hanging open and revealing his chest hair.

Dylan almost always wore business attire, even around the house, and he never went without his feet covered, be it socks, slippers, or shoes. Right now, his feet were bare.

His dark gaze flicked over her. "Sit."

Sadie resisted the urge to slap him and stared in shock. Dylan responded with silence and disregard. Standing there, baffled, annoyed, and fascinated all at once, Sadie couldn't speak for a moment.

She caught a hint of smile curving on his cheeks.

"Ah-ha!"

He grunted. "Sit."

Regardless of the way her nerves prickled at his arrogance, she obeyed, and sat in the chair next to him, ramrod straight. "I walked in here ready to submit." She shook her head. "But I've changed my mind. I don't even know you."

"Eat."

"Eat?"

He raised a brow. "You'll be hungry if you don't." Taking deliberate, measured bites of the strawberry, he raised his brows and smiled. "I guarantee you'll be one busy fiancée this evening."

"Is that a fact?" she purred.

"Indeed."

The V between her thighs warmed and tingled in anticipation, her pussy muscles contracting in need.

Trying to play it cool, Sadie selected an orange and carved the rind with a knife. She could never eat now. She was so nervous and excited, her stomach was in knots.

Sticky juice coated her fingers as she pulled open the orange.

Dylan leaned forward in his large, velvet-lined lounge chair. "I suppose you're curious how it's come to this?"

Her hands shook and her insides quivered as she sliced through the exploding pulp, making a huge mess.

"One couldn't help but wonder, all things considered."

She should slap him. She should.

But she'd fantasized about being thoroughly possessed by him for a long time. When she hadn't been secretly wishing Dylan would be stronger with her, she'd been dreaming of her cop.

She needed to experience what it felt like to *not* be in charge. To be *taken*. Controlled. Loved thoroughly.

Dylan's behavior had her nearly ready to cream her panties, not that the silky strap she wore really counted as underwear.

Her skin prickled and electric shivers danced across her breasts. Her nipples awakened, hardening into buds in preparation for his suckling, her labia swelling at the thought of being stroked.

Distracted, her hand slipped and the sharp blade nicked her palm.

"Ouch!" She shook her wrist, smarting from the pain. Real great!

Dylan smothered her hand in his and took the knife. Setting it aside, he drew her palm to his mouth. With his tongue, he licked away a tiny droplet of blood, then suckled at the miniscule cut.

Heat rushed to the injury. His plush lips upon the sore flesh activated the nerves in her palm, sending sensations straight up her arm. The long muscles from her fingers to her elbows tightened as her arousal increased, becoming needy and raw.

"You didn't give me an explanation yet," she whispered through her teeth.

Dylan lifted his head, his gaze meeting hers. He dropped her hand and stood. Reaching around, he tugged down the zipper of the flimsy crimson dress she wore. "See, babe," he grinned as her dress collided with the floor, leaving her standing in only an almost non-existent red thong before him. "The sweet side of Dylan flew home. Consider me his opposite."

Sadie shuddered. "So now you've got multiple personalities?"

He chuckled, carving her orange into two halves. "Not quite. You're simply seeing a side of me never revealed before."

He dropped half the orange to the floor, cupping the other portion in his palm. Squeezing the fruit gently, he used the knife to slash the pulp crosswise in several quick movements. The orange's blood welled and he brought it to her chest, cupping her breast.

Hooking his finger in her panties, he tugged them and they fell around her ankles. He smashed the pulpy fruit against her breast, squeezing hard. The flesh of the orange enveloped the pert bud of her nipple and droplets of succulent liquid coated her areola.

Juice flowed down her body from her chest to her stomach, sliding between her labia and along her thighs.

Slowly, Dylan slid the orange south, following the path of the nectar to her sex. He cupped her mons with the fruit, pressing the orange against her once again, but this time with more force. The fruit's essence squirted into her folds and he rubbed the orange in circles, creating pressure against her clit.

Knees weak, Sadie fought to remain standing. The orange caressed the sensitive skin of her freshly waxed bikini line and sent fireworks exploding through her. Palming the fruit, he placed a hand to each of her flaming thighs and spread her legs wider. Slowly, ever so slowly, he delved into her moist labia with his tongue, and lapped, consuming the orange's juices.

Working his way upward, he licked the sticky trail clean, his mouth working magic over her belly, her breasts. He circled her areola, tracing the outer edge of the pink bud, then enveloped the pebble. He suckled hard, driving her wild, and she had to dig her fingers into his shoulders to refrain from collapsing.

Without warning, he wrenched away and took a step back. He studied her for a moment, then ripped the remaining bruised orange with his hands, tearing it in two. He held the jagged piece to her mouth, caressing her lips.

Swallowing, she accepted the almost-depleted fruit, slowly chewing the juiceless flesh, able to taste her own desire within the smashed pulp. "I'm not sure what to think."

He took the remaining slice away, casting it aside. "Don't."

"Don't?"

"No. Just go lie on the bed."

"I—" Sadie hesitated, her jaw shaking with passion, her chest aching with reluctant pride. She drew a deep breath, yearning for his commanding touch upon her abandoned skin so deeply she could almost cry. Yet she was not prepared to let him have his way so soon. Instinct demanded she refuse him, though her body had long since accepted. "No."

Dylan's dark eyes locked with hers. "Don't think you have a choice." He cradled her jaw, slowly caressing the bone, then reached around to the back of her neck. Chills coursed her spine as he ran his fingers through her tightly fastened hair to the band securing the updo. Yanking the bun free, he let her short tresses fall in a mess around her face.

His fingers knotted in her curly locks and he drew her face to face with him. His lips hovered an inch above hers, leaving her sure he would kiss her senseless.

She could smell the distinct odor of brandy on his breath. "You've been drinking."

"Don't worry, I've sobered up plenty enough to perform." His thumb stroked her scalp. "A night like tonight isn't something a man slops his way through."

Thick tension hovered between them. Sexual. Emotional. Demanding.

Jerking her gaze away, she turned her face to the side. "I always have a choice." Her voice shook as she spoke. "I choose not to want this."

He planted a soft kiss to her cheekbone, then grasped her chin, forcing her to face him. To face her need. "Perhaps you can deny me, but do you think you can actually deny yourself?"

"Yes."

"No." He reached out, his palm cupping her juice-dampened breast, cradling the soft flesh. His thumb flicked over her erect nipple.

"Yes," she whispered weakly, despite the fact that she didn't pull away. That she couldn't pull away.

"Oh, how you are enjoying this, aren't you?" His eyes flashed in determination and he seized her by the waist. In one swift motion he threw her over his shoulder, securing her legs in his unyielding grasp.

She fought against his hold, beating his back with her fists uselessly. Pathetically. "Let me down! Now, damn it!"

Her protests were a joke, her struggles a mockery of her words. She didn't want him to release her and leave her be, not any more than she wanted him to be nice.

Damn him, he was so right about her.

Crossing the room, he dropped her on the large, pillow-covered bed. She landed in the thick cushioning lined with incredibly soft cotton sheets. He climbed over her and pinned her hands. "I'll warn you, my love: when I hopped that first plane to come after you in

Hawaii, I'd decided then I'd do the opposite of everything in my nature, but when I caught the flight to Cairo, I committed to it."

She rebelled against his hold, wishing to God her damn body would quit wanting him so she could shove him away. "That doesn't give you the privilege of being an asshole."

He ground his hips against hers, the thick length of his hard-on pressing against her dampened pussy. "But you like it, don't you, Sadie?"

She turned her head. "Of course not."

"Yes, you do." He laughed, dry humping her. His clothes were so thin, he might as well have been nude, his every muscle, their clefts and bulges, pressed against her nerve-enlightened skin. "Even now, you're dripping wet. Ready for me to drive into you. This is what you want and you know it. You need *us*, Sadie. You've pushed and pushed, and all you've really wanted was for me to force you home. No choices, no sweet talking. You want me to take you, and damn it, Sadie, I am."

Sadie couldn't prevent her pelvis from responding, even as she protested. "That's ridiculous," she said through clenched teeth.

What were truly absurd were her weak objections.

He'd *won*. Game over.

She couldn't withstand any more tension. She wanted him. She needed him. Now. Hard. Fast.

He was right, damn it, and she was ready to let him be right.

"Ridiculous? *Sure* it is," he snarled sarcastically. "Do you remember, Sadie, in Tuscany, when you asked me what my fantasy was?"

"Yes," she whimpered. She wished he'd shut up already!

"I couldn't verbalize my deepest desires then, but now I'm going to show you. I have more fantasies than you could dream of." He released her wrists and trailed his hands along her torso, brushing his fingertips ever so slightly over the sensitive skin of her stomach to the golden hairs guarding her center, then slowly returned to her breasts, enveloping the mounds in his palms. "I think you're going to enjoy them."

Her nipples beaded into tight peaks, aching with intense sensation. She was so desperate for his mouth to claim the buds, she almost grabbed his head and forced him to pleasure her as she so needed. But this Dylan wouldn't tolerate such an action.

"Like what?"

Why wouldn't he get on with loving her already? She wanted his cock in her, damn it!

"This is a start. The rest, you'll see. All night long." Grasping her chin, he stared deeply into her eyes. "That I promise."

fourteen

Dylan crushed her lips with his, devouring her, hungry to satisfy all his pent-up sexuality. He kissed her fully, thrusting his tongue into her mouth and swirling it along her inner cheeks.

Pressing her body against his, Sadie knotted her fingers in his hair and eagerly flicked her tongue against his. He considered her eagerness a dare—the harder she kissed, the harder he kissed, until their mouths were mashed together in a bruising union.

Groaning with urgent passion, he realized for the first time he couldn't blame his lack of exploration solely on his embarrassment with Dora. Patience was not easily practiced in the bedroom, and especially not by him. He wanted Sadie, he wanted her now, hard and fast and thoroughly. His cock throbbed with need, the sensitive flesh behind the tip of his rod beating as if it had a heart of its own.

With a growl, he ripped his mouth free. He caressed her body with his as he slid from the bed, coming to stand over her. This time, he wanted more than a quick fuck.

Hell, he wanted more than a slow fuck.

Like he'd warned her, tonight was going to be very different from anything either of them had experienced, and he'd be damned if he'd wimp out now, not when he had the situation in such perfect order. Never again would such an opportunity cross his path. He wasn't like Maxim. Things like this didn't happen to him every day. This was his chance to experience a fantasy as well as his chance to win his fiancée's complete, abiding love.

Panting, Sadie lifted her head, leaning on her elbows. Her sparkling hazel eyes begged him to return, but she remained silent.

He crossed the room, retrieving three of the scarves she'd so conveniently bought before her abduction. The men had delivered the bagged silky strips of fabric to him shortly after her capture. He'd known then that he'd make good use of them.

He ran the silk over his fingers as he returned to the bedside. Indeed, these were perfect. He tossed them onto the mattress.

"Slide to the middle of the bed." He swatted the side of her bare bottom. "Spread your legs. Wide."

Sadie obliged, exposing the hot pink flesh of her moist mons.

Dylan licked his lips, ravenous at the sight of her juicy cunt. Going to the end of the bed, he grabbed her left ankle, tied the silk around it, then did the same to the right.

"Hey!" Sadie protested, though without heart. She moaned as he stretched her legs open even farther and secured the scarves tightly to the bedposts.

With huge, curious eyes she stared at him in silence as he climbed over her and seized her wrists, wrapping the silk tie around them several times, then securing her hands to the headboard.

Before he shared her, he wanted to savor her sweet taste. Crawling between her thighs, he spread her labia, holding the glistening lips wide open. He dipped his tongue into her tangy, orange-flavored juices, slowly licking the length of her delicious pussy.

His already painfully stiff erection twitched and Sadie moaned, thrusting her mound against his face. Her female scent smothered him and he probed her with his tongue, sliding in and out of her tight depths as her pelvis moved in rhythm.

Gripping her hips, he ate her thoroughly, savoring his recently found ability to love Sadie orally. Nothing could taste sweeter to him than lapping at her moist folds, kissing her intimately. How could he feel any closer to her than this?

And why the hell had he waited so long?

Now that he knew her this way, he wanted to know all of her . . . every inch of her beautiful body, her every desire, her every passion.

Trailing kisses along her left thigh and hip bone, he traveled up her body to her breasts and cupped their weight. He rubbed his palms over the soft skin and squeezed, massaging the supple flesh.

"Are you ready?" He gyrated his hips against her.

Was *he* ready? He'd gone far with Sadie the past couple of weeks, but participating in a ménage wasn't breaking out of the box, it was exploding it. Could he actually do this? Fantasizing about a four-some, even planning one, was a lot easier than the actual partaking.

He shoved the reluctant, boring side of his brain into a corner, determined now more than ever.

Sadie moaned in response, sounding half drunk on lust. "Very."

A tremor shook his lower stomach and he clenched his muscles to control them. No more second guessing, he commanded himself. Do the opposite.

Sadie was about to discover how serious he'd been about his earlier vow. How serious he was about her.

"Good." He seized her mouth in one final kiss and swept his tongue deep into her throat. Breaking away, he stood.

He crossed the room, going into the small alcove that guarded the entrance to his quarters and swung open the door, nodding to his two new buddies who waited in the hall. "She's all set." Stepping aside, he welcomed them inside.

"And you?" Ziyad questioned with an all-knowing smile.

"Geared up as I'll ever be."

And he was geared up, damn geared up. In fact, if he got any more ready, his pecker would burst. "Approach her slowly," he instructed as he followed them inside. "I want to savor the look on her face."

Dylan grinned to himself. Damn right, he'd made a good decision, and he wouldn't get all wishy-washy or change his mind now. He couldn't imagine finding himself in this situation again.

He wanted this. He needed it. Sadie needed it. Their relationship needed it.

He grinned at the thought. One thing was for sure, Sadie wouldn't taste satisfaction anytime soon. Before she received any cock, theirs or his, he intended to dispel every wanton desire from her mind. Sadie had too much energy for her own good. He intended to fulfill her sexually. Hell, to wear her out. To make her tired. Complacent. *His*.

Moreover, the thought of watching two men tweak and toy with her body turned him on. After all, there was nothing he enjoyed more than seeing Sadie writhe in pleasure.

Sadie struggled against her bonds. What the hell was he doing? Why was he bringing those creeps in here? He couldn't mean to return her to her room *now*! She was naked and tied up, not to mention her cunt was exposed and dripping.

The insufferable bastard! He'd teased and turned her on as torture and now he had the nerve to send her away?

She jerked at her wrists, frantic as Dylan coolly strode to the chair he'd been sitting in when she'd arrived. With ease, he lifted the velvet-lined lounger, bringing the clearly heavy furniture closer to her bed. Then he fetched a camera she didn't recognize and sat facing her, his hands on his lap, his view directly aligned with the juncture between her legs.

Her heart beat faster.

"Do you like my new camera, Sadie?" With a sparkle in his cocoa eyes, and a sly smile, he watched intently, grating on her nerves.

What the hell did he think he was going to do with that?

"Approach her slower," Dylan commanded the men.

What?

The two men measured their gait as they advanced on either side of the massive bed. During the kidnapping, she hadn't the time to really notice their looks. In her fear, she'd pegged them as slimeballs, but in reality, the men were the epitome of tall, dark, and handsome. Dressed in light clothing, their shirts were unbuttoned and hanging open. Their large, manly frames were well muscled and hairless, their skin appearing as if it had been oiled. Indeed, they reminded her of a model on a romance book cover.

The larger man to her left was at least six-foot-four and had long, silky black hair that cascaded past his shoulders. A slight, jagged scar marred his cheekbone near his eye, making him appear dangerous in a toe-curling, intriguing sort of way. He gazed at her with hunger—ravenous, sexual need—the kind that a woman wanted to see in a man. In *her* man. But he was not her man.

The kidnapper to her right was sweeter in appearance, though that was not to say he was less attractive. He had a baby face and close-clipped wavy hair, and his smile—*damn*, he had a smile. Dimples dotted the tight muscles of his cheeks and teamed with thickly lashed eyes that could melt a woman into lust dust.

"Dylan, you better call them off! You better think twice!" She wasn't into being quiet, no matter their looks, especially not at the moment. The more she fought against the damn scarves she'd ironically purchased because she thought they were sexy, the more she exposed herself to them. Their glances toward her wet pussy were making matters worse. She stilled, taking deep, angry breaths.

"Dylan," she ground out, clenching her bound fists. "If you think I'll fall for your games twice, you're way out of your league. Send me back to that room with these men and you'll never get me in your bed again. Never!"

"You're not *leaving* my bed. Not a chance." Dylan's words were cool and irritating.

She opened her mouth to scream at him, to demand an explanation. "I—"

"Each of you, get a condom," Dylan ordered the men, pointing to the table beside the bed.

Do *what?*

The bigger man grabbed the brown paper bag from the nightstand, rummaged though it, and tossed a foil-wrapped condom to his partner.

The men stripped in tandem, dropping their clothes to the ground in less than an instant. She stared in disbelief at their naked, rock-hard bodies and mammoth cocks. Tearing open the small packages, they rolled on the condoms.

"Dylan?" she squealed, so confused. She strained against the bonds and lifted her head to look him in his eyes of dark brown. "Dylan!"

"It's a fantasy come true, Sadie." He had the nerve to wink at her. "Enjoy."

Sadie officially freaked out. Two men? Two men! Wait . . . not two . . . counting Dylan, he intended for her to have sex with *three* men? No way! The prospect was ludicrous! She said she'd thought about a threesome, not that she would actually participate in multiple-partner sex. "Dylan, have you lost your freaking mind?"

"Yes."

"Dylan, let me go!"

"You don't really want that, now do you, Sadie?"

She groaned in protest and struggled against the bonds. What in the hell was Dylan thinking? What—

"Reintroduce yourself, men. She may have forgotten your names. I want her to know them."

"I'm Nassor, madam," the scarred one told her in a velvety smooth voice, so richly accented that tingles danced on her skin.

"Ziyad," the other said. "At your service."

"Good. See Sadie, they're playing nice. You play nice as well." She heard the snap of his camera. "Tease her. Unmercifully. Do the things I told you she enjoys."

"Dylan!"

Nassor straddled her, his long legs nestling against her sides. He ran his calloused fingers over her bare belly and breasts. Unwelcome sensations shot through her body.

"Get off me."

"We're here to pleasure you."

She sucked in a sharp breath and arched against him, as if she could push his large body off her, but her efforts were weak. Pathetic.

She should insist, but deep in her heart, she didn't want to.

Nassor bent and brought his mouth to her ear, suckling the lobe. She shivered, her body awakening as she leaned into his attention.

She could feel herself succumbing. Melting. Desire and fantasies gained control of reason, and as much as the thought of a foursome seemed almost frightening, she didn't have the power or the desire to fight what was happening.

Nassor cupped her breasts, filling his palms with the flesh, and massaging them in full, rounded movements. His thumbs flicked over her nipples and the buds tightened into pert pebbles.

His hands felt so good. Damn wonderful. Tantalizing.

In that moment, all her protests collapsed. She moaned aloud and every muscle in her body tightened. His hands were that of a hard worker, rough and so unlike Dylan's. As he caressed her breasts, his fingertips created a sandpaper-like sensation over her sensitized skin.

In the background, she heard the click, click, click of the camera as Dylan shot evidence of her surrender.

She sucked in a deep breath, aware that she was sinking further and further into the situation as Ziyad crawled between her legs. He forced her thighs open and his thick fingers delved into her mons. He ran his thumb over her labia, exposing her clit. He pressed the palpitating button and ecstasy ignited through her as if he'd just flicked an on switch.

Sadie writhed in passion, her resistance long forgotten. She couldn't fathom what was happening. It was like a dream, but a damn good one, and she didn't want the fantasy to stop. Not now.

Arousal possessed her body; every one of her nerves awoke. Tilting her pelvis, she welcomed Ziyad's hand. He drove into her slick depths with several fingers, stretching her sheath to accept him as he pushed deeply within her pussy. He pumped rapidly in and out of her, driving her body wild. Ziyad wasn't playing around . . . he wanted her turned on and he wanted it immediately.

She was all too happy to oblige.

Her resistance now completely forgotten, Sadie bucked against his hand, the motions of her hips uncontrollable.

It was almost too much. Her body was going insane, passion electrifying her from top to bottom. Worse, the more she accepted the fact that she was having multiple-partner sex, the more she realized just what she was getting into. Every one of her holes would be filled. Simultaneously. The thought alone almost made her come.

Nassor tweaked her nipples, rolling the tight buds between his forefingers and thumbs, then squeezing. The painful pleasure was more than she could bear and she screamed out, begging for mercy, begging for *more*!

Nassor responded by releasing her breasts and leaning forward. He filled her open mouth with his ten-inch cock, pushing the wide rod to the back of her throat. The delicious flavor of chocolate teased her taste buds, surprising Sadie. He had on a chocolate-flavored condom! Who knew?

She suckled his length desperately, as if she were milking his rod for relief. The stroke of his hard flesh running along her tongue and cheek made her salivate. She moaned, swallowing him, wanting more of him, of the wondrous taste.

Nassor continued to love her mouth, but returned his hands to her breasts, mashing the mounds in his palms. Meanwhile, Ziyad vigorously hand fucked her cunt, pumping in and out of her slick sex so fast she almost couldn't stand it.

Having so much attention paid to her concurrently pushed Sadie to new heights; her body was soaring, her mind in disbelief at the incredulous circumstances.

Squeezing her vaginal muscles, she resisted the urge to climax. She wanted Dylan to partake, not simply watch. Damn him and his picture taking. She was the photographer, not him!

The need was too great and she couldn't control herself. She spiraled into an uncontrollable, rippling orgasm. Her inner walls convulsed around Ziyad's hand as pleasure exploded through her body.

The ultimate climax struck her fiercely, and she thrashed on the bed, reality fading out as she writhed in extreme sexual bliss.

Clutching the soft sheets above her head with her bound hands, she grasped for anything to hold onto to steady herself. She screamed, then collapsed, her body spent.

Distantly, she heard a thump. She drew several deep breaths, aware that though she'd come, this was nowhere near done with. Not if she had anything to say about it.

Dylan was getting in this bed with them. If he could go so far as to arrange to have two men fuck her, he could join them.

Lifting her head, she looked at Dylan, and noticed he'd dropped his camera. He licked his lips, his smile slight. Her eyes drifted down, observing his cock standing at attention and forming a tent in his pants.

Sadie smiled. He was turned on, big time. He liked sharing her.

His hands slid under the fabric of his pajamas and grasped the shaft, jerking it up and down. She watched him pleasure himself, amazed by how comfortable he now was with his sexuality. To think he'd kept this side of him secret from her so long.

Sadie lifted her gaze and locked eyes with him. A connection passed between them, a bond unlike she'd ever experienced. To-gether, they were pleasuring in something far greater than either one of them had dared to dream of, much less consider, at least until re-cently. Though strangers were teasing her body, she and Dylan were making love.

The men switched places and Sadie sucked in a breath, preparing herself for another vigorous round. Ziyad straddled her chest with his long, sinewy thighs covered in dark hair, while Nassor positioned himself between her legs.

Dylan remained seated, leaving Sadie to guess she'd have to drive him crazy with want before he'd get up the nerve to join them. And that she would.

Knotting his fingers in her hair, Ziyad pulled her head forward, and nudged her lips with his massive rod. The scent of his tasty fruit condom invited her and she opened wide, swallowing his banana-flavored erection.

Suckling the tip of his broad head, she slowly slid her tongue along the taut skin of his cock, tasting him, teasing him, making a show of blowing him. Though he attempted to pump anxiously into her, she prevented his eagerness with the suction of her mouth, and blew him with patience, consuming his length one inch at a time.

With his thumbs, Nassor opened her labia, exposing her en-gorged clit to his thick, expert tongue. He lapped the swollen crease of her sex, suckling at her drenched folds, then gently took her nub between his teeth, stroking the bud with his tongue.

The feel of his mouth upon her was gloriously intense. Sadie's whole body contracted as she fought the urge to buck from plea-sure, well aware that she was entrusting a stranger with a very del-icate area.

He sucked sharply then released, drawing her nerve-enflamed clit in and out while he pressed fingers into her tunnel. She spasmed and drew him deeper. She craved something longer, wider, like Dylan's big prick . . . or perhaps both men's cocks.

What would it be like? Would it be too much, taking three men at once? The notion was slightly scary, but damn, she couldn't wait. Visualizing the sex to come, she pressed her loins into Nassor's face, panting, moaning, making an eager display in hopes of rushing the men.

Especially Dylan, damn him! Was he waiting for her to pass out first?

The more she thrust and performed, the more the ecstasy swirling through her strengthened and increased.

An orgasm rose in her again, driving her even higher as she soared, teetering on the brink. How much more could she take?

She struggled to catch of glimpse of her lover as Ziyad fucked her mouth. Was Dylan enjoying this or was he anxious? Possibly regretting his choice?

She needed to know how he felt. She needed . . .

Him.

Ziyad pressed deeper, filling her throat with his thick banana cock, and forcing her to swallow him. Simultaneously, Nassor dipped a smaller finger in her sex, and then slid the sopping digit into her anus, forcing her to a precipice.

That did it!

She thrashed, crying out over her crammed mouth. "Dylan!"

The men pressed deeper, filling her more, more, more, until she couldn't accept any additional prodding. Until she was so crazy with abandon she wanted to cry and beg for relief.

She whimpered his name. "Dylan, Dylan . . ."

To her surprise, smooth fingers grabbed her toes, the soft pads of thick thumbs stroking the inner sole of her foot. She coiled, trying to escape the torturous touch, but the bonds held strong, forcing her to endure the unwanted attention. Her struggles thrust her body against face and cock.

Damn it, didn't he realize? She wanted . . . needed . . .

"Dylan!" she squealed over the rod filling her mouth, suddenly aware that it was her lover tickling her toes. He stood at the end of the bed, a pleased, almost smug, smile on his face.

"Enjoying yourself, Sadie?"

Sadie turned her head and spit out the dick pumping in her mouth. Lifting her upper body, she panted at the man tormenting her with tongue and fingers, and tempted Dylan with her eyes.

"What do you think?" She licked her lips. "You've no idea what you're missing."

He tickled the arch of her foot. "Soon, little Miss Impatient. For now, no breaks. Get back to his hard-on before it goes flaccid." His dark eyes drifted to Ziyad, who pumped his erection with his hand, then back to her. "Now."

To enforce his wish, he lightly stroked the bottom of her foot once again, driving her wild with tickly irritation.

Ziyad's mushroom-shaped head nudged her mouth once again, and she accepted him, this time sucking him slower, more fully. From the corner of her eye, she watched Dylan's observation, loving the way he gazed at Nassor eating her cunt . . . his eyes glazed with passion.

Who the hell was this new man masquerading as her fiancé?

She sucked in a deep breath as Nassor tongue fucked her until she wanted to scream. Did her fiancé have any idea what he was doing to her? She was in sexual agony and Dylan was getting away with murder! He had control of the situation, she knew he did, and he was making her suffer intentionally.

Damn him!

The men persisted, pushing and prodding her body, teasing her with the notion of more, of complete and utter fulfillment, but never supplying it.

Again she peaked, a hurricane of an orgasm blowing through her body and threatening to wipe out her willpower. Her every muscle tightened as she held on, determined Dylan wouldn't get away with such torture.

To her surprise, she didn't have to fight. It was Dylan who ended her anguish.

"Enough," he issued. "I don't want her coming again. Not until it's time."

Ziyad groaned, slowing, but continued to thrust into her mouth. Nassor abandoned her pussy and straightened. "Shall I untie her ankles?"

Nassor licked her juices from his glistening lips and Dylan nodded in agreement. "Yes." Dylan's eyes swept over her body. "Ziyad, untie her hands."

The men released the bonds and she sunk into the mattress, engulfed by arousal, but physically spent. She drew a deep breath, then another, sighing. Her eyelids fluttered and she found herself drifting. Floating.

Could she continue? She was in a fog, her body used beyond comprehension, yet so hungry for more; she couldn't stop if she wanted to.

The next thing she knew, she was stirred from her lethargy and lifted into Nassor's arms. Dylan's clothes dropped to the floor like white feathers floating to the ground, easing off his body in such smooth movements, it was almost as if he were shedding into the nude. His fingers skimmed over the mattress as he circled the bed, then lay across its center, his legs dangling off the side.

Nassor deposited her on Dylan's solid body, guiding her legs so she lay face down. She melted against the heat of his flesh, her face burrowing in the cleft of his shoulder.

Finally.

Dylan's forefinger found her spine and traveled slowly down its length. Awareness shot through her spinal cord, reawakening her body. Her pussy yawned for his fulfillment, new liquid trickling from her already slick tunnel.

Sadie couldn't wait another moment more. She needed him in her. She needed relief. *Now.* She grasped for Dylan's cock and found his hard shaft. Fisting her prize, she guided it to her slit. Dylan stopped her, caressing her bottom. "Patience."

"I can't . . ." she whimpered. "No more."

He grasped the fleshy meat of her ass, his fingers digging into her skin, and ceasing her from taking him.

"More," he growled into her ear, nibbling at her lobe. "Much more."

Oh God.

Nassor grasped her hips from behind, his calloused palms laying flat on her soft skin and steadying her. His cock danced between her legs, aligning with the crevice of her tush. In response, her anus twitched, her inner muscles squeezing at the thought of having a cock buried in her asshole as Dylan fucked her cunt.

Oh hell yes! But there was more . . .

Ziyad crawled across the bed, kneeling directly behind Dylan's head. He cupped her jaw, lifting her to face his jutting member. The movement forced her onto her knees, rounding her read end for Nassor.

How was it possible to feel so loved, so wanted . . . so sexy?

Nassor dipped his fingers into her dripping heat, and sequestered her thick, creamy juices. Rubbing the luscious liquid over the puckering bud, he entered her with his thumb, forcing her asshole to open for him. She gasped as he warmed her up, preparing her body for a much wider, much longer entry.

Again, he retrieved thick desire from her sex, and spread the moisture along his shaft from top to bottom. Spreading her cheeks, he positioned to enter her anus. Her stomach lurched in excitement.

Dylan grabbed her waist, holding her steady. He plunged deep into her pussy, quickly followed by Nassor, who filled her rectum with his immense width.

"Dylan!" Sadie squealed in delight and shock, gasping for air, the intensity of taking two cocks at once more than she'd ever imagined or expected.

Ecstasy poured through her body as she stretched to accommodate their thrusting staffs. Extreme, hip-bucking pleasure crashed through her lower half in a tidal wave. She lost control of her movements, wild with passion as she rammed and begged for more. Much more.

The two men pumped in and out of her body, fucking her slow and steady, despite her eagerness, which drove her insane. She wanted to go faster, she wanted them to let the animals deep within themselves loose upon her body and completely ravage her. She'd waited so long . . . too long . . . for such measured torture.

Repeatedly they filled her completely and pushed her to the edge. She whimpered and pleaded, becoming dizzy, almost incoherent from the wicked wonderfulness of it.

Ziyad wound his fingers in her hair. He nudged her lips with the broad head of his banana-flavored rod, quieting her begging. Happy for more, she opened, accepting him. His delicious cock slid along her tongue, igniting the sensitive taste buds of her mouth with pleasure, making every nerve in her body electrify.

Distantly, she realized what a fantasy come true this was . . . three men, ramming in and out of her every hole, driving her mad with carnal bliss, their every attention all on her . . .

It didn't seem true. Real. She certainly hadn't ever thought a foursome possible. She *still* didn't think it was possible.

Soon, she'd wake up and realize she'd dreamt all this.

Except she didn't need to pinch herself to know she could feel. Every inch of her body was alive with bliss. Her skin hummed with ecstasy, her muscles wound tight, desperate for relief.

Sadie took all the men with vigor, sucking, bucking, and fucking with all her energy. Though she fought for the freedom to take their cocks harder, faster, the men held her tight, slowly pushing into her over and over, their hips gyrating and grinding with their own desire.

They were filling her so completely, fucking her so vigorously, but still, she needed . . . she wanted . . .

"More!" Sadie screamed, her cry spiraling into a high-pitched squeal. The men slammed into her, ramming her body with their swords, satisfying her so thoroughly she thought she'd faint from the explosive force building in her. She milked their cocks, taking as much of the men as she could handle—and then some.

Her sheath coiled into a whirling tornado of ultimate satisfaction. Digging her nails into Dylan's shoulders, she belted her gratification as an orgasm exploded through her body.

Her pussy spasmed and her vision blurred, her world suddenly black as physical exhaustion claimed her.

I'll call if I need you." Dylan shook both men's hands, glancing to his snoring fiancée with an ample smile. Never had she looked more beautiful. "I believe we've worn her out quite thoroughly."

Nassor chuckled and Ziyad's eyes gleamed with satisfaction as he spoke. "I hope to find a wife like her one day. She's a good woman. Obliging."

Dylan bit his tongue, thinking the men had *no* clue how impossible Sadie was, but he played along. "I was happy to share her. Perhaps again."

Nassor agreed with a lopsided smile. "Indeed."

"Perhaps again, American." Ziyad added.

Nodding their good-byes, they strode from the room, leaving Dylan to his turbulent thoughts.

The foursome hadn't been what he'd expected and certainly not what he'd feared. There hadn't been a moment of jealousy or regret. He hadn't been embarrassed or ashamed of having sexual relations with other men. Watching Sadie writhe and squeal in ultimate pleasure had been intoxicating. Once the men had started touching her, a whirlwind of lust had swept through him, overpowering any doubts he might have had.

He felt closer to her now, closer to himself as a man, than he ever had. Than he thought was possible.

He wanted to do this again and again. He never wanted to go back to the old Dylan.

But he had to return home eventually, didn't he?

Releasing a pent-up groan, he gently bit the tip of his tongue. In the big picture, what really mattered was his love for Sadie.

Crossing the room, he gathered her unresponsive body in his arms and slid her under the sheets. He sat on the bed next to her, slowly stroking the length of her delicate jawbone and wishing he could see into her dreams.

"What will your next move be?" he whispered, his heart constricting at the thought of being left again. "Will I ever tame you, Sadie, my love?"

Did he even want to? He worried he'd gone completely wild himself.

From his actions of late, it seemed he had, from skipping out on real life to ditching his inhibitions. The past few days, when he looked in the mirror, he almost didn't recognize himself. Sometimes, he hated the new man he found himself staring at and not understanding why he would behave in such ways. Other times, he couldn't love the new Dylan more.

Sadie murmured something in her sleep and nestled her face in the pillow. Staring, he memorized her face, her beautiful skin, the way her eyelashes occasionally fluttered as she slept.

"I love you," he whispered, almost glad she couldn't hear him. It had been a long time since she'd expressed the same emotion. "So much."

He couldn't lose her. Damn it. He *couldn't*.

He wasn't positive yet, but it appeared his current plan was working. What would her reaction be when she woke? Anger? Disgust? Happiness?

Would she want another ménage?

Screw his conscience. He hoped she wanted ten more.

"Well I know one thing, love," he murmured, taking the colorful scarves from where they lay discarded on the mattress. He ran the silk fabric over his palms. "You won't be running again. Not this time."

He loved her too much to chance it.

Sadie had no idea why she'd allowed him to tie her to the bed, pretending to be asleep, even though she was wide awake and excited as hell.

Perhaps because of the tender way he'd admired her. The way he'd whispered his love. The way he'd gone to the ends of the earth for her.

Or, maybe she was simply enjoying herself more than she'd ever anticipated enjoying a fantasy. She didn't want it to end. She wanted to keep playing. To keep being his hostage, his possession, *his*.

She was well aware that any psychiatrist would declare her insane in the blink of an eye. God forbid she mention such thoughts to a women's rights activist. She'd be burned at the stake.

So her thoughts were far from politically correct and all that jazz. Secretly, she always wished Dylan would be more possessive. Demanding. In love.

She enjoyed that her boyfriend was being a jerk, but only because she knew it was a game. In real life, at home, he'd never get away with this.

She knew she *shouldn't* want such behavior from the man she was about to marry, but it didn't change the primal, raw feelings in her gut. Dylan loved her. He wouldn't let her go. He wouldn't compromise. He'd do *anything* for her.

He was willing to go the extra mile and back for their love.

Game or not, his behavior gave her more faith in him, in them, than ever before. Come thick or thin, their relationship was rock solid.

Effective immediately, her doubts had vanished.

So had her cop.

She didn't need to fall asleep to be positive he wasn't coming back. How, or why, she didn't know, but the nightmarish sex dreams wouldn't return. She was sure of that much.

She sneaked a one-eyed peek at Dylan. He stood in the open French doors, facing the setting Egyptian sun, his black robe gently blowing around his body from the evening breeze. With the way he stood and the serene appearance on his stubble-covered face, he looked more in his element, more content, than she'd ever seen him.

Happiness curled through her stomach, a twisty, tingly feeling that almost made her laugh. She was so glad for him. For them. Dylan had finally freed himself. So had she.

She loved him so much.

Reluctantly, she closed her eyes and drew in a deep, relaxing breath. She needed to get some rest. Tomorrow she had some heavy shopping to do.

It was high time she got a wedding dress. High time they headed home.

Of course, that was unless Dylan had another foursome in mind . . .

Grinning, she snuggled into the pillow and let her muscles and mind go limp. She needed to get some rest, just in case.

fifteen

At least *her* hotel had working AC! Sadie was positive she'd never woken to such a hot, dry morning in all her life. Groaning, she licked her lips, barely able to peel her eyes open. "Dylan?"

He moaned in response. "Go back to sleep."

She fluttered her lashes, feeling as if sand were in her eyes. No way could she go back to sleep. She felt like crap, not to mention grouchy as hell.

She jerked at her wrists, impatience nipping at her. She'd enjoyed these restraints yesterday, but this morning she was in no mood to be tied down. Not unless he wanted to hook a coffee IV to her arm.

Enough with the fun and games. She really needed a drink, and she really needed to go pee. A shower wouldn't hurt either. "Untie me. I need to use the bathroom." When he didn't budge, she kneed him in the butt. "I'll go in the bed if you don't get up!"

"Ugggggh!" Dylan rolled over. "It's the crack of dawn. Couldn't you let me sleep another hour?"

"You don't have to get up. Just untie me already."

With annoying slowness, Dylan sat, stretched the sinewy muscles of his shoulders and neck, then shook his head. "So you can run again? Nah. Not taking the chance. I prefer to wake up."

His bitter words were a needle in a balloon.

"You think I'm going to run *now*? Say you're kidding me." When he didn't, Sadie sunk into the pillow, deflated. She chewed her lower lip. "You're serious? You think I'd leave you after . . . that?"

Forgetting her physical needs, her mind raced with worry. Dylan sounded so distrustful it hurt.

He tossed over, kicked off the sheets, and sat. Straddling her waist, he raised a thick, dark brow. "Are you prepared to promise me you won't run off again?"

Using her annoyance as a buffer, Sadie remained silent as he worked at the knots securing the scarves in jerky movements. In time, he freed each wrist.

She jerked her hands away the moment they were released. Rubbing the skin where the bonds had been, she swallowed. Tears welled in her eyes.

To hell with pride! To hell with her fantasy! He'd hurt her feelings . . . after how he'd behaved? No way!

She shook her head in disgust. "You're supposed to trust me."

Dylan chuckled. "Are you kidding *me*?" To her dismay, he caught her hands, pinning her under him, so she was at his mercy once again.

"No," she snapped and struggled to free herself, twisting under his weight. As she turned, she caught sight of the clock. Good grief. It wasn't morning! It was four in the afternoon. They'd slept the whole day.

She wriggled against him. "Dylan. It isn't the crack of dawn, it's near sunset. Let me up, seriously!"

Dylan held her in place. "I don't give a damn what time it is. You've run off on me twice when I've come after you. I'm not taking any chances." He leaned down and murmured in her ear, his hot breath tickling the sensitive skin of the pierced lobe. "Promise you won't run and I'll believe you. Otherwise—"

Sadie licked her lips, aware that she was playing with fire. "Third time's the charm," she threw at him.

Dylan scoffed and abruptly released her hands, rolling off her. "Funny."

Lying stiffly beside her, he glared into dead space. She stared at the ceiling and released a frustrated sigh.

Damn it. She really hated it when she was wrong.

He was correct not to trust her. She *had* run off on him, yet here she was, still playing mind games.

Why was she hesitating? Her cop was gone and she was positive she loved Dylan as much as he loved her. She wanted to go home.

Sadie curled against him and leaned her head on his shoulder. "Dylan, I won't run off again. I want to marry you. I'm going home with you."

"Really?"

He sounded so sarcastic and doubtful her stomach knotted.

She couldn't take this emotional turmoil. After all they'd surpassed, she simply wanted to have fun with him.

"Yes, really." She poked at his side, desperate to lighten the mood. "Now either we're going to have more great sex or I'm off to shop for a wedding dress. Do you realize the big day is a little less than three weeks away?"

"Great sex?" Dylan hummed, drawing her tight against his torso. "I shouldn't have untied you."

"I think it's my turn to tie you up." Wrapping her legs around his, she trailed her fingers over the solid muscles of his chest. "Last night was fantastic, by the way. You told me why, but dare I ask how?"

"Maxim."

"Maxim?" Her mouth formed an *O*. When she'd decided to run off to Cairo, she'd totally forgotten Dylan's rich playboy friend and that he knew Egypt well.

"Well, I'll have to thank him." She kissed him gently on the cheek. "And thank you too."

Dylan squeezed her. "You, my dear, are very, very welcome."

Her hand on the shower curtain, Sadie listened to Dylan's smooth, deep voice carrying into the bathroom. She couldn't hear what he was saying, but she surmised he was talking on the phone. Rather excitedly too.

Perhaps he was making plans to return home. Already.

Good, she told herself, denying the way her back bristled at the thought. The way her chest tightened.

She threw back the shower curtain and stepped under the hot, streaming water, closing her eyes.

Acapulco beckoned her . . .

Mexico, the beach, the sun . . .

But no, she'd promised him, right?

Cool gulf water and hot sand between her toes . . .

What picture clue to leave Dylan next? The photo definitely needed to be something to drive him nuts searching for, so he'd lose a few days.

Meanwhile, she'd cook up a surprise of her own, a little—

Oh God.

Had she gone crazy? Lost her mind? Her senses?

A half hour ago, maybe an hour tops, she'd promised Dylan she'd stay.

She intended to stay.

She *wanted* to stay.

Working the jasmine-scented shampoo vigorously through her hair, Sadie did her best to stifle the burning itch in her soul. But not even the subtle, floral scent helped to relax her.

The reality of the foursome was soaking in, hard and fast. Until now, it had seemed so surreal. But it wasn't.

Dylan had really turned into another man.

Oh damn, and he'd taken so many photos, more than likely mostly horrid shots of her. While she might be quite talented at taking pictures, she didn't photograph well.

As soon as she could get her hands on his camera, the film was hers. Shit.

Why did everything suddenly seem so overwhelming? Suffocating?

She hadn't really promised, had she? She'd said she'd stay. She didn't say *promise*.

The vow was implied!

Damn it. This was insane.

She cranked the temperature up so high the water scalded her skin. She scrubbed her arms briskly. Why did she keep doing this to herself? To him? To them? She *knew* her cop was gone. She *wanted* to go home. To marry Dylan.

So why did she find herself so anxious? Daydreaming of escape?

With only a few weeks left before their marriage, she didn't have time to waste on doubts. Damn her nonsensical urges, she was getting out of this shower, finding some clothes, and going shopping for her wedding dress.

She wouldn't stop until she found *the* one. In fact, she wouldn't settle until she was sure she'd found something guaranteed to steal her mother's breath away as well.

Fortunately, her ankle was feeling better. Shopping and some fresh air would do her good. Not that the air in Cairo was very fresh—more like smoggy—but she needed to get out of this room for a little while. She needed a distraction.

Shutting off the water, she grabbed a towel and stepped onto the cool, marble floor. After drying off, she wrapped the soft pink cotton around her body and headed into the master bedroom.

"Dylan? I have no clothes but that red nightie. I—"

"You won't need clothes for this," he purred in a velvety, seductive tone that immediately grabbed her full attention.

Sprawled in a towel-covered bed, his massive body was a human sundae of fruit and whipped cream. He'd carefully arranged sliced strawberries over his loins, creating a trail from his nipples to his cock, which stood proudly, undoubtedly ready for her tongue.

"Oh my gosh!" Sadie dropped her towel and her hand went to her mouth. "You're dessert!"

"Breakfast, actually. I thought after last night you'd be hungry." His offer was smooth as honey. She curled her toes, eating up the sight of him.

She raised a brow. "My other fantasy?"

"You didn't think I'd allow it to go unfulfilled, did you?"

"I didn't think—" Sadie couldn't restrain her giggles. "I always imagined I'd be the one covered in food."

His eyes pointed out a large wicker basket on the nightstand filled with fruits, whipped toppings, candies, and even chocolate syrup. "You will be, after you eat. Ladies first."

"No fair! You get chocolate!" She crossed her arms.

"Mmm . . . Get over here, start licking, and you might be in for a surprise."

So much for her wedding dress! If she didn't know better, she'd think Dylan set this up deliberately to sabotage her.

"*You*! You know I was supposed to be looking for a dress so we could go home."

"We have twenty days until the wedding . . . there's more than enough time. We've been gone this long, and hell, we won't exactly be returning to a bunch of smiling faces either. We might as well have our fun while we can."

Sadie's lips curled in satisfaction. "Now I like the sound of that!"

She ran to the bed, leaping on the mattress. Little bits of whipped cream sprayed through the air, splattering the wall as she landed, but she didn't care. She didn't *have* to care.

Going right for the kill, rather than wasting time on his chest, she licked along the edge of his sweetly coated private regions toward his erection. To her delight, her tongue discovered a layer of rich, creamy chocolate spread under the whipped topping.

"Chocolate!" she cried.

Dylan grinned, knotting his hands in her hair, and drawing her head to the tip of his erection. "You didn't think I'd disappoint you like that, now did you, babe?"

"You know me too well," she murmured.

She swallowed his cock and the syrup covering his great length, her tongue working overtime as she licked him clean.

From his perineum to his balls to the very tip of his mushroom head, she devoured him. Up and down, round and round, she used her tongue in every manner possible, swirling and flicking around the hard shaft that jerked every time she hit a sensitive spot. She gobbled up the strawberries, holding some in her mouth and running them along his shaft.

She consumed all the sweet stuff until his rod was squeaky clean. The taste lingered as she blew him, taking him all the way to the back of her throat, never more turned on or delighted by giving head. The fact that he'd done this for her was beyond sweet. Beyond love.

Thick desire dripped from her pussy, running down her damp thighs. Her clit pulsed for attention, her labia swollen and hot with arousal.

Dylan's grip on her hair tightened and he drew her upwards, away from his cock, to the whipped cream trail she'd skipped. Following his lead, she consumed the remainder of her breakfast, over the flat of his six-pack stomach, dipping her tongue in the tiny cavern of his navel, and upward, to the fine clefts of his built pecs. She flicked her tongue over his nipples, toying with the tiny, hard beads.

"Do you like that?" she asked.

"What do you think?" His fingers dug into her scalp, wrapping the strands of her short hair hard around his digits, as if the action would bring him some measure of control.

"Ahhh . . ." Suckling his nipples, she drew the erect peaks between her teeth, and he groaned. His hips bucked against her, demanding entrance.

Not a chance!

She shifted her lower half and continued her licking and teasing. Releasing his grip on her hair, he grabbed her bottom, and aligned her pelvis with his sex.

"I want you. Now," he demanded in her ear.

Sadie arched, refusing him access. After all, it wouldn't be fair to end this before Dylan fed, now would it? Not at all. Not a chance.

She humped his cock without allowing him entry, grinding his rigid rod against her engorged folds. Her pubic hairs created friction and heated the passion between them. In response, her vaginal muscles constricted, hungry to be fulfilled.

Much as she wanted to slip him deep inside of her, she didn't relent until she'd licked away every speck of cream and chocolate from his torso, and even then she was having so much fun torturing him she didn't want to stop.

She gyrated against his cock in exaggerated movements, loving the way he groaned in protest, the way his fingers clenched her skin, as if he were holding on for dear life.

Ecstasy built in her. The more heightened her desire became, the more uncontrollably her hips flexed. An unexpected orgasm seized her, shaking her world as her pussy rippled with pleasure. She peaked, screaming, her nails digging into his shoulders.

Close to passing out, she collapsed on top of him, resting her head in the crook of his shoulder. Squeezing her ass, Dylan slapped each cheek, and then tossed her off him. "My turn."

Sadie felt like a puddle of lust. The thought of his tongue upon her body, mimicking the attentions she'd favored upon him, was intoxicating.

"Mmm . . . can't argue with that." She stretched, hands above her head, and opened her body to his will. Her clit pulsed, her sex starved for more attention. Reaching down, she played with the bundle of nerves, robustly applying pressure to the dripping bead.

Dylan rolled over, grabbed the basket, then straddled her. Shaking the can of whipped topping, he sprayed the foamy cream over her breasts. Her nipples tightened almost painfully in response, squeezing into tiny, sensation-inflamed buds.

Slowly, he moved downward along her body, covering her in the sticky liquid, and laying strawberries unsystematically on her body.

"Did I mention I love your wax job?"

"Don't bring that up," she quipped. "I'm enjoying this, so it's not a good time to argue."

"Oh, but I love your skin, Sadie, so creamy, smooth. I can't wait to lick every inch of it, especially your legs and . . ." His movements drifted downward, and he placed a strawberry over her mons. "Your cunt."

He kissed her there, making her shudder from both his words and action, then continued garnishing her.

His sweeping touch was oh-so-sensual, and with each breezy connection of his fingers and her stomach, each spray of the topping, each fruit planted, her muscles quivered with passion.

By the time he finished decorating her, she didn't want to be eaten; she desperately wanted his thick, hard cock in her. She panted with need, trying so hard not to squirm on the bed and ruin all his artwork.

His tongue connected with her body, sweeping over the flat of her stomach. She arched, tingles rippling over her skin as he licked. Pausing at her navel, he dipped into the button and swirled, then kissed and sucked his way upwards, to her breasts.

In a maddening, slow effort, he devoured the sweet meal he'd made of her, lapping at the cream and gradually working his way to her nipples. Cupping each of the mounds in his hands, he encircled her left areola with his mouth and suckled.

She felt like a queen, having so much attention paid to her. Never had she imagined her fantasy would be this sensuous or arousing. Hot, fiery desire burned over her skin with every stroke of his fingers and tongue. Her cunt tensed with a surge of pleasure and she reared against him.

"Harder. Suck it harder," she begged. "Please, Dylan."

Increasing his hold on her nipple, he drew the pebble between his teeth so severely that the action was close to painful, but in such a damn good way. She moaned and dug her nails in his back, scarcely able to withstand any more oral torment, her body slamming against his in desperation.

Dylan switched breasts, issuing the same harsh treatment to her right nipple. Mind-possessing heat undulated through her, swelling her sexual organs.

"Dylan please . . ." She pushed against him, needing the agonizing foreplay to end. Now.

She wanted his cock in her and she refused to wait any longer.

"I'm still hungry." Chuckling with amusement, Dylan kissed along her stomach, licking away traces of the cream he'd already devoured, and slowly chewing any strawberries he came across.

Sadie opened her mouth to protest, suddenly aware it would do her little good. The more she pushed him, the more he pushed back.

The wait for him to reach the juncture between her thighs was pure, utter agony, but finally his lips found her mons.

Placing his palms on her upper thighs, he spread her legs open and gobbled at the sundae, his tongue flicking and rubbing along her clit. He ate her clean, from front to back, not shy in the least about where he lapped.

Pushing a strawberry slice down, he ran the fruit along her folds and over her tunnel. He drove it deeper, sliding it across her perineum, then to her anus. Grabbing the strawberry with his teeth, he flicked it across the puckering bud, driving her crazy.

Sexual voltage shot through her in tiny, electric currents. He dropped the fruit, spreading her with his fingers, and delved into her cunt. Swirling his tongue in circles, up and down, back and forth, he pleasured her in every way imaginable with his mouth.

The room faded; reality faded. Sadie became nothing but a ball of panting passion as a powerful orgasm gushed from her, her vaginal muscles constricting with such force, she almost couldn't withstand the ecstasy.

Dylan slid his hands under her ass, lifting her bottom. Sweeping his tongue along her labia in wide, slow strokes, he continued to lap at her juices until she collapsed on the bed.

He shifted to his knees, aligning her pussy with his cock, and drove into her with one full thrust. Their bodies united and came together in a frenzy. Her arousal ignited once again, bursting with pleasure as he speared her, bucking in and out of her. The bed shook under them, creaking as if it were close to collapse.

Driving her to another climax in no time, Dylan buried himself deep within her. His seed filled her with warmth and he stilled, his hands squeezing her bottom.

Slowly, he released her and flopped on the bed. He took her hand in his. "Delicious." He planted a soft kiss on her palm.

Sadie stared almost blankly at the ceiling. For the first time in her life, she was truly stunned beyond words. She inhaled and exhaled while she tried to regain some sort of logical thought.

"Wow," she finally managed, then gasped, her head still muddled.

Dylan chuckled. "You're panting."

"I think I just lost and gained five pounds all at once."

"No loss, no gain. You can't complain."

"Complaining is the last thing I intend to do."

Finally, her mind cleared and she sat, suddenly aware of what a total disaster they'd made of the bed—hell, of the room. Whipped cream and chocolate were smeared all over the towels he'd laid down, but unfortunately, he hadn't thought to cover the walls or floors. The whipped topping had made it as far as the ceiling, though how she could only guess.

What could she do but laugh? The mess had been so worth the fun they'd had.

Standing, she tiptoed to avoid several withered strawberries. "Want to take a shower with me?"

"Lead the way," he growled, his dark eyes locking with hers once again.

Well, what do you think?"

Sitting in his lounge chair, Dylan jerked his gaze from the screen of his Palm Pilot to Sadie, who twirled around in a fringed, bright turquoise–and-orange tunic and balloon-legged pants. A shawl hung from her shoulders. Around her neck, she wore an intricately beaded necklace, and in her hand, she carried a gold, sequin-decorated silk bag.

The sight of her dressed in the very vibrant clothing chosen by Nafrini brought a smile to his face. The outfit was so not Sadie, but she looked damn cute and damn sexy.

Dylan consumed the sight of Sadie, thinking twice about his desire to leave the house today.

He chuckled, humored by the way her ridiculous clothes turned him on. He certainly hadn't seen many Egyptian women dressed like that. Hell, he was surprised Sadie had even dared to put the clothing on.

Nafrini's plan, perhaps? Buy her something so outlandish she'd never want to leave the house?

Nafrini was brilliant. She'd handled every detail for him, and with such flair. When he'd told her what his fantasy woman would look like, he'd expected a dolled-up Sadie in a red dress. He hadn't expected what looked—and felt—like a new woman.

If it hadn't been for Nafrini, he'd never have considered that, once they'd kidnapped Sadie, she'd have no fresh clothes. But once again, Nafrini had handled matters beautifully.

His gaze drifted downward to her open sandals, unable to help himself as he imagined sucking on each long, slim, and ultrasexy toe. "I think the sight of you will make me smile all day."

"Do I look that silly?"

"Absolutely not. You look that good."

She blushed. "Oh. Well, in that case, look away. You aren't conning me into bed this time, buster." She ran her fingers through her hair. "I'll tell you what. I'll wear this, and you turn the camera over to me."

"Not a chance."

Her hands went to her hips. "Dylan, I want . . . No, I demand to see those pictures of the foursome and decide which are keepers. You know I don't photograph well."

He should have seen this coming. Dylan shook his head, not willing to negotiate his beautiful pictures being destroyed. Though she loved to smile for the camera, every time she developed pictures of herself, she threw half out. "I'll love every photo and I'm keeping them."

"I'm taking the camera and getting that film. Wait and see." She flashed him a false smile. "I'll just double check my curls and be off."

As she disappeared, he tore his eyes from her alluring form, his cock half hard from the sight of her. He had to get his dick calmed down. More sex would likely make his prick raw.

Physically, he was as satisfied as he'd ever been in his whole damn life. Hell, he was more satisfied than he'd imagined he could be.

But mentally . . . emotionally . . .

Shit.

Suffice to say, there was room for improvement. Lifting his Palm Pilot, he scanned over Bill's e-mail once again, thinking of all the messages her father had left on his phone. Then there was Mike.

Damn.

He'd ceased all communications when he'd hopped the plane to Egypt and hadn't regretted the action once. Even now, he'd checked his e-mails only out of sheer necessity. Not desire. Much as he didn't want to fool with business and family interaction, he knew he had to deal with certain responsibilities, though he couldn't wait to turn the Palm off.

He *could* wait to go home. Funny, but now that he'd been away so long, he was beginning to realize how right Sadie was. His life was boring and bogged down with responsibility. He couldn't remember the last time he'd just let loose. Now that he had, he didn't want to stop. He supposed he was an all-or-nothing sort of guy, and right now, he was all for more sexual fantasies.

Reading over another irate e-mail, he groaned and set the Palm aside, calling to Sadie. "Forget about shopping. Let's go see the pyramids."

Shit on responsibility. He'd answer e-mails tonight.

"Really?" Walking from the bathroom, she stared at him with a funny look, her brows furrowed. "*You* want *me* to put off something in regard to our wedding? I thought you'd be rushing me onto the first flight to America you could book."

"Nah." He shrugged. "As I said earlier, we've been gone this long. We might as well enjoy ourselves before the storm hits, right?"

Sadie's eyes widened before her features melted into a smile. "Right. Of course." Crossing the room, she slid into his arms, sitting on his lap. "If that's what you want, I can go shopping tomorrow, and we'll spend the day together. But—"

"Sounds great." He cut her off, not wanting to deal with any *buts*. He wrapped her in his in his arms, enjoying her soft body against his.

Maybe he was confused in many areas, but he knew one thing for certain: he never, ever wanted to let her go.

sixteen

In her daydreams about exploring Egypt, she'd pictured riding camels into the desert and traveling for miles on end to reach the pyramids. Instead, as she walked outside into the brilliant sunlight and oppressive dry heat, she discovered a taxi waiting to drive them to their destination.

Immediately she recognized the vehicle as one of the "service" taxis her hotel manager had warned her about. Apparently, like most tourists, Dylan had no idea about the scam artists, and he'd be none too happy when he heard the steep charges for riding in one.

She placed a hand to his arm. "Sweetie, this is a service taxi. They cost twice as much."

He opened the door for her, ushering her in. "But they're twice as roomy."

"Not quite," she muttered, sliding into the seat. What was with Dylan?

The driver murmured a greeting in Arabic, and Dylan slammed the door shut, directing him to the Giza Pyramids.

While Sadie wouldn't call her fiancé cheap, he did *not* like being ripped off. Ever. Whoever this man was, he was not Dylan. Sadie sighed and gazed out the window in silence, exhausted from trying to put a finger on the changes within her lover.

In less than ten minutes, they arrived at the pyramids. Dylan stepped out, holding the door open for her. She scooted across the seat and stood, astounded by the vast stretch of flat desert.

As Dylan negotiated a price with the driver, Sadie leaned on the vehicle and bit her nails, nervous about dealing with the new Dylan. While he didn't care for paying a high price or being ripped off, she'd never known him to haggle as he was now.

His odd behavior worried her. Suffice to say, she'd been a tad shocked when he'd suggested she tour the pyramids with him today. She'd expected Dylan to toss her over his shoulder and dash to the airport the moment she'd agreed to stay. Now he acted so nonchalant about their return, she could think he didn't care if they caught a flight home ever. His behavior didn't make sense.

In fact, for the past couple of days, *he* didn't make sense. She knew she'd really pushed him with this game of hers, perhaps even pissed him off, but she hadn't expected him to become a different man.

Did he think she wanted him to change?

Did she want him to change? Worse, could she honestly say she didn't like the transformation?

She gulped at the knot in her throat. *No!* No way. She didn't want to change him. Honest to God and cross her heart, she loved Dylan, just the way he was: hell, she loved him *because* of who he was.

And that was exactly why she was not leaving him again. Not this time, not even if the dreams came back.

Dylan settled on a price far higher than she would have paid, and thanked the driver. With a wide grin, he took her hand. Together, they faced the pyramid towering over them. Her every intense thought was immediately forgotten as she stood in awe of the great wonder. "Wow."

"I feel like a speck." Dylan took a few slow steps forward, as if he was afraid to approach the massive limestone structure. His dark eyes widened. "Now I get it."

"Get what?"

"My parents," he murmured.

"Huh?" Sadie wiggled her brows at him, then shook her head. "You're being silly." She strode forward, itching to place her hands on the sand-colored rock that workers had fashioned thousands of years ago. "I can't believe this was built in a time before electricity. Just look! We should climb it, Dylan. Can we go inside?"

Dylan caught her arm and drew her to him. "My parents. You think they're boring. Stuffy."

"You don't exactly disagree," she scoffed, but softened, realizing no one enjoyed having their parents taken down a peg or two. Hell, she knew that feeling too well, all things considered. "Look, I like your mom and dad, I do, Dylan. I just don't want to *be* your mom and dad. But I'm sorry if anything I've said has upset you."

Frantically, he shook his head in protest, as if he had a fire lit under him. "No!" He pointed to the pyramid. "They're not boring! They *do* have fun—quietly, secretly, yes—but Sadie, they do have fun."

"Okay . . ."

"Standing here, under this great wonder, isn't it exhilarating? Don't you just feel like the whole world is suddenly this exciting, interesting place?" He lifted her by the waist, swirling her round and round.

Sadie squealed in agreement and threw her head back as he spun her. "I wish I were a bird and I could fly to the very tip, and look down on the world," she cried out, feeling high on life as he whirled her. Finally, they became so dizzy they fell to the ground together.

Dylan helped her regain her footing and blew out a deep breath. "My parents, they come here every year."

"I didn't know that."

"This year was delayed because of our wedding. They like to come in the spring, before the weather is too unbearable. It's like this huge, once a year 'date' they go on. Though we occasionally took our family vacations to Eygpt, I never got to go along on their annual trip."

Sadie steadied herself, her mind beginning to put two and two together. "So what you are saying is . . ."

Dylan smiled the hugest, most dimpled smile she'd ever seen on him, looking satisfied with himself for whatever he was about to share.

"I know the answer, Sadie. The solution." He grabbed her hands and drew her close. Placing her palms on his chest, she stared up at him. If he had an answer to every uncertainty she'd felt in the past month or so, she'd sure like to hear it.

"You see, we can settle down, have kids, and live a complete life. But the key is that we can always have *our* 'thing' Sadie. We don't have to die because we get married." Staring into her eyes, he grasped her chin so that she couldn't look away. "Sadie, my parents come here because it makes them feel alive. In love. God knows what the hell else they do, the life-loving sneaks, but we—"

Sadie snickered. "Well, as I said before, they did make you."

"Funny." Dylan rolled his eyes. "Seriously, what is our thing?"

The answer struck her. Her mind twirled with realization. He was right about his parents. He was right about them.

"Acapulco," she murmured under her breath.

While Acapulco in a literal sense certainly wasn't their thing, it was where she was headed next. This game, it was their thing, tried and true. If they took a quick adventure like this once a year, every year, for the rest of their lives, how could their marriage ever be boring?

Standing here in Dylan's arm, she was ever so happy, but she wouldn't be satisfied, not until she left him again.

After a full day of exploring the pyramids, Sadie should have been tired. On the contrary, energy pulsed through her body, and she could hardly remain on the bed next to Dylan or focused on his attention.

She didn't need rest! She didn't need sex! She needed to pack!

Now that she was certain she was leaving him again, but for all the right reasons, she struggled to contain her excitement. Their game was too fun to end here in Cairo and she was eager for one last fling.

She snuggled against Dylan and spread her legs for him. He slipped two of his fingers between her labia, pressing her clit. Rubbing the bead, he whispered in her ear. "Climb aboard. Ride me." He pressed his fingers down harder, licking her lobe. "I'll give you control."

She might be eager to leave, but how could she resist such a request?

Her pussy damp and ready to sheath him, she straddled Dylan and pinned him to the bed. "Those men still around? I'm thinking we should invite them in."

"Nope. Sorry. You'll have to settle for me." He wrestled his hands free, bringing them to the small of her back, and trailed his fingers along her spine. "But don't worry, I don't plan on making anything easy."

His thumbs settled on the crevice of her ass, deliciously stroking back and forth as his hand splayed across the lush globes.

"As if you have control of anything right now, sucker." She seized his hands, throwing them back over his head, and holding them firm. "I do believe I'm the one on top."

"Oh yeah?" He raised a cocky brow at her. "You better make it good."

"Damn good," she purred. Leaning over him, she trailed nibbles and kisses down the arch of his neck, biting whenever he tried to pull his hands free.

The hardened buds of her nipples rubbed over his hairy chest, creating electric shocks from her areolas to her mons.

She captured his mouth in a hungry embrace, devouring his lips and sucking on his tongue. He tasted so damn good, she wanted to consume him.

Since she couldn't in a literal sense, she lifted her hips, driving him into her full force. She fucked him, thrusting his cock deep into her sex. Her labia and clitoris rubbed against his pubic hairs, causing delightful friction.

A quick, mind-blowing orgasm burst through her. Her lower regions quaked with pleasure. Collapsing on top of him, she released his hands. He reached around, cupping her ass, and plowed into her three more times, filling her with his semen.

As soon as he finished, she rolled off him, resisting the urge to giggle. It was time to get moving.

Drawing a deep breath to steady her excitement, she stood and walked towards the bathroom. His camera sat on one of the dressers near the door, and she made like she was picking up her purse, discreetly stealing it.

He would *not* be saving any gross pictures of her, only the sexy ones.

Going into the bathroom, she cranked on the water. The ten minutes it would take her to shower felt like a lifetime. Never had she been antsier. Her mind was going crazy with plans.

She just hoped Dylan liked his surprise.

She quickly showered, then dressed in a pair of breezy slacks and a satin tank top. Her hair was a mess, but she didn't care. It was always a mess.

Hurrying from the bathroom, she tossed her camera-laden purse over her shoulder. "I'm headed to the Khan."

He raised a brow, stretching his lithe muscles so that his body equaled the length of the large bed. "Now? Fuck me and run?"

She shrugged, trying so damn hard to play it cool. "The air is less smothering in the evening. Besides, I can't settle down."

An insinuating grin spread on his face, dimpling his cheeks. "Come here. I'll give you something to do."

She crossed the room, not wanting to leave without a quick kiss. But *not* sex! "Another orgasm? I think I've already had quite the healthy dose today, Energizer bunny."

"Oh bull. No such thing as too much sex."

"Good-bye, Dylan." She pecked him tenderly on the cheek, her lips lingering on his stubbly jaw before she pulled away. She straightened, drew a deep breath, and planted on a smile. "See you soon."

She walked briskly from the room, her heart lurching with a hint of fear, but thudding in exhilaration. Her heels clicked over the marble floor as she raced for the front entrance, pulling the folded note from her bag.

Slowly, she opened the letter. After dinner, she'd scribbled it in the bathroom with a half-dead ink pen and then stamped it with a brilliant lipstick kiss. The faded scribbles on the wrinkled stationery looked pathetic and the crimson lipstick had more of a hooker effect than the loving gesture she was going for, making her regret having to leave this as her good-bye message to him.

But it was the words that counted. Not the ink. Not the prostitute-red lipstick.

Holding her breath, she glanced at the note.

Dylan, my love,

Though this may look bad, I swear I have not left you again, not in the sense you're likely thinking. I promise marriage and your love is all I want, and I am not breaking my vow to you. This is not about running from you, but with you. I have left for Acapulco and you'll find me there, waiting for you in the garden. One last time my dear, come and get me, for we have discovered our "thing," and this is it.

Love always, Sadie.

Sadie folded the letter with a sigh. Was she doing the right thing? Of course she was.

They needed this one last fling, some sex in the sand, some fun in the sun, because as Dylan had stated repeatedly, when they arrived home, the shit would hit the fan. She considered the trip to Acapulco beautiful weather before a storm.

Next year—and there *would* be a next year—Dylan would have to put in for some vacation time prior to her vanishing. That way, they could play without worries.

She carefully laid the note on the telephone table in the entry-way, her hands lingering over it for only a moment, then she rushed out the door. After she found her wedding dress, she'd catch the next flight departing from Cairo, no matter where it was headed. After all, she didn't want him catching up with her too soon.

Staring at the ceiling, Dylan groaned and wished he could sink into the mattress and disappear. He should've put off checking his messages yet another day. The number of calls from Bill on his cell phone was scary. Her father was certifiable.

"Maybe I should inform her that I don't want us to turn out like *her* parents," he muttered to himself. "Damn."

Dylan shook his head. After scanning over the large number of remaining calls he needed to listen to, he decided he'd simply delete them and start fresh. He couldn't take listening to one more piece of sexual advice. In the last message, Bill had suggested he change his underwear to boxers.

Not going to happen.

What would Bill come up with next?

Dylan almost dialed the airport, intent on arranging their flight home, but curiosity got the cat. After all, the most recent message from Bill was less than ten minutes ago. While he probably wanted nothing, as usual, Dylan couldn't help but worry.

With his crazy father-in-law on the loose, his business partner literally steaming, and clients demanding their money back, it was no wonder he was concerned. He'd be glad to get home and sort this mess all out, even if it meant accepting that he no longer had a career.

He highlighted the call and pressed the green ON button.

"Dylan. Bill here. Sadie called me about an hour ago and I've tried to call her back repeatedly. She's not answering that damn phone of hers again. Anyway, Sadie's mom says the wedding plans are a go, not to worry, and enjoy your last stop in Acapulco. Do me a favor though, and scoop me up a handful of sand for my collection. See you on the thirty-first." He paused, chomping loudly on what sounded like tobacco, then spitting. "And boy, that girl better be coming home knocked up or we're taking you to the doctors. If you haven't listened to my other messages, you've missed out on a ton of good advice, so quit ignoring me and get to it."

Dylan barely heard the last half of the call. *Acapulco?* Bill had heard from Sadie an hour ago and she'd said they were headed to *Acapulco?*

No freaking way!

He leapt out of bed and ran into the hall, taking long strides as he sprinted to the front door. If she'd left him another damn picture clue to follow, he'd—

His heart sank. Skidding to a stop, he stared at the folded note sitting alone on the table by the door, and felt sick.

She was gone. Again.

Drawing several deep breaths that did little to suppress his anger, he stared at the note, wishing his gaze alone could make it catch fire. Damn her! She'd promised him.

He'd trusted her!

Obviously, a bad decision on his part.

He snatched the letter into his hands and tore it open so fast he ripped the paper. His eyes scanned the words, his mind disbelieving.

. . . this is not about running from you . . .

Right. That supposed to make him feel better? Balling her note in his fist, he threw the crumpled mess at the door.

How could she? Damn it! She knew he needed to get home. Enough was enough! He'd really had it this time.

The paper bounced off the wood and pattered to the floor below his feet. Frustration knotted his every muscle as he stared at the trashed note from his runaway bride, fighting the intruding notion that maybe, just maybe, he was looking forward to catching up with her.

Running his hand through his hair, he groaned. Damn it, Sadie had really gotten to him with this game, and in ways even she couldn't imagine.

Deep in his heart, he knew they'd progressed, that this time was different from the times before. That his fiancée was simply having fun with him.

Even harder to grasp was the reality that he liked it. That he wanted to go get her.

But annoying questions loomed in his mind: If she wasn't content by this point in the game, would he ever truly satisfy her? Would she ever stop running? Would the game ever end?

seventeen

There are no flights to Acapulco for two days?" Sadie drummed her fingers on the counter, feeling like a rubber band about to snap.

"No. No flights to Acapulco."

She winced at the bland, repetitive reply in accented but understandable English from the ticket clerk. "You've got to be kidding me. You are, right? Seriously, I need to get to Mexico. Anywhere in Mexico. Just get me there. Please."

The pursed-lipped man with angry, beady eyes had already informed her that the last flight to Acapulco had left early this morning. Twice.

But she didn't want to believe her terrible luck.

Had she called . . .

Damn it, she should have been on that plane! After shopping for hours, she'd finally found the perfect wedding dress, an airy, white silk gown that wrapped around her body. The lush design accented her waist with gold embroidered trim and sported a train that trailed six feet behind her. But trying on so many dresses, on top of their earlier trip to the pyramids, had worn her out, and she'd been too tired to even phone the airport.

Instead, she'd spent the night in her hotel room, admiring the way the soft fabric of her gown wrapped and clung to her every curve. How different it was from any wedding dress she'd ever seen. In it, she felt like a goddess, and she was positive Dylan would see her the same way. As for what her mother and soon-to-be-mother-in-law would think, well . . .

She didn't need to fret about that right now. She had enough to worry over. "You're absolutely positive?"

"Yes, ma'am," he reiterated in a much harder tone. Someone groaned from behind her.

The pads of her fingers thumped against the glossy countertop. This was *so* not good. For all she knew, Dylan had found her note right after she'd left. He would've had plenty of time to have caught the flight to Acapulco this morning. He could be well ahead of her even now.

If he hadn't already left, he could still arrive at the airport any moment. Catch her in the act. Stop her from leaving.

Sadie blew out a frustrated breath. She should have thought this out a little more, bought the tickets first, or . . . or . . . something, darn it!

Now she'd never have time to hatch out her plan to surprise Dylan with a sexual fantasy, as he'd done for her. With her luck, he was probably plotting yet another crazy way to get her. Heaven help him if he tried to kidnap her again.

Not good. Not good at all!

Or was it?

The thought of another one of his surprises wasn't *that* discouraging. Surely she could suffer whatever blissful escapade he put her through. But darn it, she'd wanted the upper hand in the fantasy this time!

"Ma'am?" The ticket clerk glared at her as if she were dense, awaiting her attention with clear impatience.

Behind her, someone in the long line moaned in protest.

"Come on, already!" they called.

She winced, hating that she was being *that* person.

But she didn't know where to go. What to do. "There's nothing—"

"No, ma'am," the clerk snapped, his tone very annoyed. Lifting his chin, he eyed her like she was scum. "Please step aside if you cannot book another flight."

"But—"

"As I've explained numerous times, Mexico is one of our less popular destinations. We do not have flights going out daily. What is fact I cannot change."

Sadie looked to the clock. Three already. Her fingers drummed faster. "Okay. What *do* you have? There must be a flight heading in the vicinity of Mexico that will be taking off soon."

He stared at her for a moment, then turned to his computer, his fingers tap-tapping on the keyboard at lightning speed.

"Very soon, please," she added.

Without even glancing at her, he read from the screen. "We have a first-class seat available on the next flight to LAX. It leaves in an hour."

"Los Angeles?"

The man behind her stomped his foot, groaning at her question.

The Californian city wasn't even close to Acapulco, but it would have to do. What other choice did she have?

"Fine." She nodded.

She chose not to dwell on the price of a first-class seat to LAX or that once again she wasn't paying for it. She whipped out her parentally provided credit card, choosing to ignore the fact that, while long ago she'd vowed not to depend on their lotto wealth and hadn't since she graduated from college, she had used the Visa ten times since the beginning of this trip.

"I'll take it." She handed him the card, reminding herself that her parents liked—no, loved—when she blew their money. Better for her to spend it this way than for her mother to buy her another tacky two-thousand-dollar purse, wasn't it?

As the receipt printed, she glanced beyond the ticket counter, her gaze sweeping the crowded airport for some sign of Dylan. Even on tiptoes, she couldn't see hide or hair of him in the busy lobby.

A pen drummed on the counter. "Ma'am? Please."

She quickly turned around and signed the receipt he laid in front of her.

A moment later she had the necessary papers in hand. She nodded in gratitude, handing him her luggage to be checked. He quickly tagged it, tossing it down the chute behind him.

"Thanks. Sorry if I was difficult," she apologized, feeling slightly guilty for being *that* person.

He lifted his brows in a cocky manner. "Indeed."

"Asshole," she murmured under breath. The clerks at the Department of Motor Vehicles were less miserable.

She turned to walk away. The moment her hand landed on the handle of her carry-on, her mistake slammed through her. Her camera! Oh no! No, no, no!

She always carried her camera on. She never packed it. X-ray machines could damage the film, not too mention its value. But she'd had so much to lug throughout the airport, she'd placed her camera bag in the suitcase just until she had her bearings straight.

Panicking, she whirled around. "I have to have that back. My camera—my film—is in there!"

He shrugged. "Too late."

"But my camera!"

"Too late."

"But—"

"Good day, ma'am." He glared at her in warning.

Seething, Sadie snatched her carry-on and stormed away.

Great! Fabulous!

Anxious to get through customs and pout in a corner until her flight was boarded, she wheeled her smaller luggage, packed solely with her neatly folded but still wrinkling wedding dress, toward her gate, worrying over her camera, all the while looking over her shoulder for Dylan.

Dylan rolled in his hotel bed, sifting through the many brochures he'd grabbed from the front desk when he'd checked in, searching for a clue as to where Sadie might be. In her letter, she'd said he'd find her in a garden.

A garden. Great hint, Sadie.

It was bad enough the little thief had stolen his camera. But her clue was ridiculous. Acapulco was a beach destination bursting with restaurants and nightclubs. Aside from the flowers lining many hotel beds, he had no idea where he'd find a garden or his fiancé. As far as he could figure, she had to have meant some sort of nursery or nature park. But nothing like that was featured in these tourist guides.

Dropping the useless pamphlets, he slid on his sunglasses and walked from his hotel room. After he locked the door, he circled the deck surrounding the beachside pool. Beautiful tanned bodies in minuscule bathing attire strutted all around him, half-dressed, sexy young women clinging to men old enough to be their fathers, sipping fruity drinks, laughing, swimming, enjoying each other.

Everyone was having a ball, everyone except him. He was alone and searching.

Again.

Dylan suppressed his annoyance and located an empty table. He took a seat under the wide umbrella and stretched his legs.

He should have seen the signs. He should have figured her out. After all, she'd mentioned Acapulco while they were at the pyramids. But he hadn't had a clue.

When it came to Sadie, there was no rhyme or reason. Married or not, she'd always do what she wanted. She was right about one thing: she couldn't be like his mother.

But he wouldn't change that for the world.

He loved his wife-to-be, loved her regardless of her quirks, loved her even though he had no job to return to, considering his partner had already suggested a spilt.

That was too late to change now. His job didn't matter anyway, and besides, he was better off starting his own firm, a smaller one, where he had no one to answer to but himself.

He needed to find Sadie, not so he could go home, not so he could rush their marriage, but simply because he wanted her in his arms once again.

He waved to a waitress, a young Mexican woman dressed in a pink uniform who came bearing a complimentary drink and a menu.

"*Hola.*" She smiled widely.

"Hello." He handed her back the menu without looking. "Tuna salad and a beer, and don't make it a light. I don't suppose you have time to answer a touristy question?"

She raised a brow, her gracious smile growing wider, though it hardly seemed possible. "*Si*, señor?"

"I'm looking for a garden."

"A jardin?"

"A mucho big garden."

"*Si.* I think you want Jardin Botanico de Acapulco, perhaps? Is a big garden outside of Acapulco." She pointed north. "Is five dollars."

"Oh. Sure." Dylan reached for his wallet to give her five dollars, not sure if he'd gotten the information cheap or was being ripped off.

The waitress laughed and waved her hand. "No, no. Jardin charges five dollars to admit, you see?"

"Oh. Oh, okay, yes I see." He laughed at himself, tossing the cash on the table for the tip, thinking she'd get the money regardless.

"The front desk can give you directions to Jardin Botanico, if you please." The young woman stepped closer, so that her legs aligned with the side of his chair. Her thigh pressed against his arm.

Nervous at her sudden closeness, he gave a quick nod, and looked out over the beach at the crashing waves. "Thank you."

To his shock, she bent, purring in his ear, her hot breath caressing his earlobe. "I do not charge for advice, señor, but there are other things you can tip me for besides food service."

"Oh." Dylan straightened. "*Oh.*"

He clutched his lemonade and took a gulp.

Her hand slid over his shoulder, slowly, seductively. "You are alone. I can keep you warm tonight, señor."

He spit out the sour drink, choking. Good grief, for a seemingly sweet young lady, this prostitute was throwing herself at him. She must have seen the cash in his wallet.

He quickly shook his head. "No thanks. I'm engaged."

She looked to the empty seat across from him. "Pity."

Granting him one final sexy smile, she sauntered away, moving to the next table.

Dylan glared at the vacant chair she'd just eyed. *Pity.*

Leaping to his feet, he decided he wasn't hungry after all, and headed to the office for directions.

*L*adies and gentlemen, I'm afraid our scheduled, intermediate stop at JFK airport will be extended. Due to severe thunderstorms, takeoff to LAX airport will be delayed an unknown amount of time and . . ."

Sadie bolted upright in her seat, her panic drowning out the pilot's announcement.

No way! This couldn't be.

Extended? But why? Who cared about some silly storms? She didn't see any lightning. The plane wasn't shaking. What the hell was the problem?

She flopped in her seat with a heartbroken sigh. She had no way of knowing where Dylan was right now, but this was not what she'd had in mind when she'd left him.

She'd wanted to feel the spray of saltwater on her skin, to watch a brilliant sunrise, to get a tan for her wedding.

To have sex on the beach. In the ocean. In the pool. Everywhere. Damn it.

Didn't these people know what an inconvenience they were causing? It was ridiculous! Absurd!

Sadie gulped and blew out a deep breath.

Deep down, under all her frustration, she knew the delay was for the lives of everyone on this plane. She should be thanking the air traffic controllers for protecting her, not cussing them.

But being thankful simply didn't mingle with her current mood.

No, after almost five hours on this plane, first-class seat or not, she'd had time to reconsider the way she'd left Dylan. Time to realize he might not have been thrilled to go on another chase. Time to once again wonder if he was even going to come after her.

Damn it.

She spent the rest of the landing cussing and swearing under her breath, thinking of the wedding dress crammed above her in the storage unit. Of their film, which was possibly now ruined by the x-ray machines. Of the fiancé she was not with. Of the sex she was not having. Of all the things she couldn't control sitting in this damn seat while landing in her home city of New York, the very last place on earth that she wanted to be.

Damn it.

Matters couldn't get worse than this.

The hot, humid weather clung to his skin and he wiped a bead of sweat from his forehead. Shifting uncomfortably on the hard wooden bench, Dylan waved away bugs in irritated strikes. Brilliant colored flowers and lush green foliage bordered the trail he sat along. Birds filled their air with their song. He'd listened to their beautiful music for so long, the tweeting had become irritating noise.

Where the fucking hell was Sadie?

A butterfly fluttered in front of him and he swiped out, attempting to catch the insect by its brightly colored wings. But the butterfly was as elusive as his fiancée. Flying before him, teasing him, then flitting away again, before he had time to react.

Of course, while catching a butterfly wasn't impossible, you couldn't keep a butterfly. They weren't pets. You either had to release the creature or it would die.

Perhaps he was going about the game all wrong with Sadie. No matter how many times he caught her, she flew away.

Dylan stood, glancing around the garden one last time, as if Sadie would be hiding in the dense foliage or somewhere else nearby. No surprise, she wasn't.

He couldn't wait here any longer.

He *wouldn't* wait here any longer.

With a deep sigh, he strode from the park. No way would he return to wait for her another day. If his little butterfly wanted him, she could catch him.

Retrieving his cell phone, he dialed Sadie's number, determined to tell her as much.

eighteen

Matters had become worse, in fact, a whole hell of a lot worse.

Sadie stalked the length of her hotel room. How could they have lost her luggage? *How?*

Since severe thunderstorms were forecasted to blast the area overnight, takeoff had been delayed in New York until morning, and all the passengers had been given hotel rooms.

But the damn idiots had lost her suitcase, leaving her with nothing but a wrinkled wedding dress and a bad attitude. Sure, she could go home, at least pick up some of her clothes. She certainly didn't need to stay at the hotel.

Bottom line, she didn't want to go home. She wanted to go to Dylan. Not to mention the risk going to their house would bring. The last thing she wanted was to be caught by either set of their parents.

What now? What if they didn't find her luggage? She refused to leave New York without her suitcase. No way. Not only was her favorite camera in it, but also the film from Dylan's ménage photo shoot.

Lots and lots of negatives of her in the nude, up close and personal, panting from orgasms . . . taking their three cocks . . .

Ughhhhh! She stomped her foot in frustration and threw herself onto the queen-size bed. The hard springs creaked under her weight and her back immediately protested. She loathed a firm mattress.

This totally sucked.

She'd wager Dylan was already in Acapulco and probably pretty damn pissed. Her incessant calls to him had never made it past his voice mail, so either he was out of range, or intentionally ignoring her.

She needed to get to Mexico ASAP, which meant she had to get her luggage back and fast. Rolling over, she grabbed the landline phone from the end table and hit redial, calling the airport. She'd been making an effort to keep her cell line clear all day, hoping the airport would call and give her good news. For once.

On the third unanswered ring, her cell went off, and she quickly hung up the other phone.

Maybe this was it!

She leapt to her feet and snatched the phone from the dresser, answering quickly. "Hello?"

"I'm leaving."

Her heart skipped a beat. Her stomach flopped over.

Dylan? Was *leaving*?

She ran her hand through her hair and straightened. "Wait, what? You can't leave."

"You heard me Sadie, I'm leaving." His tone was flat, not happy, but at least not angry. "If this was your idea of a joke, ha-ha. If this is a new twist in your game, ha-ha."

"It wasn't, I swear. I—" Sadie gripped the phone, scared by what his words implied. Had he not understood her letter? She was just having fun, but she wasn't uncommitted.

"Not this time, Sadie." He cut her off before she could explain. "You said we were going home. That you weren't scared of marriage anymore."

"We are, and I want to marry you. I do. Just like I promised." Sadie gulped, wondering if she'd dug herself a ditch bigger than she could climb out of. "I just wanted to enjoy one last fling with you. I thought this game could be our thing, remember? Like we talked about. We've had fun, haven't we?"

"Well, I was enjoying the chase, right up to the point where I realized you aren't in Acapulco, my little butterfly." He paused for too long a moment and she agonized. "Chasing you around the world has been something else. I've enjoyed every minute. Sure, I can see this as our thing. Certainly. But we can't run forever, Sadie, and I thought you were ready. Now I wonder if you'll ever be ready."

"I am. I promise. I am."

He scoffed, a gesture that stung like a wasp's attack. "Yeah, well, you spend all day outside in hot weather, in a bug-infested garden, the thrill of the chase burns off. I want my fiancée, but apparently, my fiancée does not want me."

Sadie held back tears. "Believe you me, Dylan, I want to be with you."

He chuckled. "Oh, so now you miss me, little butterfly?"

"A lot."

"Good, good." His voice softened, lowering a notch, and becoming velvety, seductive. "Prove it."

"Dylan, just listen to me."

"Where are you?"

"New York."

"Ironic," he murmured. "I thought you wanted to be with me."

"I do! If you would just listen to me—"

"Like I said, prove it."

Her sadness fled at the change in his tone, replaced with an acute desire to please him.

Wondering what on earth he'd suggest, she licked her lips. "How?"

"Touch yourself, little butterfly. Touch yourself like you did back in Hawaii. Moan for me."

Arousal coiled through her at his suggestion and warmed her center.

"Is that want you want, baby?" she purred into the phone. She sat on the edge of the bed, kicking off her shoes, lying back, and stretching her body.

"I sure do," he demanded, his sensuous tone leaving her no room for refusal. "I want you to come for me, right now, wherever you are, whatever you're doing."

"I'm in bed."

"What a shame."

"Not from my point of view." Sadie propped her feet on the edge of the mattress and slipped her hand into the waistband of her slacks. "Tell me what to do."

"Slide your fingers into your pants, slowly now, and run them along the thin strip of hair covering your pussy."

Sadie followed his directions, her fingers grazing gently over her skin and hair. Tingles danced across her belly, like tiny little Amazonians worshiping the beat of a drum.

Her slacks restricted her movements too much so she unbuttoned them, kicking them off. As they landed on the floor, she slipped her hand under the satin of her thong, again stroking the narrow length of pubic hairs protecting her center.

Her cunt watered in response, desire flooding her flesh and over-flowing onto her thighs.

She continued to do nothing more, nothing less, than caress her fingers gently over the sensitive area, stroking, teasing, with a hair's-breadth touch.

"Mmm," she moaned, impatient to slip her fingers deeper, but awaiting his command. Her hips rotated, anxious to rock to the beat of fulfillment. "Dylan, masturbate with me. Let's make love over the phone. Touch yourself for me."

"Tell me what to do." Hoarse and raspy, his words came out in a growl.

"Grasp your dick in your fist," she commanded him, her fingers twitching in eagerness as she imagined his big hand wrapped around his shaft. "Stroke it. Slowly now, no rushing."

He groaned in response, his voice breaking as he spoke. "Slip your fingers between your pussy lips. Are you swollen with want? Quivering?"

Relieved, she followed his lead, sinking her fingers into her engorged, soaked folds. Her pelvis bucked involuntarily as she waited for further instruction.

"You could say that."

"Are you wet?"

"Oh yeah."

"Press your clit, babe . . . in big wide circles . . . and tell me how it feels." His breath labored, coming heavily, making it clear he was vigorously working his cock in his hands.

She rubbed the tiny bud, taking the liberty of alternating her finger movements, up and down, in and out, so that the little bundle of nerves exploded with sensation.

All along, she pretended it was his hands upon her, and her hands upon him, pleasuring, loving, united. Despite the distance between them, their desire melted into one, driving them to ecstasy not normally found in masturbation.

"So . . . good." She ground her teeth. "So damn good."

"But not as good as me?"

Sadie lifted her hips, needing more, and wishing he were close by to give it to her. "Never as good as you. I wish I had your big cock inside me, thrusting in and out, so hard, so fast. Can you imagine my wet cunny wrapped around your shaft?"

"Shit yes." Panting, he gasped at her suggestion. "Your pussy is so tight. Can you feel me, deep inside you, loving you?"

Sadie drove three fingers into her vagina, plunging the digits in and out of her slick tunnel in rhythm with his heavy breathing. "I feel you," she whimpered. "I need you."

Her hips pulsed against her hand as she pictured Dylan on top of her, her face in the expanse of his wide, built chest, his arms propped near her head, rocking to the rhythm of his thrusts. Slow and easy, he'd pump into her, his pelvis grinding against her labia, smashing her center, the coarse hairs of his sex rubbing the sensitive flesh.

"I need you too." He released a sudden grunt and fell silent. After a moment, he spoke again, his tone calmer. "I love you."

He'd clearly climaxed—at his own hand, but by thinking of her. The thought of him desiring her so intensely pushed her over the edge.

Her vaginal muscles shuddered, constringed, and burst, an orgasm releasing through her body.

With a sigh, she relaxed into the mattress, and curled into a ball of spent ecstasy, wishing he were there to hold her. "I love you too. I miss you."

He cleared his throat. "Then come find me."

Alerted by his suggestion, she rolled onto her back. "Find you?"

"I won't be in Acapulco. I'm going to go stay in a castle and if Dame Fortune is on my side, double my money. Wish me luck, little butterfly."

Dylan hung up, leaving her breathless, her mind whirling with passion and problems.

Enough already! Dylan pulled his ringing cell phone from his pocket and turned it off. He refused to answer and she refused to stop calling.

Shouldn't his battery be dead by now? She'd called at least a hundred times today. Though he'd ignored her each time, she kept right on.

Speaking to her was sweet torture. The simple sound of her voice melted him into mush, and he knew if he gave her a chance to convince him otherwise, he'd never leave Mexico. She'd beg him to stay, to wait, and like a fool, he would, right up until the moment when she ran away from him again.

No. Not again. Not the way he saw it.

"We are now boarding coach passengers. If you're seated in rows one through five, please . . ."

Dylan listened to the flight attendant rattle off rows until she called his, then he grabbed his carry-on and strode from the crowded waiting area to the gate. He boarded the plane, all the while reminding himself he'd made the right decision.

What else could he do? Sit there in Acapulco, awaiting her command?

He was turning the tables. If this was going to be *their* game, she could play along as well.

This time, Sadie needed to come get him. You bet he'd be hidden well, too. No easy clues. No quick solution. She was going to have to work to find him, just as he'd worked to find her.

He was setting his butterfly free . . .

Listen, you jerk. For hell's sake, listen to me! Do I have to come down there? If there was a bomb in my luggage, you'd sure find it!"

Sadie slammed down the phone before she said something even worse than the stupid comment that had just slipped out. Frustrated didn't even begin to describe how she felt at the moment.

After several deep breaths, she dialed Dylan's number—*again*—ready to throw a tantrum as his voice mail picked up.

"Dylan!" she screeched then hung up. *Ugh!*

Why wasn't he answering? If he was flying across the big blue, to England or Ireland or who knew where, she'd likely give birth to a very large cow. There'd better be a castle in Mexico, damn it.

How the hell was she supposed to find him from that silly clue anyway? It wasn't as if there was one castle in the whole world.

She could never pinpoint anything from what he'd said. Never!

If only he would answer, she could explain to him that she was stuck. Not that she had any idea where to follow him to if she weren't.

Why wouldn't he answer?

She hung up and dialed the now-memorized number for JFK airport. They didn't answer either, she guessed because they were avoiding her.

Giving up, she flopped on the bed and stared at the ceiling. This was not good. What was she going to do? That camera . . . those pictures . . .

God. Her mind reeled with everything that had gone wrong the past couple days.

After several minutes, a loud knock sounded at her door. Not expecting it, she practically jumped from her skin, leaping from her bed to answer.

Dylan? Could she hope?

Sadie threw open the door and stared at a uniformed officer who frowned down upon her. "Sadie Williams?"

Not even close.

Suddenly aware of her attire, a hotel robe and nothing more, she clamped her arms over her breasts. "Can I help you?"

Her mind rushed to her many sex-filled dreams of her cop, her face burning with embarrassment.

The police officer kindly averted his dark eyes. "We've received a report that you threatened the airport, ma'am."

Sadie took a step back. "What?"

Was this another one of Dylan's tricks? It had to be. She'd bet the cop was a male stripper.

Sadie ran her gaze over the officer's length, noting his NYPD uniform, his radio, and especially his handcuffs. She had to hand it to Dylan. The guy looked very real. Authentic. She was tempted to play along, come onto him, to see how far Dylan had paid him to go.

The cop cleared his throat. "You made a statement to JFK airport that there may be a bomb in your missing luggage."

Oh shit, he was real!

"Oh no!" Her heart took off like jackhammer in her chest. She was really in trouble! "I swear, I wasn't serious. I was being sarcastic. Mouthy. Stupid. They lost my luggage and I just want them to find it. Oh God, I'm sorry."

He nodded slowly, looking dead serious. "I understand, ma'am, I do. In fact, I've been through the same thing. Lucky for you, I happened to be in the vicinity and I immediately recognized your name. You donate a lot of money to police charities. But these are serious charges."

Actually, her *parents* contributed a lot of money to police charities, not her. She supposed they thought they were saving her soul by donating money on her behalf.

But they may have just saved her butt. At least, she hoped.

"Charges?" *Damn, damn, damn . . .*

"You can't get away with this."

Something in her clicked. *Her* cop said that. And he was right. How could she have ever . . .

Shaking her head, she put aside the thought. She couldn't think about *him* at the moment.

"Oh God. Please, officer." Sadie swallowed the large knot forming in her throat. "I didn't mean to cause such a commotion. I just really need that suitcase back. I have some *very* private belongings in that bag."

"I understand, ma'am, and it's only because of your upstanding name that I am going to let you off with a strong warning and speak to the airport on your behalf. But this is serious. Don't call them again or you will be facing serious charges."

"Okay." She nodded, her heart slowing, her hopes of ever recovering the incriminating pictures quickly diminishing. "But what about my luggage?"

"They will call you if it's found. Otherwise, you can file—"

"A claim through TSA. It's out of the airport's hands. I know," she sighed. "I don't want money. I want my luggage."

"Don't think there will be any more warnings."

"I understand." She was tempted to slam the door in his face, she was so close to tears, but she stopped herself. She gripped the wood in a painful grasp. Can't shoot the messenger, right? Besides, it was very nice of him to give her a warning. "I'm sorry for your trouble and I won't call again, I promise. Thank you."

He granted her a measured smile. "Keep the donations coming and have a nice day, ma'am."

"You too." Sadie shut the door and sank against it, drawing her knees to her chin. She wrapped her arms around her legs and hugged herself tight.

What now? She couldn't call the airport. She couldn't reach Dylan. She was stuck in this awful hotel room with no clothes and no choices.

What's more, she finally saw what she'd been running from all along. Her desire to be single. To be free. When she'd left New York, she wasn't ready to commit. Had she married Dylan, she never would have gotten away with it. She—*they*—would have failed. It would have been a crime.

But the dreams were gone and so were her hesitations. She no longer felt as if she were giving up her life, but starting a new one. A better one. There were no walls between them, only love. And unfortunately, distance.

All she wanted was to go home, but New York wasn't home. Dylan was.

nineteen

After an evening of blackjack and slots, Dylan showered and threw on his briefs. Sipping a glass of rich, warm brandy, he settled on the bed with his cell phone.

Sadie had filled his voice mail with desperate, angry messages. He listened to her plead in two of them, and explain herself in another, frowning as he realized he'd presumed too quickly.

So she hadn't been toying with him in Acapulco after all. How could he have guessed she'd been rerouted and her luggage lost?

What a damn shame. He shook his head, worried about his pictures. He couldn't believe she'd checked the film and camera.

Still, he decided, he hadn't acted too fast. Their game had needed a twist and he'd provided it. Hopefully, everything would work out.

He deleted the remainder of her messages and laid back, sipping his drink. It was time to give Sadie her next clue.

He selected her number and hit send.

She answered in half a ring. "Dylan?"

Her voice instantly turned him on. "I'm thinking about you."

"Well, that's nice. I'm pacing the floors."

"Much, much too boring, my dear. Why don't you come and get me then?" he suggested.

"Where?" she begged. "Please, Dylan, tell me where to find you."

"Some people come here to get married, Sadie. Some come to win. What better place to end this game of ours?"

"Dylan—"

Las Vegas?

Dylan was waiting for her in Vegas!

Suddenly, all his hints, the few that he'd given her, made sense. Though she couldn't recall the name of the hotel, she did remember one that was shaped like a castle.

Yes, Vegas it was.

Exhilaration pumped through her veins, from her head to her toes, and she leapt onto the bed, jumping up and down. "I found him, I found him!"

The mattress creaked under her weight and she stumbled, crashing to her knees. She drew a sharp breath and commanded herself to calm down.

Now that she'd pinpointed Dylan, the urge to throw on some clothes and catch the next flight southwest overwhelmed her. How easily she could go to him, take his hand, and his name, and end this game. Be home.

Except, how could she? Without her luggage, there was no way she could up and leave.

She simply couldn't. She was stuck.

Rolling over, she screamed into the mattress and pounded the protesting springs. *Stupid, stupid, stupid!* She should have never left Cairo! She should have stayed! She *could* have stayed!

Shoulda, coulda, woulda. She hadn't.

She punched the bed one last time, groaned, and flopped over. It was time to face facts.

Dylan was in Vegas. She was in New York. Her luggage had been missing for two days and counting. Realistically, she'd never get that suitcase back, and even if she did, the film would likely be ruined. There was always a chance—hell, matters could work out perfectly even in the next hour—but her hope was slight . . .

Every moment she spent in New York while Dylan called the shots, she was losing ground. Losing precious time.

Why shouldn't she just go? Did she really care so much about some sexy photos of her?

Of course she did.

God forbid the pictures landed in the wrong hands and ended up on the Internet, or worse. Besides, she cherished those memories, even if she had intended to throw out the bad shots.

If only she could call the airport. Maybe they'd found her suitcase. It could be on its way even now.

Yeah right.

With their level of substandard service, she'd be lucky if it showed up in a month.

Standing, she paced the floor. Back and forth, back and forth she walked, driving herself crazy with her indecision. Her heart squeezed at the thought of being with Dylan, of creating new memories, of marrying him.

How could she possibly stay here another day? How could she stand another night without Dylan?

She couldn't.

Screw it.

There was no way she could wait and maintain her sanity. No way.

Tonight, she'd reasonably call the airport and make arrangements for her luggage delivery, and then get some much-needed rest.

Tomorrow would be a big day. She'd have to purchase some new clothes and toiletries for the trip, considering she had none (barring going home, which she refused to do).

After that, she was off to Vegas to marry her fiancé.

twenty

Sadie grabbed two simple cotton shirts and a blouse from the department store racks and slung them over the jeans resting on her arm. Determined to find some suitable undergarments and be gone before someone she knew spotted her, she headed to the lingerie department, walking dangerously fast through the aisles.

She'd chosen to shop at Kohl's, knowing there would be no chance of running into her family, but still, she was on edge. Glancing at her watch, she was disappointed when she saw it was already two. Hell, she hadn't even stopped for lunch. Why did it seem like the simple shopping trip was taking a lifetime? She didn't care what she wore or how she looked. She only wanted to go to Dylan. To marry him.

Of course, she couldn't very well head to Vegas with only one set of dirty clothes and a wrinkled wedding dress.

Booked for takeoff at six, she only had a couple more hours to shop, get a bite to eat, and make her way through security. It wasn't much time, but she would make it. Not even a tornado and two-inch hail would stop her from getting to him now. She thoroughly intended to arrive in Vegas by this evening and be married by the morning.

But then, she hadn't run her decision to elope by Dylan, though surely he'd agree. Why wouldn't he?

She stopped at a rack of sassy, pink baby-doll nightgowns trimmed with white fluff. Perhaps she should purchase a slinky outfit for their honeymoon.

Not these, though. While she thought they were pretty, they were also too cutesy. She wanted something racy, black, and bold.

She scanned the many lingerie racks for something more suitable, surprised when her cell phone began to play the loud maddening jingle she'd recently programmed it with. Flipping it open, she was thrilled to see the number on the ID was Dylan's.

Smiling, she continued to browse the nightwear selections. "Heya, handsome, I'll be in Vegas by this evening. Where shall we meet? I'm thinking a wedding chapel, preferably tacky as all get-out. Aliens or Elvis or—"

"I want you to strip. Now."

Sadie stopped in her tracks, her fingers lingering on soft silk. "I'm in a department store."

"Even better," he growled. "I've always wanted to try sex in public."

"Ha! Fat chance." Sadie shook her head and dismissed the idea. "Besides, you're not even here with me, so how is that going to happen?"

Or was he?

Could this be another twist in his game? She whirled around, searching as far as her eye could see.

Maybe he was sneaking up on her even now. Maybe he'd never gone to Vegas. Maybe this was all a ruse. Maybe . . .

"Masturbate for me, babe. *With* me."

Oh that. Darn.

She'd hoped too soon. Not that she minded phone sex—on the contrary, she loved it, especially the mind-blowing kind they had—but she'd been hoping for real flesh and bone Dylan this time around.

With a sigh, Sadie resumed looking at the lingerie. "I told you, I'm at a store. I can't."

She didn't like the route this call was taking. If she knew Dylan, which she did, he'd persist. Worse, she'd likely give in to him, and with her luck, get into a ton of trouble for it. She'd end up missing her flight and her plans to marry him tonight would be screwed.

No, she didn't like the odds at all.

"Oh come on, you can."

"I'll be damned if I end up in jail. I'm coming to marry your ass."

"Oh, you think so?" He acted surprised, as if he hadn't chosen Vegas as their next destination on purpose.

Of course he had!

The perfect black-lace camisole presented itself and she snatched the satin top from the rack. "Hell, yes."

With matching thong, the black-on-black lingerie was exactly what she wanted. Flirty. Daring. Mischievous.

Dylan chuckled. "I don't recall agreeing to that."

"Huh?" Drawn back to their conversation, she quickly realized he wasn't talking about the camisole, but their wedding. "You have to."

"I don't know . . ." His velvet voice trailed off with a sigh. "Will you touch yourself for me? Right now?"

"What!?" She shuddered in anticipation as heat coiled in her abdomen. Instantly, her body yearned to agree to his whim, though her mind knew better. Much better. "No . . . not . . . not here, Dylan, please!" she stuttered, sounding weak in her resolve.

"Don't turn me down." He made a tsk-tsk sound. "Step behind a rack or something. I want you so bad, I can't wait. Not another minute. Don't you know how much I miss you?"

"But . . ." Sadie swallowed as arousal spread through her body, a wildfire of need. Dylan sure didn't have to say much. The pitch of his suave, seductive voice made her sweat, like an ice cube melting into naught but a puddle. She longed for him, for his touch, in such an animalistic way, she could hardly breathe.

While her mind insisted *no*, her body insisted *yes!*

Yes! Yes! Yes!

The thought of sneaking an orgasm in the midst of shopping was too good to be true. Pleasure, clothes, and pleasure, not to mention the thrill . . .

How could she pass it up?

She had to, damn it.

But she couldn't.

"No *buts*, Sadie. No protests. Simply go into the dressing room." His tone became more forceful and demanded she obey. "I *need* you so badly, don't you know that?"

A deeper desire, more emotional than simple lust, warmed her heart, traveling south to her womb. Her eyes focused on the swinging doors that led to the dressing rooms. Did she dare?

No way!

Do it!

She couldn't!

Do it!

Could she?

Clutching the camisole to her chest, she ran her tongue along her gums and bit her lower lip, debating. "I can't even believe I'm considering your crazy suggestion."

She knew better than this. She did. Trouble was, her body didn't. Her heart didn't.

"Please," he urged.

Sadie groaned. Her hardened nipples rubbed the lace of her bra and sensation shot through her. Dampness coated her inner thighs. Her need for him pulled at her, arguing that expressing love, in any form, was a beautiful thing.

She shook her head, her will disintegrating in the face of all rationale. "Devil."

Dylan chuckled. "Devil's bride."

Despite rhyme and reason, she found herself stalking to the dressing room at full speed.

Surely she'd end up in a world of crap for this.

So she'd better climax like a tornado, damn it.

She slammed through the swinging doors, thankful the attendant was absent and she didn't have to check in. A stall hung open at the very end of the row, and she rushed to it, locking the door behind her.

She pressed her back to the wall. "Fine. I'm in here," she whispered, wondering if others graced the room.

"Good girl."

She rolled her eyes. "Bad boy."

"Turns you on, doesn't it?"

Sadie cracked a smile. "Yeah."

"Strip." His tone was smoother than chocolate, compelling her. "I want you to touch yourself for me, to imagine it's my hands running along your skin, loving you."

Eager to please, Sadie unbuttoned her jeans. Propping herself against the wall, she lifted one leg onto the bench, and slid her hand under the fabric of her silk panties.

Pressing her eyes shut, she conjured an image of her lover, imagining his fingers upon her body, loving and touching along her torso to her center.

Dipping her fingers into her moist folds, she stroked her swelling labia.

"That's it," he coached. "Tell me what you're doing, little butterfly."

His new pet name for her made her heart skip a beat. She pushed her hands farther. "I'm touching myself, just as you'd touch me."

"Where, Sadie? Tell me where. I need details."

"My . . . my clit, Dylan, I'm pressing it, rubbing it, just the way you do . . ." she breathed, teasing the bundle of nerves harder, faster, her slit yawning to be filled.

"I wish I could place my lips to your cunt and kiss you." His words reached through the phone to turn her on more than her hands ever could. "Taste you."

Sadie's hand movements increased, and she cradled the phone, slipping her other hand into her shirt. Rubbing her fingers along the lace of her bra, she found the outline of her pert nipple and traced the bud.

"Can you imagine my mouth on you?"

Oh damn, could she ever. She escaped to the stroke of his tongue, the pinch of her clit as she imagined him claiming it with his teeth and suckling.

"I'm touching my breasts as well."

"I love your breasts," he murmured. "Your nipples. They're perfect."

She slipped her fingers under the fabric of her bra and found her nipple. She stroked the sensitive flesh, creating bursting delight through the soft mounds. Her chest heated, flushing.

She tensed as throbbing centralized in her clit, making the nub electrify. "Oh damn."

Pleasure undulated through her body.

"That's it." His breath became shorter, flaunting that he was masturbating as well. "Slip my cock inside you. Take me."

Sadie moaned unintentionally as she slid two fingers into her dripping heat. Her thumb pressed her clit and applied pressure to the sensitive button. Slowly, she pumped her digits in and out of her unfulfilled sex, wanton with the need to feel him deep inside her, stretching her to the max, his head stroking her g-spot.

She released another gurgle of pleasure, this time louder, all too aware that she could potentially be heard by other women in the dressing room.

Yet nothing could stop her from continuing the passionate phone call. Embarrassment, shame, not even trouble with the law could curtail her desire for Dylan. Perhaps her mind could protest, but when he commanded her body, she obeyed.

"Tell me how I feel deep inside you." Dylan's demands were oil on a flame. She pressed deeper and upward, her fingernails raking her tender, swollen g-spot.

"Good. Damn good." Her hips thrust to meet the movements of her hand. "But not as good as you."

"But I am there, sweetie, loving you. Feel me. Thrust faster," he urged, his voice becoming powerful. "Lift your hips higher. Take your fingers deeper."

"Yes," she agreed, mesmerized by his commands and the thought of his hands upon her excited body, his cock deep inside her pussy. She followed his ordered motions, tilting her hips so that she could fully plunge her hand into her cunt, ramming against her G-spot with vigor.

"Don't forget your breasts. I love your breasts."

Slowly, gently, she twisted her tight nipples between her forefinger and thumb. Already wrought with arousal, the attention to her nipples drove her over the edge. Her body tightened, her skin enflamed, her every nerve awoke.

"*Mmm* . . ." Sadie tried desperately not to scream, to contain the orgasm bursting through her, but nothing could contain the intensity of the climax. "Dylan!"

"That's it, come for me, little butterfly. Come," he encouraged.

His tender epithet made her feel so feminine, and she blossomed, her orgasm releasing.

Calming, she sucked in a deep breath. "Why are you calling me that?"

"Because like the butterfly, you cannot be captured, you just keep eluding me. Flitting away."

"Not this time," she whispered.

His heavy breath fell as he clearly followed her climax. "Then come to me," he gasped with distinct finality. Instantly, she knew he'd hang up.

"Wait!" she cried. "Where will you be in Vegas?"

Frantic, she freed her hands, wiped them on her jeans, and stood. She clutched the phone, hoping he wouldn't hang up. "Please, Dylan."

"Gambling for your heart."

What did that mean? Didn't he know he already had her love?

"My heart has always belonged to you. You've won it fair and square."

"Not yet, little butterfly, not yet. I still need to win this game of ours."

"It was never about winning, Dylan. It was about the chase. The thrill."

"Maybe for you, but I'm a guy. For me, a game is always about winning, and the stakes have been high in this one. I want my prize."

His answer brought a smile to her face. True, that. He might be an extraordinary man, but he was still a man.

Picking up the camisole, she held it in front of her. No doubt, it was a fit, the same as Dylan was to her. "Oh? Your prize?"

"You."

"And once I'm yours?"

"This is a game that shall never really end, as you've already agreed. There's always something to be bartered for in a marriage."

She thought of all she'd won the past few weeks and raised a brow. "Indeed."

After a short pause, Dylan cleared his throat. "You thanked me, Sadie, for setting up the foursome, but I never relayed my appreciation to you."

"For what?" Sadie laughed. "Dragging you halfway around the world?"

His voice softened. "I'd die, wither up and disappear, without your passion. Pain in the ass you may be, but you free me. You make me the kind of man I want to be, instead of wishing and wondering my life away. So thank you."

His touching gratitude squeezed her heart. Tears welled in her eyes and her insides turned to mush.

Never had anything he said meant more to her.

Her voice shook as she spoke. "I love you, Dylan."

She could feel his smile, his warmth, right through the phone. "Then come love me in Vegas."

Dylan hung up.

Using her shirt, she dabbed her tears of happiness away and redressed. She drew a deep breath, slung her purse over her shoulder, and stepped from the stall with a brilliant smile.

She had a fiancé to catch.

As she walked down the corridor to the exit, a plus-sized woman standing in front of a large, three-panel mirror, examining her *way* too small clothing choices, turned and glared at Sadie as if she were Lady Godiva herself.

She shook her head. "Disgusting."

Another woman joined her, coming to stand at her side, her eyes screaming in judgment. "Absolutely sick."

Heat rose to Sadie's face, embarrassment flushing her every pore, followed by quick anger.

Sure, the way they glowered at her and spoke was no one's fault but hers. Well, she could blame Dylan, but nonetheless, these ladies hadn't asked to overhear her masturbating.

Maybe it was the condescending way they looked at her, or perhaps their revolted tones, but antagonism rose in her. Her reaction was totally inappropriate, but she didn't care. The words burst from her mouth before she could stop them.

"Yes, the way those pants squeeze your hips is rather disgusting. You may want to pull that fabric out of your ass." Sadie smiled wryly at her. "Then have some sex. It may help you develop a better sense of humor."

Sadie strode from the dressing rooms with her chin up, not sorry for her actions or words, and not looking back once.

Vegas or bust, baby!

twenty-one

Sadie stepped from the cab onto the sidewalk, dragging her newly purchased luggage behind her. Awed, she stared at the Excalibur hotel. A Vegas-style Arthurian castle, it came complete with moat and drawbridge.

White with multicolored roofing and numerous towers, the busy hotel almost made her feel as if she were walking into a magical kingdom. *Almost*, except for the Vegas nightlife buzzing around her, loud and in her face, not to mention the awful, dry heat of Nevada.

She and Dylan had been to Hawaii, Tuscany, and Egypt. Why hadn't they gone anywhere cool?

Next year.

She heard the jingle of slot machines and happy cheers in the distance. A smile broadened on her face and she followed the noise. Where the gambling was, she'd find her fiancé.

Lush red carpeting greeted her as she strolled inside. Her heart ached to dash through the hotel until she found her lover, but she resisted. Impatient as she was to find Dylan, she decided to get a room and shower first. She couldn't very well drag her suitcase into the casino.

When she thought of all the time they'd wasted apart, she wanted to scream. How silly Dylan had been for not listening to her, trusting her. Of course, what goes around, comes around.

Admittedly, she was glad their game would be ending. Right now, she wanted nothing more, and nothing less, than to be with him.

She paused en route to the lobby, debating. Wouldn't it be more logical for them to share a suite? What a waste of good money to pay for a separate room. Plus, he didn't want to have to squander time lugging her belongings from room to room.

Maybe, *maybe*, Dylan had been smart. If it had been her, she'd have left a key at the desk for him.

On a gamble, she bypassed the kiosks intended for self-service check-in and approached the desk.

The clerk dazzled her with a wide smile. "Welcome to the Excalibur!"

She couldn't help but laugh at the young man's enthusiasm. "Sadie Williams. Dylan Burton, my fiancé, should be expecting me."

"Do you have a room number?"

"No."

"Oh, um . . ." The clerk's face creased as he frowned, dampening Sadie's hopes.

He turned to the keyboard, his fingers going a million miles an hour over the keys.

"Is everything okay?"

The young man lifted his head, looking rather guilty. "Oh yes. Sorry. It's my first day."

"Oh. Well then, is there a key for me?"

She shifted, anxious to get moving. She was now in the same building as Dylan, yet not with him. If she wasn't wasting time worrying over a shower, she could already be wrapped in his embrace. Headed up to his room. To get married.

But that wasn't going to happen. She refused to make love, or get married, while smelly.

"Oh." The clerk studied the screen, his eyes darting. He gave a quick nod. "Don't know how I missed that. Yes, you're in room three-twelve."

Sadie sighed with relief. "Good."

He fetched a card key, and five minutes later Sadie was in Dylan's empty suite, showering.

Thank God she'd made herself pause long enough while speed shopping in New York to buy something beyond jeans and tee shirts. She would never have felt comfortable greeting Dylan in the casino so casually attired, and moreover, being dressed sexy gave her confidence. Despite her impatience, showering had been worth the time.

Wiggling the hem of her short, tight black skirt into place, Sadie fluffed the curls in her hair one last time and walked into the richly decorated casino. Neon lights in multiple colors flashed everywhere, accompanied by the melodic music of the slots, the jingle of coins, and bartering of money for a good time.

Sadie scanned the crowd. Good grief.

Dylan was a needle in a haystack. The last thing she wanted was to mistake the wrong man for him, as she had in Tuscany, though she truly felt like pouncing on every possible Dylan she noticed until she found her fiancé.

Sadie paused under an impressive, sparkling chandelier, contemplating which way to go. What was Dylan's game? Slots? Blackjack? Poker? Keno?

He'd mentioned something on the phone. What had it been?

Oh. He'd said he would double his money. Not much of a clue, but she doubted he'd be doubling anything on slots. She'd check the tables first, and then worry about the rest of the games.

Walking briskly, she made her way through the casino, caught off guard when she spotted her lover at a roulette wheel.

With two women pasted on either side of him.

Stopping in her tracks, Sadie stared at Dylan in shock. The trashy looking bleach blonds in hot-pink leather practically humped his legs, their bodies pressed dangerously close to his. Almost immediately, Sadie dubbed the women Barbie One and Barbie Two, though the original Barbie doll definitely had better skin, even if it was plastic.

What the hell did Dylan think he was doing?

Wait. Maybe it wasn't Dylan. Maybe she was mistaken, like in Tuscany. She had to be, right?

Nope. She could smell him—the way the spicy scent of his signature cologne mingled with his natural musk. The way he moved, the way he laughed, the man was Dylan, clear as day.

The bastard!

Sadie inched closer, casually planting herself within earshot of the threesome, a mere foot or two behind her unnoticing fiancé. Her confidence protested the sight of the women and their exaggerated curves. The way their plastic tits—oversized, overfirm mounds far too high to be natural—molded to his torso.

Stupid women. Didn't they know they were ruining their backs?

Dylan continued playing roulette, as if the tramps were nothing more than two ornaments attached to his body.

Sadie resisted the urge to scream and saved her lung strength for the impending confrontation.

Who the hell did Dylan think he was, anyway? Where did he get off?

She'd—

"No more bets," the dealer called and spun the wheel. The ball fell into a red slot. "Sixteen."

"That's you again!" Barbie Two squealed, jumping up and down.

Acting like quite the cool cat, Dylan accepted his payoff, and slid more chips onto another number. Barbie One trailed a hand along his shoulder, then stood on her tiptoes, whispering in his ear.

What the hell had the slut said? Shit!

Dylan brushed Barbie's hand away and shook his head. "Please. I've already said no thanks. Repeatedly. I've tried ignoring you and if I could walk away right now, I would. I told you, I'm engaged, and I'm not interested."

A whoosh of relief burst from Sadie's lungs, her heart missing a beat or two. What had she been thinking? Sure, the situation looked bad, but she knew Dylan. He hated bleach-blond hair. She should have trusted him.

"But . . ." Barbie Two grabbed Dylan's tush, digging her greedy fingers into his ass.

Her cue.

"*But* he told you. He's engaged. To me." Sadie stepped forward, shooing the woman away. "Go on, don't make this get ugly."

Barbie One rolled her eyes. "Come on, Val, he's a waste of time anyway."

Barbie Two, aka Val, nodded in agreement, shooting Sadie an evil glare. The two sauntered off, hips wagging, likely in hopes of landing some other fool.

"Ah, my savior." Dylan turned, his eyes praising the sight of her. "It appears I'm winning all the way around tonight."

"You almost won my foot in your ass," she snapped. "What were you doing, letting those women paw you all over?"

"No more bets," the dealer barked again then spun the wheel. "Nine!"

Dylan sighed at the loss and shrugged. "They wouldn't take no for answer, believe you me. I seem to attract whores like flies to honey lately. What is it? The tan?" He pointed to a generous stack of chips in front of him. "Anyway, the flies' honey."

"Ahh . . ." Stunned, she glanced at the pile of chips he beamed over. "Say what?"

"I've been raking in some cash tonight. I'm just playing roulette for fun. Earlier, I cleaned up at the blackjack tables. Made them shut down."

She cleared her throat, not really giving a damn about the money, but the flies it was attracting. "Should I read into that earlier sentence? Whores are becoming a problem?"

He laid down more money after losing the last spin. "Not exactly a problem."

Sadie's eyes widened. "*Not* a *problem*?"

Apparently, Dylan was having the time of his life.

He laughed. "I had a waitress throw herself at me in Mexico as well. You should have been there."

She trusted him. She trusted him. She trusted him.

That didn't mean she couldn't be protective as hell when it came to whores, though, right? "Interesting. And how did you respond?"

Dylan chuckled again. "Do I hear a jealousy bug?"

Attempting to keep a plain face, Sadie shrugged and turned away. "No. Absolutely not."

He brushed a curl over her ear, his fingers stroking the lobe suggestively. "Good. Because I was going to suggest we take those nice ladies to our room, you know, and all have a good time. After all, you had three men in Cairo."

A waiter serving cocktails walked past her, and she snatched a glass, drinking the fiery liquid quickly. The rum and Coke burned as it washed down her throat.

"I'm not sure . . . I'm not . . ."

"No more bets," the dealer interrupted, spinning the wheel. "Five!"

Dylan raked in more winnings with a wry grin and shifted his stance to face her, his elbow resting on the table. "I'm teasing, Sadie. But boy, talk about the kettle calling the pot black."

"Wait a minute. That's not fair." She jabbed him in the arm, poking his well-formed bicep. "Quit it."

He caught her hand and drew her face to face with him, whispering, "But truly, would you do that? Have a foursome with two other women?"

"With the right women, at the right time, and at the right place, maybe. *Maybe*," she stressed. "Let's just say I'm not shooting the idea down."

His brows lifted keenly. "Fair enough."

Enough of the chitchat about other women—she had better things in mind to do with her man. Wrapping her fingers around the thick muscles of his upper arm, her nails pressed into his skin, and she tugged him away from the table. "Come on. Let's go to our room."

He resisted, not letting her budge him. "Can't babe. Look at the streak I'm on."

Great! His stupid streak! Who knew when that would end? It seemed he'd been lucky since he'd arrived in Vegas.

Frustration snaked through Sadie, taxing her patience. "So? Screw it! Come on. I want to be with you."

Dylan stared at her like she was a nut job. "Are you crazy? A few more wins and a good investment, and we can run away to the islands."

Throwing her head back, Sadie groaned.

"Except we plan to have lots of kids and settle down in our nice, new, big home, so no islands for us. Not for at least thirty years."

"Oh, right." He played with several chips, running them through his fingers and dropping them on the pile. To her dismay, he placed yet another bet.

"Oh, right?" Sadie stomped her foot. She hadn't rushed all the way here for this. She wanted to get married, damn it!

A wry grin formed on his face as he intently watched the wheel. "I'm teasing again."

She sunk her nails into his skin, pulling him harder. "Dylan! Come on. My parents are rich. I'll give you double what you have there. Just come on!"

"Patience. Just give me ten minutes." He patted her hand, and returned to the game, leaving her standing there ready to implode. Not that it would do her a damn bit of good. She could probably strip in the middle of the casino and he wouldn't want to retire. He was obsessed with winning.

With a sigh, Sadie accepted defeat.

But defeat could only be tolerated for so long. Ten minutes, fine, she'd put up with the short wait. But if he pushed for any more gambling time, she'd have a cow. A large one. While she didn't want to make a scene, she would if she was forced.

Time wore on, and she watched him, the way his eyes sparked with the thrill of raking in more chips, the way he exuded confidence. He was having such a damn good time, which pulled on her conscience.

His ten minutes dragged by, and with each extra passing second, she tried to be generous. Loving. After all, he *was* winning.

But then he kept winning. And winning. And winning.

No matter the money, her staying power wore thinner and thinner by the second. So thin, her ability to wait with a smile for one more moment snapped. He'd said ten minutes, not two hours! Enough!

Reaching down, she seized his cock, smashing her hand against the bulge. She rubbed her palm inward, to his balls. His wide eyes locked with hers as she squeezed the taut sacs.

"Wrap it up, or I swear I'm dragging you from the casino, and with no fortune."

Dylan nodded in agreement, looking dumbfounded. "Okay."

twenty-two

Damn slow thing." Dylan pressed the button for the elevator twice more. "Come on already."

Sadie grasped his shirt and pushed him against the wall. She'd wanted Dylan sexually a thousand times before, but never like this. Never this starving, do-or-die need that wouldn't let go, wouldn't relent.

After all the waiting she'd been through in the casino, she couldn't stand another moment of physical denial.

"Damn, Dylan, I have to have your big cock in me." She tore at the buttons of his shirt, working her hand under the fabric. She ran her fingers through the coarse hairs covering his chest. "Let's do it in the elevator."

"If one ever comes." He hit the button again and again.

Someone standing behind them chuckled. "Vegas." Laughing, the man walked away.

Sadie paid the stranger no mind, only caring about one thing. Getting Dylan's pants off.

She suckled his lower lip, drawing the flesh between her teeth, then releasing. Her kisses were ravenous, her desire not to be denied.

"I can't wait." She pressed her torso against his length, grinding her hips to his. "I need you. Now."

His pelvis rocked against her, mimicking her motion. "Vixen."

"You wouldn't have it any other way."

She molded to him like a magnet to steel and slipped two fingers inside his waistband, caressing the edge of his pubic hair.

Reaching around, Dylan cupped her bottom, squeezing both cheeks before lifting her. She wrapped her legs around his waist, her hands encircling his neck. The thick, rigid length of his cock stood proudly between her legs, heating her upper thigh.

"Push the button again." With her teeth, she clamped down on his neck.

Clumsily, Dylan searched for the button and hit it several times. A moment later, the elevator finally arrived. Carrying her, he stumbled through the open doors, selecting the top floor. He backed himself against the control panel, his fingers incessantly hitting the button to close the doors, even as they slid into motion.

The moment they clicked shut, Sadie slipped from his embrace, her body sliding along his until her feet met the floor, then she dropped to her knees. Ripping at the fly, she tore open his pants. His slacks dropped to the floor and she dove into his briefs, pulling his long shaft free.

In her palms, she cupped his balls, her thumb caressing the base of his erection, encouraging further growth. To her amazement, he widened and stretched under her ministrations, standing even taller.

Caressing the thick vein along the soft underside of his cock, she kissed its wide tip, and then slowly suckled the tender spot behind his crown.

Dylan moaned and grasped her upper arm. "Babe, we don't have time for savoring."

He vigorously attacked the elevator buttons, hitting every floor, then holding the doors shut.

"Mmm . . ." she protested as his left hand clamped around her forearm and drew her to her feet. "But you taste so good."

"I fuck better than I taste." He grasped her waist, yanking her against him, his hands sliding down to squeeze her ass.

"Prove it."

In one quick movement, he lifted her, and she wrapped her legs around his waist. Locking both hands and feet behind him, she secured her body to his. He reached under her skirt, pulling aside her thong, and his massive hard-on pressed against her wet mons.

The mushroom-shaped head rubbed along her slit as he cupped her bottom, positioning himself to drive into her ready and waiting sheath.

With one strong thrust, he plowed into her, demanding her body accept him fully. Her nails pierced the skin on his shoulders as she cried out. Their bodies clashed in fury, their hips grinding and pumping as they pawed at each other.

All she wanted was to feel him, to savor every square inch of the man she loved. She never wanted to let him go. His hair, his face, his jaw, his neck . . . she ran her palms all over his body, worshipping her soon to be husband.

He thrust his cock into her tunnel, his hands kneading the fleshy muscles of her rear, squeezing each cheek, then releasing. Oh God, it was—

Ding! The elevator door opened, halting their furious lovemaking. They paused midfuck, their gazes flying to the door.

A brawny security guard rested his hand on the sliding door, preventing it from closing. His deep eyes, eyes almost as black as her cop's, *devoured* the situation. "What do we have here? Are you guests of the hotel?"

"Yes." Dylan pulled his softening sex from Sadie, lowered her to her feet and fumbled to get back into his briefs. "Room three-twelve."

Quickly, she straightened her skirt, and together they shifted to the back of the elevator.

"Not anymore." The guard stepped inside and closed the doors. "Even if this is Vegas, we don't allow that type of behavior."

Sadie's heart skipped a beat, and without thinking, she acted on impulse, stepping forward. "Wait."

The last thing she wanted was trouble. Getting kicked out of the hotel wasn't that big of a deal, but what if he called the police? She didn't want a rap sheet—she was going to be a wife, and one day, a mother.

Besides . . .

The situation was perfect. The security guard was perfect.

In uniform and with a built, muscular body that rippled with strength evident even through his short-sleeved shirt, not to mention his dark coloring, he reminded her so much of the cop who once haunted her dreams.

Judging from the bulge in his pants, he measured up in the sexual department too. So what if he wasn't a real police officer, he was close enough. What better way than to kiss the nightmares a final good-bye than a hot threesome between a cop and her fiancé?

All he could do was turn her down. After all, they'd already been caught in the act. Asking wasn't a crime, was it?

She wouldn't do it without Dylan's full cooperation though. Looking her fiancé in the eye, she silently asked for his approval. He did not disappoint. With a sly grin, he gave a quick nod and whispered, "Go for it."

She placed a hand on the officer's well-formed bicep, her fingers lightly caressing his tan skin. "Instead of kicking us out, and all that nasty stuff no one likes to deal with, you could say screw your duty, and come screw me."

She flashed a beaming Dylan a quick wink and then pressed closer to the officer, molding her body against his.

The security guard stared straight ahead, his body stiff and aloof. "Excuse me?"

She trailed her fingers along his back and grabbed his butt. "Are you shy?"

He gulped. "No."

She looked down, observing the growing tent in his pants. Indeed impressive.

"Stop the elevator and join us," she purred, squeezing his ass cheeks again. "You know you want to."

His tongue darted from his mouth in temptation.

"Jeez, you're hot. Damn." His eyes swept over her body, then halted abruptly as he shook his head. He put up his hand as if he could command away his attraction. "I'm working."

"So?" She ran her hands from his back to his front and cupped his swelling cock.

"So . . ." His protest disappeared as she squeezed more firmly and he sucked in a sharp breath. "Shit. I've never done anything like this before."

He appeared ready to detonate, but that didn't slow Sadie. Massaging his balls, she teased the base of his hard, easily ten-inch shaft with her thumb through his pants. "What do you say, officer?"

He groaned in answer and Sadie knew she had him.

Her fingers fluttered over his sex and she stepped back. "You can stop the elevator, can't you?"

His hands shook as he reached for his keys then with a quick insertion of one and a turn, he halted the elevator with a sudden lurch. He turned to her. "This better be worth the risk of losing my job."

"It will be," she promised and grasped him by the shirt collar. "I guarantee."

She yanked the buttons to his crisp light-blue shirt open, and revealed his chest, her eyes roaming over the built pectoral muscles that lay under a carpet of black hairs. "Perfect. So damn perfect. What's your name, officer?"

"Jon."

Pulling Jon by his shirt, she backed up until her bottom pressed against Dylan. His lengthy rod nestled the cleft between her ass cheeks.

Leaning down, he gathered her into his arms and nibbled at her neck.

"Slide this over his cock." Dylan presented her with a condom. "But first, suck him off."

Accepting the protection, Sadie tore the plastic wrapper open. Dylan grasped her shoulders and pushed her to her knees, his hands tangling in her hair.

The security guard's fingers intertwined with Dylan's and wrapped around her messy tresses, tugging at her scalp. Their hold ignited the nerves in her head. Tingles danced across the tender skin as they gently guided her.

She fumbled with the button at the waistband of Jon's uniform, so eager, so excited, she could barely function. Finally, the fastening popped free, and she tugged down the zipper, digging her hands into his boxers.

She found his meaty rod, strengthened and stiff from his arousal, and drew the shaft forth. Kissing the tip of his wide head, she trailed her tongue along his length. Suckling, pecking, even nibbling, she devoured his cock, tasting every inch of him.

The grasp on her short hair increased, urging her on, driving her wild. Acutely aware that *both* men observed her, she performed to please, herself as much as them.

She adored that Dylan enjoyed watching her. That it turned him on. That he had such faith in her loyalty he didn't blink an eye to share her.

Trust—the true test of a relationship. Dylan loved her without petty jealousies and insecurities. Their love was now as strong as steel. Unbreakable.

Jon rocked in her mouth, his hips thrusting from instinct. Swallowing him fully, she allowed his cock to slide down her throat until her lips met his balls. Pleasure tingles did the salsa on her tongue, her already aroused body yearning to be touched, to be filled.

She cupped Jon's balls and cradled the soft sac in her palms. Stroking the sensitive flesh, she trailed her nails over the thin skin. Jon groaned and his grip on her hair increased.

The vein along the bottom of his cock pulsed, threatening an orgasm and Sadie slowed, backing off. Holding the condom at the tip of his shaft, she slowly rolled the protection over him, engulfing his sex in the ribbed rubber.

Dylan scraped his short nails over her prickling scalp to the base of her neck and across her shoulders. His palms rested on her biceps as he drew her to her feet.

Turning her to face him, Dylan slid her shirt and skirt from her body, allowing the clothing to drop to the floor, leaving her exposed and bare in a very public place. Her skin set afire with awareness. Exhilaration.

Jon scooted closer and pressed his cock to the small of her back, while Dylan's erection lay hot against her lower belly. Sandwiched between them, she gasped, every inch of her body alert with the knowledge of how she was about to be fucked, two men at once: double the pleasure, and double the fun.

Eager to take both their cocks deep inside her, she laid her head on Dylan's chest, her nails piercing the skin of his shoulders as she pressed her bottom to Jon. "Please. I can't wait anymore."

Dylan could not believe this was happening. Unplanned.

Slowly, Dylan's fingers stroked Sadie's arms, thoroughly enjoying the way Jon's eyes studied her body, the way his cock pressed against her ass cheeks, the way this stranger was hard and ready for *his* woman.

His prick danced between her thighs, brushing the thin strip of pubic hair that covered her center. The taut skin of his hard-on was stretched thin from arousal and the vein along the underneath of his shaft throbbed from intense need.

Lifting Sadie, Dylan pulled her legs around his waist. With one forceful thrust, he drove into her wet pussy, sinking deep in her snug channel.

Sadie moaned and wrapped her arms around his neck, pressing her warm, soft breasts into his face. Inhaling deeply, he hugged her tight, supporting her body.

He spread her ass cheeks wide, revealing her to Jon. Dipping a finger into her wet sex, Dylan drew forth her creamy desire. Placing his finger to the officer's dick, he slid the juices along his condom-covered shaft, lubricating Jon to enter his fiancé.

Jon tensed under the ministrations and Dylan smiled. "What happens in the elevator stays in the elevator."

Their eyes locked.

Both of them were out of their box, feeling strange about it, and yet so gloriously aroused, forgetting their inhibitions was easy.

After a moment, Jon returned his smile and positioned his lower body against Sadie's. Aligning his cock with her anus, he eased his way into her tight rectum.

Sadie's sharp nails sunk deep into Dylan's shoulder blades as she accepted the man's width. Her back arched, her muscles tightened. Finally, when Jon was completely inside her, she relaxed with a whimper.

Her body melted into his and she whispered in his ear. "I love you, Dylan."

That was all he'd ever wanted. Ever needed.

Sadie gently kissed Dylan's ear, then trailed her tongue along the sinewy muscles of his neck, and onward to his collarbone.

The men pumped slowly in and out of her, their thick cocks repeatedly filling her lust-driven body. She moved against them, eagerly accepting their length, her body driven wild with pleasure.

Jon reached around her left hipbone and placed a hand over her mound. His fingers delved into her slick folds and found her swollen, pulsing clit. He pressed the nub and gently rolled it, pushing her past the point of reason. Her world whirled as she cried out, drawing deep, sharp breaths as she attempted to prevent the orgasm that was threatening her far too quickly.

Clutching her bottom with one hand, Dylan balanced her against his torso and cupped her right breast, massaging the firm flesh deeply. His fingers rolled her nipple and stroked electric sensations through the pert bud.

His hot lips nibbled her neck, sucking a trail along the corded muscles to her shoulder, drawing her sensitive skin between his teeth and then releasing.

The attention to her breasts, her shoulders and neck, her clit, in addition to the thick, long swords thrusting in and out of her moist tunnels, drove her mad. It was all so much to take, almost too much to handle, but not nearly enough. She bucked against them, her body lurching with ecstasy, somehow screaming for more, though she could never take it.

The men held her in place and forced her to withstand the unbearable pleasure. Their hands and mouths were everywhere all at once. Her squeals escalated into screams.

"Shhh . . ." Jon commanded. "People will think someone is being murdered."

His fingers pressed harder on her clit, as if to torture her with the fact that she needed to be quieter.

Sadie writhed. "Screw them."

Jon thrust hard into her. "I think I'd rather screw you."

"Nibble her earlobe," Dylan urged Jon. "It drives her nuts."

Jon leaned forward, whispering, his hot breath tantalizing the area with promises of carnal teasing and torment. "Quiet now."

His cock plunged deep into her anus as his teeth claimed the top of the nerve-infused cartilage, and drew her ear into his mouth. He suckled gently, his tongue stroking the sensitive skin.

Working his way down, he kissed, licked, and pulled at her ear, detonating the burning fervor that possessed her body. Dylan drove deep into her womb then stilled, grinding his hips against her enflamed labia and Jon's toying hands.

Squeezing her eyes shut, Sadie held tight to Dylan, her fingers clawing into his skin as she fought to contain her screams. Hardly able to breathe from the exciting, powerful waves, she gasped for air, close to hyperventilation, her world blurring. Her body was possessed. Afire. Explosive.

Every inch of her craved their touch, delighted in their hands upon her, their cocks deep inside her, yet her mind rejected their ministrations. The passions burning through her body were too much. Unbearable. She couldn't take anymore.

But how could she call a halt to such glorious ecstasy? Much as she was going crazy, she needed this sweet torture . . . she needed relief . . . she needed . . .

An uncontrollable orgasm burst through her body, spiraling out of control. She became a siren of bliss, lighting like a billion matches set off all at once, tightening, constricting, and discharging.

Her world went black for a brief moment as she collided with release. Gasping, she fell against Dylan's shoulder, clutching him for support.

The grunting men continued to thrust in and out of her, their cocks moving in steady rhythm.

Jon climaxed first, groaning and jerking as his hot semen filled the condom within the taut confines of her rectum. His whole body stiffened and then relaxed. After several moments, he slowly eased himself free of her body.

Dylan lifted her legs higher and held her thighs securely as he plunged in three more times. His fingers knotted in her upper leg muscles and he bellowed, his face contorted in what looked like pain. With several quick, powerful jerks, he came, filling her pussy with his cum.

Dylan went limp, and for a few moments, they stood there, leaning against each other, panting from their orgasms.

Lifting her free from his body, Dylan slid her to the floor. Sadie collapsed in a heap, still dizzy from the intense activity. Finally, her head cleared enough for her to speak. "Wow." She ran her hands through her tangled hair and she winked. "Good job, boys."

Dylan lifted his upper lip in a wry smile. "What a lucky night."

"You can say that again," Jon agreed.

Sadie laughed and stood on shaky legs, gathering her clothes. The men joined her in dressing, none of them quite sure what else to say. They quickly clothed themselves amid the silence, awkwardness taking over.

Jon fastened the last button to his shirt and then went to the controls.

"What floor are you on?"

"Third."

The elevator lurched back into motion. Sadie straightened her hair, then folded her hands in front of her, biting her lower lip.

A quick glance at Dylan revealed he felt the same way—giddy from the fantasy, more in love than ever, and likely to explode in rolling laughter at the outrageous, unbelievable position they'd just found themselves in.

It took all her will not to explode and make a fool of herself. It was clear from Jon's red face that he now felt uncomfortable and she wanted to save him any embarrassment. He'd been quite the sport, after all.

The elevator glided to a halt, the display above highlighting their floor number.

"Thanks." She held out her hand and he accepted it, shaking as if they were nothing more than business acquaintances.

Dylan nodded his regard and they stepped from the elevator. Turning, she waved as the doors glided shut behind them. No sooner than they closed, she fell to the floor, laughing harder than she'd ever laughed before.

Tears welled in her eyes, her stomach aching as the muscles contracted and released from her humor. "Can you believe that just happened?"

"Only with you, Sadie," Dylan chuckled richly, magical happiness glowing in his dark eyes. "Only with you."

"He was hot, too. Can you believe our luck?"

Dylan scooped her from the floor and into his arms, cradling her against him. He nuzzled her face, calming her. "We should head back to the casino and make good use of this night."

He walked down the corridor, toward their room.

Her mind protested at the thought of more gambling. She had much better plans. "I think our luck is better spent getting married."

With a sparkle in his chocolate irises, he rolled his eyes. "Sure. Waste away immense fortune for a piece of paper."

She playfully hit his chest with a balled up fist. "You think I'm a waste?"

"Hardly. I lost my job over you, you know!"

"I'm sorry," she whispered, feeling guilty yet glad at the same time.

"It doesn't matter. You do."

He'd gone through so much just to be with her. She'd never doubt him—*them*—again. "We'll start a new life together, a better one."

"Nothing could be better than just being with you." Juggling her as he walked, he caught her hand, and lifted her higher, pulling her into a kiss. His lips fiercely embraced her mouth, brutally passionate as his tongue slipped between her teeth and tangled with hers.

A moment later, they reached their room. Slowly, he lowered Sadie to her feet. Backing her against the door, he never once released her from the kiss as he slipped the card key through the slot. Devouring her, he cupped the back of her head and his fingers wrapped around her curls.

After much fumbling, Dylan shoved the door open and the two of them stumbled inside, their mouths still attached, their hands searching. He pinned her against the wall, trapping her.

The embrace was hungry, almost bruising as he kissed her, his tongue reaching deep into her throat. She grabbed it with her lips and suckled the tip, not letting go.

A guttural groan escaped his throat and his eyes flashed open. "Heaya," he attempted to protest.

Relinquishing her suck-hold, she grinned and sidestepped him.

"Damn." His tongue ran along his reddened, swollen lips. "Hellcat."

"Don't you know it?" Sadie walked around him, reexamining the hotel room. The first time around, she'd rushed to the bathroom, showered and redressed, without thought to much else, and she hadn't considered her surroundings.

Truly, it was a wonderful room to begin a honeymoon in. Decorated in warm tones, it sported a king-size bed and hot tub, which was located in the corner of the room, in a castle turret.

She couldn't wait to get started on happily ever after with Dylan, but there was that sexy camisole she'd purchased. She shrugged off her skirt and top, and turned to face him.

"Mmm." His ravenous dark eyes roamed her body from head to toe. "I'll tell you what. Hop in the shower. I'll order dinner and meet you there."

Sadie unfastened her bra and released her breasts. The sudden freedom was heaven and she drew a deep breath, adoring the way he stared at her open-mouthed.

"Try out the hot tub yet?"

He shrugged. "A soak in a spa is no fun alone."

Down went her thong, dropping to the floor in an instant. "Well then, we shall have to remedy that." With a wink, she headed off to the bathroom. She had the sneaking feeling she was washing away one sexual escapade to get dirty from another.

"I won't argue with that," he called after her. "When you're done in there, you'll find me in the spa. Heaven knows the food will take forever. Room service always does."

"I'd like a big dinner. I'm famished." She paused at the threshold to the bathroom, looking back over the room, and her fiancé one last time.

He looked too damn good to pass up—or lose again.

Forget the sex. They could enjoy each other in the hot, bubbly water of the spa *after* they'd said their vows. She wanted to get married and she was in a hurry. A big one.

Nodding, she graced him with a seductive smile. "Perfect. This room will be the perfect start to our honeymoon."

"Start? You're always on the run, babe." He chuckled and shook his head. "And where shall our honeymoon end?"

"At home, dear. Where else?"

"Good. I was afraid I'd have to tie you up again."

"You can do that anyway."

twenty-three

She didn't know why she'd put it on. She only planned to take it off after they ate. Yet, the dark, flirty camisole and thong made her feel sexy. She wanted Dylan to see her in the outfit, if only for a second.

And a second it would be. She couldn't wait to get to the chapel and take his name. She figured they'd soak in the hot tub and relax until their meal arrived, then eat and dress. Within the hour, they'd be getting married.

After one last look in the mirror, Sadie crossed the room to the spa turret, standing on the lower step and inhaling the steam.

Dylan soaked in the hot depths of the water, his arms spread, and body limp. His eyes were half open, his smile lax, his muscles like Jell-O from the massaging bubbles assaulting his body. She imagined she would look similar after consuming a giant dark chocolate candy bar dipped in caramel—pleasured . . . fulfilled . . . relaxed . . .

Wait. Too relaxed. Dylan was falling asleep!

She didn't have time for him to snooze. Reaching into the water, she flung some at his face. "Hey!"

His eyes flew open. "I was just thinking about you."

"You mean you were just dreaming about me."

"No." He cocked a smile as he straightened. "Well, maybe. Hey, you wore me out."

"The night's barely started." She spun around, showing off her outfit. "What do you think?"

"It looks damn good on you, but it would look even better off."

"Oh," she pouted. "You want me to strip?"

"Yes, please."

"Well, okay, baby, since I love you so much." She pulled the camisole from her body in slow, sultry movements, deliberately prolonging the removal, with the absolute intention of driving him nuts.

Once the flimsy top was over her head, she tossed it aside and hooked her fingers into her black, lacy thong. Inching the underwear down, she slid them over her hips and ass, then her thighs.

The panties fell to the floor around her ankles, and she stepped free, leaning on the tub. Her arms pressed her breasts together, presenting the lush mounds to an openmouthed Dylan.

His eyes studied her. "You are amazing."

She flashed him a foxy grin. "I know."

"Brat."

She shrugged and stepped into the spa. "When the occasion calls."

Sadie sunk into the hot depths, sliding alongside his body. A jet massaged her back and applied delightful pressure to the tense muscles surrounding her spine.

She nudged his foot with hers. "So, what wedding chapel shall it be?"

When he only answered with a grin, she waggled her brows. "I thought an Elvis ceremony would be neat, though I heard there are joints where you can dress up as aliens and get hitched."

His toes slid between hers, entwining their feet. "I think I saw one that did *Star Trek* weddings."

"Not a chance."

"Oh come on. It's my favorite show."

"Yuck." She shook her head in disgust. "I may love you, but I don't love *Star Trek*."

"Brat."

"When the occasion calls." She wriggled her foot against his. "I think it's gotta be the traditional Vegas wedding—Elvis. Anything else wouldn't be right."

"Traditional?" Dylan snorted. "What we're having at home will be traditional."

"Except we'll already be married." Sadie stood, already tired of soaking. She was too antsy to sit still and definitely too antsy to wait for dinner. The threesome hadn't worn her out as it had Dylan. To the contrary, she buzzed with energy, and she wanted to put the liveliness to good use. "Come on. Let's quit wasting time. I want to get married."

He caught her arm, looking a little put off. "You're serious?"

"Well, what did you think?"

"That you were kidding around." With a gentle tug, Dylan drew her back into the hot tub and onto his lap. His hard cock pressed against her buttocks, threatening more sexual fun.

Fun as it sounded, she didn't have the patience at the moment.

She wriggled free from him, turning in the water. Kneeling in front of him, she looked him dead in the eye. "No. No, I'm not *kidding*. I want to get married, Dylan. Tonight. Now."

He frowned, his eyes heavy with thought. "But what about our wedding at home?"

"What about it? We'll still have it for our parents. After all, it's really their wedding. Let's have our own. One that's just for us. Just for our love." She rose from the water, allowing the moisture to cascade from her body all over him. "Win the game, Dylan; win me. Make me your wife."

With that, she stepped from the spa.

"When you put it that way . . ."

An hour later, holding a bouquet of rather pathetic-looking pink carnations, Sadie walked down the aisle of the cheap chapel to the sound of recorded music.

Impatience had gotten the best of her once again. She'd happily tossed aside the notion of an Elvis wedding when she'd realized she'd have to wait. Simply to get on with the elopement, she'd opted to choose a tacky but less popular chapel.

Half-melted candles lit her way to Dylan, who stood in his usual business attire next to the minister under an arch of faded artificial flowers. She wore her wrinkled wedding dress, feeling no less beautiful in the white silk. The gown trailed behind her over the worn red carpet, reminding her how out of place she was. Despite her surroundings and attire, Sadie felt surprisingly elegant.

For all her panic attacks and hives a month earlier, she was now pointedly calm. Ready. She was through with worrying. Her life with Dylan would be good. Better than good.

Great.

Why? Because he loved her and she loved him.

If they could work their way through the past several weeks, then no doubt they could work their way through anything. And if trouble arose, they always had their game to fall back on, now, didn't they?

She stepped under the garden arch and Dylan locked arms with her. Taking his hand, she squeezed. "I'm ready to become Mrs. Dylan Burton."

He winked. "You better be."

The cheesy music ceased playing as they turned to the minister. Hand in hand, they faced their future. Their destinies.

To Sadie, it seemed the vows had barely begun, and suddenly, she was Dylan's wife. He swept her into a quick, hot kiss and sealed the deal. She kissed him back with all of her love, their mouths entwining in bruising passion.

When their lips finally broke apart, she stepped closer, nuzzling his face.

"Ready to start the honeymoon?" she whispered in his ear, then retracted, watching for his reaction.

His eyes sparkled with false defiance. "I do believe we've already taken our honeymoon."

"Darlin'," she winked. "That was just the prelude."

Turning on her high heels, she lifted her skirts, holding up the billowing fabric as she jogged down the short aisle.

"Hey! Where are you going, Mrs. Burton?" he called after her.

Sadie threw caution to the wind. After all, they'd only live once.

"Come and get me!"

epilogue

Sadie jumped at the surprising knock on her front door. Who the hell could that be? She wasn't expecting anyone, or anything, for that matter.

Leaving behind her half-packed suitcase, Sadie walked to the foyer, praying it wasn't her mother-in-law checking up on her. Again.

Victoria Burton was driving her crazy, constantly calling and stopping in, after a year still terrified they'd disappear again.

And that they would.

Sadie loved her family, even her in-laws, and she enjoyed the life she and Dylan lived. It wasn't always fun, but it was never, ever boring.

Shortly after they'd arrived home from their adventure of a year past, Dylan started his own firm, and they'd sealed a pact. At least once a year they'd escape and forget responsibility, as long as the game was preplanned and for two weeks.

So far, they'd kept their impending vacation a secret from his parents, so they wouldn't be locked in the basement and held hostage. Her parents, on the other hand, had been sending over baby-making gift baskets daily.

"Yes?" Sadie peered through the peephole, surprised to see a delivery man in brown uniform. A nametag clipped to his front pocket revealed his name was Ted.

"I have a package for you, ma'am."

Sadie frowned. She wasn't anticipating any deliveries. Her parents again, perhaps?

She opened the door, bemused when she saw the size of the large box. It was at least a yard long and two feet wide, and she was completely stumped as to what the package might contain. Surely she wouldn't have forgotten ordering something that large.

God help her if it was for babymaking.

"I'll need your autograph." Ted handed her the electronic clipboard.

She signed and returned it. "Thanks."

"No problem. Have a nice day."

"You too." As the man jogged down her front sidewalk, she pushed the package inside. The telephone rang, interrupting her efforts, and she grabbed the portable from the hall table. "Hello?"

"Did you get my package yet?" Dylan asked nonchalantly, like his question wouldn't startle her as it did.

"This is from you?" she asked, staring at the box, clueless.

"Open it up and take a look at what I found."

Puzzled and excited at the same time, Sadie tore at the clear tape, ripping the supersticky adhesive, until it all came free. A moment later, she yanked open the flaps.

No way!

Sadie stared in shock at her long-lost suitcase. "Oh my gosh, Dylan, but how?"

"I made a few calls when we arrived home last year. Made some threats, asked some favors. You know, the usual," he chuckled. "Mob connections."

"Funny! Wait . . . you've had this a *year*?" Sadie blinked, almost too stunned for words. She'd never dreamt she'd set eyes on this suitcase again and he'd had it all along? "I can't believe it." Her surprise quickly transformed as she recalled all her stress over trying to recover the damn thing. "You turkey! I chewed out quite a few people at TSA over my denied claim."

"Guess they knew what they were doing after all."

"Guess so," she muttered, half annoyed and half thrilled. "I cannot believe you kept this from me."

"Hey, babe, I have a client coming in, but you have fun now . . . and I'll see you soon. Real soon," he promised. "Enjoy."

Despite that he'd let her fret for a year in silence, his gesture had been pretty damn sweet. Sadie cracked a smile. "Thank you, Dylan."

"Love ya."

"Love you too."

Sadie hung up and tossed the phone aside. Pulling the suitcase free from the box, she tugged open the zipper, revealing the contents. Mostly clothes, but still, some of her favorites, and there was her camera, and . . .

The film!

Sadie snatched up the rolls and stood, running toward her dark room. This was perfect. Screw their plans for Cancun. Dylan had the time off and she had something better in mind.

A few hours later, she studied photo after photo of their sexual adventure, from the birds in Hawaii, to close-ups of her body as she climaxed, to her pathetic shot of the ground as she'd fallen and sprained her ankle in Tuscany.

Oh heavens, and their foursome.

They'd all developed fine, and to her shock, looked fabulous. Waving her hand in an attempt to cool her instant arousal, Sadie contemplated the two Egyptian men pleasuring her body. Wouldn't it be nice to see them again?

Her breath increased and she forced herself to look away. She'd save looking at those pictures for when Dylan was around.

Smiling from recollections of the trip, she selected several favorites, her mind racing in full gear as she reconsidered their vacation plans. No doubt, Dylan had expected her to when he'd arranged for the luggage to arrive today.

Quickly, Sadie decided on a new itinerary. It was time for a chase down memory lane.